I0632165

Heart on Battery

Lunnaria Trilogy III

Luiza Dobrzynska

I am once again surrounded by memories of EPIPHANICS.

Consciousness dulled under the influence of sleeping pills and painkillers. Stuck between sleep and consciousness. Flesh fused with metal, someone else's hair on my head. Who am I? A doll made of scraps, a broken toy witch a team of silent mechanics worked on. I have more in common with my android than any other human. This can't be seen from the outside, so I'm able to pretend that I'm just an ordinary woman. Would I be able to accept the kind of life that Leon Beavis Hampton has chosen, supported by machines for so many years, incapable of the slightest movement, dependent on others for everything?

He hides within lava tunnels, only a small fraction of which has been mapped. Even though mining exploration of the Moon has been going on for so long, we still only know a select few parts of our satellite — the ones most industrially attractive. And these, too, have many secrets hidden from us. Hampton takes advantage of this, hiding his useless body and brilliant mind from a society where permanent disability is virtually unknown. From an early age, people are taught that it is not worth living a life which is a burden to the government or your family. The vast majority of us have never seen and will never see someone unable to care for themselves, who needs help with the most trivial daily activities. Someone like the owner of Romain Corp and a dozen other companies, mostly on Earth.

Perhaps he cares about staying alive after all. Maybe even more than me, someone who, despite that monstrous attack, looks, moves and acts like any average person. I am a cripple, but few people know that fact. This is probably why I am more attracted to Inspector Cavanaugh, who terrifies his surroundings with his old-fashioned eye implants and scars, than to someone closer to my own age. The longer I live with all these implants, the less I feel like the woman I used to be.

Citizen Hakat, I owe my life to you, but sometimes I feel like you take back payment for this debt with usurious interest...

I

Number one? That's some joke. Which one of them would that be? Stunned, I moved my gaze from the brown-haired woman to the man lying in bed, and struggled to contain myself enough not to open my mouth in surprise.

"Don't look at me" the speech synthesizer squeaked.

I stepped back involuntarily. This is the first time I've seen a person in such a state that, if not for the readings on the monitor, you could assume he is dead – and then suddenly this terrifying mummy spoke to me through the interface. It's strange to hear a human voice, to guess its emotions and at the same time to know that the speaker cannot even move his mouth. I knew that such auxiliary methods existed, but I never thought before that they could be used outside of specialized hospitals. And that someone could use them permanently, and not only during the rehabilitation period after an accident or serious illness.

Number One looked at me condescendingly kindly. The A0 mark on her forehead left no doubt – in front of me was someone who belonged to the strict elite, the one in a hundredth thousands of mankind. IQ above 220 points. Compared to her, I was a chimpanzee.

"I..." I began dully and stopped, feeling my mind is completely blank.

Scotty, laughing, patted me on the back.

"Take a seat, you'll faint from all these emotions."

Under the gaze of the beautiful woman and the old man lying in bed, my legs were starting to give away. However, I did not dare sit in such an important company.

"Come on, my dear. Don't just stand there," Number One said. "I'm a person just like you, you don't have to stare at me like that."

She had a pleasant, deep voice. I looked at Scott, he pulled up a chair for me and almost forced me to sit down. He sat on the second one.

"What is Your Excellency doing here?" he asked.

"I'm hiding, what else? They've discovered a doppelganger on the Central Island, and are currently cleaning up over there. The Chief of Arms smuggled me to the Moon, and the good-natured Leon hid me on his barge... because this is not a permanent structure, my dear, but a type of underground ship. It moves through the lava tunnels like a submarine in the sea."

"Citizen Hakat?" out of the corner of my eye, I saw Scott's jaw drop. He clearly didn't expect that.

"That's correct. He is the only one I can trust."

"Problems on the Central Island? Really?" I asked as my boss chewed on this information, completely destroying his understanding of what the situation within the highest echelons of power looks like.

"Not any more than usual. It's never peaceful there. Would you like something to drink?" Number One pressed a button on the table.

A young man in a white coveralls entered the room. I felt my eyes nearly pop out of their sockets. If it weren't for pitch black short hair, I'd be sure it was Monty! A second later it dawned on me. It must have been one of Karpinsky's test models, numbered 1 through 26. As far as I remember, Monty was number 27, and according to the scientist, he was the most advanced.

"Randy, get us three caffetinos and a box of cookies," Number One instructed him.

Three caffetino and a box of cookies, the android repeated, then turned abruptly and left. His voice was dead, mechanical. It looked like a robot, though...

"Is this one of Dr. Karpinsky's creations?" I asked.

"Yes. There are more of them here. They care for Leon," she replied.

"They are precise, well trained and don't ask stupid questions," the speech synthesizer creaked. "Henry did a great job. It's a shame he didn't go a step further."

"Are you talking about transferring a human brain into an artificial body?" I guessed.

"That would be something, wouldn't it? Unfortunately, all attempts were unsuccessful," I got the impression that he would let out a sigh if he could.

"There's something I don't understand," Scott said, rubbing his left visor. "Well, actually I don't understand anything. Mr. Hampton, since I am not mistaken about your identity, may I be completely honest?"

"Go ahead. My sensitivity tolerated worse things," I think I was right when I attributed a sense of humor to this man. It was difficult for me to understand how this was possible in his situation, but still...

"First, how did you manage... all this?" he made a circle with his hand.

He couldn't better express his thoughts, but we all understood what he meant.

Android Randy brought a tray with three steaming cups and a tin box of cookies. He placed all of it on the table, which was moved to the center, then went over to the bed and raised the headrest slightly. He also touched several controls on the synth panel.

"Don't be so surprised," Hampton said, his voice much clearer. "Randy has had a communications chip implanted. I can give him orders mentally. Inspector Cavanaugh, your question requires a very long answer."

"I'd be glad to hear it," Scott sipped from his cup and moved his visors a little. It was the equivalent of raising an eyebrow. I followed his example and felt amazed, too. I've never had the opportunity to drink caffetino with such a velvety rich taste before, even in the rector's office at the Medical Academy or on the Central Island during training. Although, it's not like I was that spoiled back then, but sometimes Hakat invited me to a coffee shop for members of the government. Even there they didn't serve anything this delicious.

"First of all, I'll say that I have been following your investigation from the very beginning, so don't be surprised that there are things I know very well. I also think you deserve an explanation. Not because I owe you them, but because they will help you in the further stages of the investigation," the eyes of the man lying in bed twitched slightly in the rhythm of the voice coming from the synthesizer. The realization that he was truly a living person, unable to communicate with the outside world or take care of the most basic needs without the help of machines, was nearly unbearable.

"So, let's begin... There's one thing that will surprise you, I'm sure. You were raised in the cult of IQ, so to speak, and so was society as a whole. However, having a high IQ number is no different from having a computer of the latest model. It's useless if you don't know how to use it properly. Many of the A0 class, whom the respected head of the world government here," Number One bowed her head a little, "belongs to, don't know how to. Of course, such an inconvenient fact is hidden from the public, but this extremely gifted by nature group of people usually have some serious problems."

"That's impossible," I blurted out.

"Oh, it's possible, miss..."

"Juliet Ankes. They call me Leeta."

"Leeta. That's nice. I understand that it's hard to believe, but A0 are often alienated, unable to establish normal relationships with other people. They are often forced to be locked in seclusion for the sake of themselves and others. Sometimes they are very unhappy and cannot use the tools given to them by nature. I'm doing this introduction so that you can understand something."

"I don't belong to class A0. Not even A2. However, I have been gifted with the ability to make the most of what I have, or rather, I worked for it myself. Ever since I was a child, I've always hated when someone was better than me. I didn't rebel or stomp in anger then, as you might have expected, but instead worked like a madman. Thanks to this fact, I was able to almost always defeat those who were intellectually much superior to me. As a teenager, I founded my little industrial empire long before the disease that confined me to bed began to unfold. When this happened, I was already a world-wide magnate. Every member of my family, doctors and friends, expected me to apply for euthanasia while I could still hold a pen between my fingers. But I didn't want to die. I had big plans, but this stupid sickly body stood in my way. I decided to fight."

"That's honorable, but it goes against the foundations of our society, and you know that," Scott drank his caffetino again. I did as well.

"I do," Hampton said calmly, "but I didn't care. It was my life, and I wanted to make my own decisions. After all, what is a body? A human being is the brain, everything else is just a cover, another tool that you should know how to replace if it doesn't meet your standards. Not throw everything in the trash."

I thought about my implants and pursed my lips. Hampton continued:

"Needless to say, my fight from the very beginning caused heated controversy. There was only one person on my side. He helped me move all my assets to the Moon Company and build a whole network of partners. Also to create properly equipped hideouts in various corners of the silver ball. When, at last, my consciousness was trapped in the now useless shell of my paralyzed body, I had the power to rise above the law."

Cavanaugh flinched slightly. I understood his conflicted feelings. As a law enforcement officer, he could not calmly listen when someone went against it, even in defense of their own life. But he remained silent and continued to listen.

"Money is power, because you can buy anything, including people, no matter how that may sound. I had a legion of scientists working for me, most of whom were smart enough to confound the greatest minds of all time. I was choosing them carefully from the very beginning. My employees had to be ambitious, reserved and greedy at the same time. It's easy to command ones like that. I wanted strength not for the sake of power itself, but for the opportunity to get a new body. All my actions served this purpose. Locked in that decaying shell that you see before you, I could only think, and I used this opportunity with a passion that you could not even imagine. Many of the lunar technology solutions used by all parts of the Company were created in my labs. I submitted the ideas. My scientists had to put them into practice.

Henry Karpinsky was one of my most promising acquisitions. He didn't care about profit, but he would sell his soul to make his dream of creating artificial intelligence come true. Not one like Randy, who still makes for an excellent nurse and butler either way. No. Karpinsky wanted to create a person with an independent mind, not limited by anything. Robotics laws were not for them. He wanted his creation to have free will over whether to help a person or not. So that they could kill if they only wanted to. At the same time, he believed that an android could have morals that would prevent them from doing such things. I sponsored his research, demanding that he simultaneously tries to connect a living brain to a mechanical body. This condition was unnegotiable."

Scott nodded and grabbed a cookie.

"Cyborg. Humanity's eternal dream. Unfortunately, impossible to achieve. Karpinsky was working on it. Experiments on living people... it's forbidden, you know that?"

"Experiments on volunteers. All signed the corresponding papers. From a criminal law perspective, you cannot do anything, inspector. They were mostly fugitive criminals, seduced by good pay and the promise of impunity, or terminally ill people."

"No matter how good the pay, who would let their brains be cut out?"

"You would be surprised. Laboratory F was their last shelter, their last chance to escape from law enforcement. I know what you're both thinking, and yes, we were deceiving these people. We promised them a complex plastic surgery that would make them unrecognizable. And they were... in a way."

"That's horrible," I whispered.

My thoughts returned to what I had seen in the laboratory, and my body trembled.

Number One listened quietly, without emotion, sipping her coffee. She must have heard about it all before.

"Indeed, Miss Ankes," Hampton agreed with me. "Nearly all experiments, of which results we take advantage of even today, were horrible. Information about the limitations of the human body, about the effects of many drugs, about the effects of extreme therapy... all this was learned in death camps, killing thousands of men, women and children, often in very violent ways. In many cases, the criminals got away with it. After the war, they were taken in by the governments of great powers. In exchange for the results of their research, they were guaranteed impunity and a prosperous life. Pharmaceutical companies that used the opportunity to test their drugs on human guinea pigs also took no responsibility and continued to run their bonanza.

Yes, Karpinsky's research took many lives. However, they were mostly voluntary. We deceived only criminals, not petty thieves, but real human garbage, trying to escape the death penalty. In any case, their fate was doomed."

"That's not for you to decide," Scott interrupted.

"And for whom is it? Judges? They are people just like me and you. They don't issue sentences out of conviction, but on the basis of penalty points. I can do that too."

"But you have no authority."

"An academic matter. Officially, I do not, but unofficially I did receive permission."

"Whose?!"

"Mine," Number One said calmly.

We looked at her in surprise. She was sitting at the table, her legs crossed, calmly sipping her caffetino. For the first time since I saw her, I could see something bad on her handsome face.

"Your Excellency..."

"Hardly anyone wants to accept this, but there is such a thing as a greater good."

"But... human rights..." I began, stunned.

She looked at me with a condescending smile. I suddenly realized that I had underestimated her age. She was at least as old as Scotty.

"What humans, child? Ones who rape little children? Ones who kill a family of several for a golden bracelet or a point's card? No, that's not human. By committing the worst of crimes, you lose your civil and even human rights. Until people realized that, crime in the world was uncontrollable. When Act 531 was introduced, it immediately began to decline."

She was speaking the truth. I learned about it in school and never thought about it, but now it was all presented to me in a monstrous light.

"Of course, one can digress whether anyone should be allowed to experiment on such social waste," she continued, "but I've seen the papers they signed. They knew all the risks associated with the experiments, so the case is legally closed. And as for morality... well, that changes, my dear. Public executions, sexual mutilation of women, lobotomies and much more were previously considered to be moral. On the other hand, no one back then would be able to comprehend that today it is moral to classify people according to their intellectual abilities or to euthanize underdeveloped children."

I looked at Scott helplessly.

"Unfortunately, that's the way it is," he muttered reluctantly. "That's why I couldn't accuse Karpinsky. If I found a point, believe me, despite my personal sympathy for this guy, everything would have ended very differently."

"With a great harm to humanity," Hampton said. "Sometimes you have to look further than the tip of your nose, Inspector."

My boss got up and walked over to Randy. He carefully examined him from head to toe, touched his face and hands.

"Genius," he said finally, "but it's still just a machine."

"Unfortunately, you are right. Although for me it's still a great convenience."

"That communication chip," I remembered. "I heard about it being implanted in clones. I get the impression that the work at Lab F didn't end at attempts to build the perfect human replica from microprocessors."

Hampton was silent.

"The clones were a mistake," he said at last. "Dr. Oenas was walking different path than Karpinsky from the beginning. She wanted a normal, but healthy human body for me. She believed that there was nothing wrong with using FGC [1] for our purposes, since until recently they've still been used as organ transplant reservoirs. Transplanting a brain into a body obtained this way was beyond her abilities, so she tried... something else. She stimulated an intentionally deactivated gene that determines the formation of the frontal lobe and the fold of the cerebral cortex. Then she implanted a chip inside it... just like it's implanted in the spine of people after a spinal cord rupture. It is creating miniature living nerve connections with cybernetics."

"And that's how she created Mr. Brel," Scott muttered sarcastically. "Congratulations."

"At first, Brel worked without issues. He was made from my DNA, so I expected him to be like me. I was wrong. It was not me, it was someone else entirely. It got out of hand at some point. He somehow blocked the chip and started working on his own. He decided to take over the management of the Romain Corporation."

"How nice. I think you deserved something like this, though," Cavanaugh said with rough harshness. "No offense, but you're the worst kind of scum. You must be thinking that you can do whatever you want, don't you? Because who could stand up against the rich?"

I saw that he was getting very fired up, and I perfectly understood why.

---

[1] Fast Growing Clone – a living reservoir of replacement parts, fitted for the recipient.

Number One just smiled without taking her eyes off him. She seemed to be enjoying it all.

"Calm down," she said finally. "You're worrying about all this for no reason. You forget the guiding principle of the police: when there is no violation of the law, there is no crime. And in this case, there is neither one nor the other. So this matter doesn't concern you. Your job is to uphold the rule of law in Lunnar, not engage in moral judgment on actions that do not fall under the criminal code."

Her voice grew a little harsher, taking on a tone that said: You must be forgetting who you're talking to. Scott took a deep breath, pulled himself together, and sat back down in his seat.

"Forgive me, Your Excellency," he muttered.

"May I ask something?" I intervened, taking advantage of the silence.

"Go ahead," she looked at me with her dark eyes.

She seemed as motionless as the robot in the corner, who was much like Monty. The positive impression she made on me in the beginning turned to ashes. I began to feel afraid of her.

"Never mind Mr. Hampton and his scams. I'm interested in something else. Who are you hiding from and why are you here? Until now, I've had the impression that Central Island was armed enough to keep the members of the government safe. Although I only saw the Outer Circle, I don't think even a mouse could slip through this protection."

Number One raised her well-groomed eyebrows.

"I'm not worried about mice," she replied coldly, "there are more serious threats. You should be aware of this, since you've been part of one."

"You know about that…" I whispered.

"But of course. My assistant and my second deputy died in the attack, which injured you. I was not there, although I should have been."

"Why?" this was a riddle that tormented me from the very beginning. What could the most important person on Earth be doing in a decrepit alley on the outskirts of Palm Springs? One so poorly protected at that?

Number One nodded to Randy.

"More caffetino. Best bring the whole pitcher. We'll be here for a while."

"How long?" Scotty asked sharply.

"The Chief of Arms will decide that. He will be here in an hour or two."

I froze. Scott's left hand gripped the arm of the chair so tight that his fingers turned white.

"What if we decided to leave?"

"I wouldn't recommend that," Number One smiled coldly. "Randy is not the only robot here. For now you must stay. So, should I continue or not?"

I restrained myself with an effort of will. My thoughts went to Yamato waiting in the rover. Did she know about him? Slowly, pretending to straighten my hair, I pressed the button hidden in my earring. This was one of our internal security functions. If Yamato picked up the signal, he knew it meant an order to immediately return to Lunnar and hand over command of the police to the military. Lois Ann Siris will know what to do next.

"I'm sure you're surprised that someone would even expect me in that forbidden place," the woman sitting opposite me continued. "I'll say that it was a rather unpleasant affair. And I would have been in that alley if not for Citizen Hakat, who nearly forced me to send my assistant where I was supposed to be in person. He had to take the initiative, because I wasn't able to think logically. He suspected a deadly ambush from the very beginning. As it turned out, he was right."

She paused for a moment because Randy had just arrived with the jug and refilled our cups. After a while, she continued:

"I gave the order to take you to EPIPHANICS. You were on your deathbed, it was the only place where they would be capable of helping you at all."

"Thank you," I whispered. Given the enormous cost of my treatment, this seemed like a funny word to use, and I knew that.

"No need," she said shortly, "I did it not for you, but for myself. I needed testimony from someone who saw the bombers. The fact that both Hakat and I knew who to blame would be pointless if we didn't have witnesses."

Legal basis, article 29 of the Criminal Code, section 8, rang in my head. *The law applies to all persons, and everyone is equal before the court, regardless of class, social status and function.* In court, Number One's word would mean the same as an unskilled worker's of class C3, if it were not for the ability to present objective evidence, or at least the results of a memory scan. And someone's subjective belief that they know the whole truth cannot be used as evidence.

Cavanaugh nodded. Perhaps he was thinking the same thing. He has already calmed down. His visors, previously protruded, returned to their sockets.

"Your Excellency, if I may, you are speaking without explaining the key point. Not that I'm trying to be intrusive, but you've decided to tell us about this yourself, and you are keeping silence on something that is extremely important. Why did you put yourself in such danger?"

"You're quite witty. This hideous construction that replaces your eyes prevents one from seeing your class symbol, but I know that you are A2. I have no idea what someone of your caliber is doing in the police, but that's none of my business. As you make your bed, so must you lie in it. Either way, you are a veteran of the best investigation team in the world. So, go ahead and solve this mystery. Let me give you a hint. When the president of the government was being elected, my candidacy was not approved unanimously. There were also those who expressed doubts. What do you think, why was that?"

He smiled. He took a sip of the caffetino, which had already cooled down slightly, and grabbed another cookie.

"You are a woman, Your Excellency," he said, "and a very attractive one, if I may point out, not just smart. But every woman, stupid or wise, has or may hypothetically have one weak point, biochemical in nature. A child."

Number One put the cup on the saucer.

"You know how to hit the bull's eye," her face suddenly aged a good ten years. "I had a son."

She fell silent and my feelings changed color again. Now, compassion has sneaked it. I, too, began to understand what actually happened in that small alley behind an abandoned shopping center, where my life had changed dramatically. If the public car hadn't broken down... if I had waited for a replacement... if only I chose a different route...

"I'm very sorry, Your Excellency," Scott in a serious tone. "So, the plan failed, if I understand correctly."

"There was no plan. I was ready to give the kidnappers what they wanted, but Hakat prevented me from doing so. Instead, he sent my assistant, Janice Osborne, disguised as me, and Mark Plesner as her bodyguard. They both died, not that the ruse was discovered. They were murdered before they could even get out of the service rover with manually-operated explosives. It was not about the information that I could exchange for my son, but about eliminating me. And Citizen Hakat guessed that flawlessly."

"And... the child?" I asked in a trembling voice.

She looked at me with dull eyes, and under the power of that gaze I huddled in my chair.

"Garrett's body was found two days later. According to the pathologists, he was already dead when the ransom message was sent to me," her voice was firm but calm. "The ones you've identified unfortunately didn't say anything. Their arrest was unsuccessful. An autopsy revealed that they had implants with poison. Who activated them remains a mystery. And to this day," her voice suddenly broke, "I still don't know who killed my sweet little boy."

Scott turned chalk white in a split second. I guessed that he must be thinking about his own child, about whom – as I guessed from the semi-statements said in our various conversations – he never knew. I saw his jaw tremble and I saw him try to control himself with all of his willpower. Then he got up, walked around the table and unexpectedly hugged Number One. He wrapped her in his arms, hugged her, and she burst into tears, as if she were not the most important person on Earth, but an ordinary, average woman.

"Calm down, my dear," Hampton said. The synthesizer did not convey emotions, but I had no doubt that he really felt sorry for his guest. He was not a bad person, only determined by circumstances that could not be called ordinary. "Crying won't help you. Whatever happened is irreversible. But you are still responsible for humanity and have access to everything that may either improve it or destroy it. You must be strong."

Number One pulled away from Scott and sniffed as she searched her purse and pockets for some tissues. I gave her mine.

"I usually don't cry," she apologized, ashamed of her own weakness.

"Now you understand why some people doubted your candidacy," Hampton went on. "Once it would've been called anti-feminism, but in truth it's a logical and cold assessment of someone's capabilities. For purely biological reasons, men are less likely to lose their heads in such a situation."

"Oh, shut up," Scotty growled.

A rhythmic screech came from the synthesizer. I realized that it was laughter.

"Unfortunately, talking is all I've got left, and I rarely have with whom, not counting the androids, technical support, doctors and my corporations, with whom I usually communicate via instant messages. Social conversations must be what I miss the most."

I thought about Monty. He was much more advanced than Randy and similar robots, which must have been out here somewhere. Nevertheless, the thought of being doomed to his exclusive company wasn't nice. There would be a basic problem of what we could even talk about. The loneliness that Leon Beavis Hampton experienced must have been frightening.

"I saw your previous place," I said. "The one next to the lunnit mine. It's very nice. Maybe you'd want to go back there? I'm sure it could be done."

"Miss Ankes, for me, the beauty of the place where my bed is placed is as important as Hawaiian garlands for a pig in a feed yard," he replied. I must have been right in suspecting he has a sense of humor, although I couldn't understand how he could keep it in such a dire situation. "I don't get out of bed, let alone my room. Further rooms are decorated by my staff, who try to sweeten their accommodation next to the living dead. For me it doesn't matter."

The inspector looked around the room. So did me, for the first time since I came here. So far, all my attention has been absorbed by Number One, who was now sitting with my tissue in hand, trying to wipe off the smudged makeup. She examined her face in a hand mirror and was still unhappy.

"Now I look like a witch. Randy, bring me some clean water in a saucer."

With the help of water, she finally wiped off the remains of lipstick and mascara, then skillfully applied foundation and began to work on highlighting the eyes with a pencil.

"Please, let me," I suggested, standing up.

She looked at me, handed a travel kit with makeup and tilted her head a little. I quickly did some standard makeup, as Mabel taught me. It's funny, I never learned how to improve my own beauty, but I was really good at doing it for other.

"Women..." Hampton squeaked. "You see, Cavanaugh, they don't change. Whether a physical worker or Miss President, they will take care of their beauty first, even during a global apocalypse."

"You have a point," Scott agreed. "I've read memoirs from the times of the ecological disaster. Everything collapsed and burned, there was nothing to eat, and pure water was worth its weight in gold, a tragedy for all time. And what did I see, among the notes about bandaging the wounded or the difficulties of preparing the most modest meal, written by those who had to live until help arrived?"

I found some soap, and since it was raining today, I was finally able to wash my hair.

Jim and Minnie are getting married today. Myra made paper flowers for the bride's wreath, the veil will be made from an old curtain.

Today we obtained some coal for darkening our eyebrows, and Sissy fished out childrens' crayons from the rubble. After licking, they can be a good substitute for lipstick and eyeshadow.

You get my point? All this was written by women who survived the death of their loved ones, saw terrible tragedies and fought to live each day.

I was listening to them with one ear, working hard on Number One's face and smiling discreetly. I didn't take these words as criticism. It has been proven a long time ago that feminine activities, ridiculed for centuries, such as cosmetics, hair-styling and petty gossip, are a great psychological discharger. It is thanks to them that the so-called 'weaker sex' turned out to be stronger in extreme situations. The global tragedies that left men mentally crippled and often unable to live a normal life didn't turn women into wrecks. It was them who built new life on the ruins and tried their best to create a family for the future children. This is probably why they went crazy less often.

Scott Cavanaugh was well aware of this. Sylvanas Evans said that of all the police chiefs she knew, he was the only one who hired women more often than men. Even when he still had full choice – because in Lunnar he was, of course, very limited. There you simply take what you can get, and that's it.

"Children add superhuman strength," tears escaped from under Number One's eyelids again. I carefully dried them with a powder puff. "Thanks to them, women were always capable of extraordinary deeds. Today this is less noticeable, because the state decides everything for you, even whether a child can be born at all."

I couldn't help but think about Marika Yovovitz and her disabled son. What did her and everyone like her feel when they heard the unfavorable verdict of the doctors? I never wanted to have a child myself, but I could still imagine it.

"Unlike you, men, we descended from the tree of evolution," Number One quickly recovered. "Because of that, we need something more in life than drinking in front of the TV, burping and talking about asses. And be done with this offensive topic."

"Hardly offensive, Your Excellency. And haven't you offended us now?" The inspector chuckled.

The atmosphere has become less heavy. With a few brush strokes for the shadows I finished my work and gave her a mirror. She looked at herself, checking the sides of her face with the extension.

"Not bad," she praised me. "You have a talent for these things. What are you doing in the police...?"

"It was Citizen Hakat's idea, Your Excellency."

"Of course... he always thinks of something that you then don't know how to handle. And only later does it turn out that he was right," she lowered the mirror with a sigh. "Sometimes I have trouble understanding him, but thanks to him I am still alive."

Scott muttered something incomprehensible. He found it difficult to reconcile his carefully cultivated hatred for his brother-in-law with the woman's words, and he tried his best not to continue the topic. I felt that he would like to shout in her face everything he knows and guessed, but he remained reasonably silent. It was not the time or place. It was a good thing, since the next moment the door opened and Constable Yamato entered. Behind him was the Chief of Arms in full uniform with a pistol in hand, accompanied by three commandos.

Yamato had very unusual expression and avoided looking into our eyes. But Hakat looked like he had a genuine desire to tear us apart one by one. Especially Scott.

"Do you really not know how to restrain yourself from sticking your nose into other people's business?"

"I am responsible for everything that happens in Lunnar and its mines," Cavanaugh said calmly. "This includes the tunnels. If you forgot, we've had to chase out more than one criminal from one of the closed branches. How was I to know that this particular shelter was built under your auspices?"

They looked at each other for a while. Then citizen Hakat pulled up one of the chairs, put down his pistol and sat down.

"Caffetino?" Number One raised the pitcher questioningly

"Something stronger. I had a long day, and now I have to deal with these comedians. Damn circus."

Another squeal came from Hampton's bed, acting as laughter. That this man still felt like laughing...

"Dear friend, I've warned you that politics make for a tiresome hobby."

"It's not always that I have to deal with cases such as last time, Leon," Hakat gratefully a small glass filled with amber liquid from Randy's hands. "Though I admit that I've been close to leaving this hellish job behind more than once."

He took a long sip.

"Is the island safe yet?" Number One asked.

"Currently, yes. We've found and eliminated the doppelganer. The fact that he slipped through this far shows the improvement of duplication techniques by…"

"By who?" I couldn't resist.

He glanced at me briefly.

"You are incredibly curious, my dear," he smiled, "you should know that politics require balance. If someone is in charge, there must be someone trying to disbalance them. This is how it's always been, because the ruling of the entire Earth is greedy business."

Maybe he was right, although I don't know, why I would know anything about that. After all, this information is not publicly available. The society knows only that there is a Global Government, consisting of the brightest minds on the planet, and nothing else. There is a widespread belief that there is harmonious cooperation and agreement between politicians responsible for certain sectors, because how else could everything work so smoothly? Now I learned that this is not at all the case and that a quiet but no less merciless struggle is going on in the highest circles of power.

"Do you at least know who the danger to Ms. Num....is? I mean, Her Excellency?" I asked.

He soaked his mouth with alcohol again.

"I do and don't know," he replied. "Until now, all leads turned out to be false. Well, maybe that's not entirely correct, since I took care of those who were corrupt, but the identity of their boss remains a mystery. One thing seems certain, that he has no personal access to the Central Island. He is someone from the outside."

"That's good then, isn't it?"

"Perhaps, Leeta. Although not entirely, since he managed to find other ways, through people weaker than they should be. We need to be more careful with who we hire."

He stared at the floor, and I would bet that he was thinking of Mabel. I was curious when he would ask me about her and I tried to quickly think of what I would tell them. However, every possible answer I could think of was shattered by the realization that I am a terrible liar, and the Chief of Arms knows perfectly well when someone isn't honest. All I could hope for was that he wouldn't ask.

"What are the chances that the same person is trying to get to Number One and is messing around Lunnar?" Scott turned the cup in his fingers and looked passionately at Hakat's glass. He himself would've probably loved to have 'something stronger', but couldn't afford to do so in the line of duty. He finally took out his frustration on Yamato, who shifted from foot to foot and didn't know where to look. "Officer, sit down damn it! How could you let yourself be taken by surprise?"

"Ted, didn't you get my signal?" I added reproachfully.

"Boss, but this guy has an entire army," Yamato muttered. "There are three A28 armored personnel carriers and four Viper-class rovers on the surface, armed so well that they could try to take over the Moon Company headquarters if they wanted to. I was caught at the exit to the main lane. I didn't stand a chance."

"And you shouldn't, kid," growled Number One. "This is not some 'guy', it's the Chief of Arms. He eats types like you for a snack and doesn't even notice."

"Seriously?" Yamato stared at Hakat.

I don't know how it happened, but the sight of his good-natured surprised face struck me as unexpectedly funny, which made me laugh. To pull myself together, I tried to finish my caffetino and choked. Scott slapped me on the back with his open hand.

"Take him outside and watch him closely," Hakat told his silent bodyguards. "We'll be talking here for some time."

As he left, Yamato looked at me questioningly. I turned my head. It was better not to say anything he might later accidentally tell.

Scott waited for the commandos to escort the officer, then turned back to the Chief of Arms.

"All right, what about my question?"

Hakat shrugged.

"That's your job to find out," he replied succinctly. "Let everyone do their own job, and the world will be a better place."

"If that was possible, then it already would've been," Cavanaugh said.

"Our opinions on this topic differ," the Chief of Arms didn't allow himself to be disturbed. "That's not the only thing, of course, but never mind that. You don't have to agree, ladies and gentlemen, you just need to listen to me, and I really hope you understand that. Now you will politely return to your station and never tell any living soul about this place. We'll be moving it soon either way."

"But..."

"Don't interrupt me, Agent Aneks. There is no 'buts'. I know what you want to say, and technically you're right. Only that sometimes there is a so-called higher cause. Have you heard this term?"

"Yes, I have. During my studies on Central Island, several lectures were devoted to derogations from applicable law and situations in which such derogations are permitted. One of them is the so-called *casus libera mentis*[2]. It's a small but important sub-clause in the Public Health Act."

When a person possessing full intellectual capacity and public rights is severely disabled by illness or accident, but still refuses to consent to euthanasia, he cannot be forced to do so by any form of pressure.

---

[2] Case free mind (latin).

Leon Beavis Hampton's mental health was perfectly fine. He also had enough money and connections to prevent legitimate heirs from taking over his business, which was what usually happened in such cases. He was still running his empire himself, which was undoubtedly rather strange... I had my doubts about how the court would react to this, but everything indicated that there were no legal issues. The rightful heirs, who had such a fortune pass by them, were either bribed or silenced and didn't sue for incapacitation. They could've done so without any risk and even had a good chance of winning. But they didn't.

The thought of a trial that didn't take place set off a chain of associations in my brain, and I suddenly remembered Harry Johnson. Brel was a nearly perfect copy of him, and if he was made from Hampton's DNA as his clone... then who is Johnson?! Where did he come from and how did he gain so much power? I almost said these questions out loud, but I restrained myself.

"You must never reveal your whole hand to you opponent," Scott said as he taught me the rules of fisbin, a challenging card game popular in Lunnar. "It's best that even your partner doesn't know the full extent of your power."

The Chief of Arms didn't notice my dilemmas. He was looking directly at Scott, whose scarred lips pressed into a tight line and whose implants protruded dangerously out of their mountings.

"What are you playing at, Karl?" he suddenly abandoned the official language. "You knew about Laboratory F long before it collapsed. You can't fool me. You didn't mind at all what happened there. And you, Your Excellency," suddenly he turned to Number One, "didn't care either. What you cared about were the results of a study that could not be officially conducted or sponsored."

"They closed the laboratory with a big bang, but only when the news about it somehow leaked to the public," it suddenly became clear to me, and I took the word from him. "Scientists like Karpinsky and Oenas have ensured legal immunity, they're simply taken by government and the matter becomes quiet. I understand Mr. Hampton, though I'm not trying to excuse him, but... you?"

"Agent Ankes!" the Chief of Arms cut me off sternly, and when I became silent, he smiled coldly. "Research in the field of artificial intelligence is a key program of the ministry of human development. We won't fly to the distant stars if we cannot figure this matter out. A dozen or several dozens of socially marginalized rejects is a very low price."

"I wonder what their opinion is."

"Nobody cares about that. New medical technologies were tested on ones like them in countries where they didn't care about human rights. It is you in particular, Leeta, who should appreciate such research and the ruthlessness of scientists, because it was thanks to them that the implantation technology was developed, which returned your human appearance. Would you like to know what you looked like when you arrived at the clinic? I have a photo, I can show you."

I shuddered. I didn't want to know what that attack turned me into. It wasn't aimed directly at my person, but I suffered from its rebound. One could say I was lucky. Of two people who came to the meeting instead of Number One, almost nothing remained. Yes, I was saved by results of work the progress of which was morally questionable. Against all logic, I suddenly felt guilty. Everyone was looking at me, expecting answer, as if I had suddenly become the most important person in this isolated refuge.

"Whatever happened, we can't take it back," I said after a while. "Denying the results of research obtained in any terrible way will mean that these people have suffered and died in vain. However, this doesn't mean that we should imitate former criminals for the sake of scientific development. We consider ourselves better than our ancestors, so we should fight for a future where we really are better."

There was silence for a while. Then Hampton, or rather his synthesizer, spoke.

"You're right. But please understand where I'm coming from. When you're in my position, it's easy to be... a little egoistical. As for my defense, I can say that I had no idea how far Karpinsky and Oenas really had gone. I used the results of their work, but didn't delve into the details."

"Most of their experiments did not actually see the light of day until the lab was destroyed," added Hakat. I had the impression that he also was trying to find an excuse. "We had no idea that these experiments could be fatal."

"Do you know how many there were?" I have asked.

"Not exactly. Most of the brains we acquired came from the hospital morgue, which is the good part of the news."

"What about the bad part?"

"We are aware of at least two deaths caused by the experiments. The rest are unclear since they include terminally ill patients who signed consent in hopes of salvation."

"Disgusting," Scott muttered.

"Yes, but completely legal. Everyone has the right to donate their body to science, even during their lifetime. And the rest is just a logical consequence."

He was definitely right. The laws governing medical practice or research were not well known to me, but I had a general understanding of them, like anyone who graduated high school would. Except that in addition to these laws, there were internal codes of ethics for each industry and professional ethics committees to ensure that they were followed. That's why stories such as the experiments carried out at Laboratory F usually don't take place. Usually...

You cannot set boundaries to science, Karpinsky once wrote to me. *People have tried to for thousands of years. Religious, legal and ethical barriers were erected, but scientists overcame all limitations, consumed by a thirst for knowledge. No one and nothing will ever change that fact.*

This uncompromising approach led to the development of a remote-control chip, a prototype of an artificial brain, and later of androids like Monty. I didn't know whether it could've been achieved otherwise. I was hoping it could be. However, of that I had no proof.

II

The situation was at least unusual. I had no doubts that if any other police officers, military personnel or even ordinary people were in our place, their fate would be decided. We were needed. Citizen Hakat knew how far we were able to go and what we could or couldn't do. He needed us, which meant something, although if he had any doubts whatsoever, he would not hesitate for a second. There are no irreplaceable people, especially in the game he played. He once let me know that he could've became Number One himself. This meant that when it came to IQ, he was at the very top. Neither I nor Scott could compare with him.

Leon Beavis Hampton built his industrial empire, even though without machines adapted to him, he wouldn't be able to even move a finger. Despite his ingenuity and determination, he needed help, and Hakat offered it to him. He appreciated the capabilities of this horribly disfigured man and supported him with his own goals in mind. Wealth is power. The Moon, with its resources, provided unlimited opportunities to earn a fortune, but for this it was necessary to be in a constant battle with large corporations. Romain Corporation was one of the smaller ones, and so far insignificant, but its influence grew.

Did the Chief of Arms need Hampton? Maybe he wasn't necessary, but convenient. He did most of the corporate work for him. Hakat could have done it himself, but given his responsibilities in government, he didn't have the time. While Hampton, on the other hand, had too much time. He had already proven his genius and tenacity by running the family business, so there wasn't much of a risk. And that's how Romain Corporation came to be. An outsider would not be able to associate it with the Chief of Arms, even if their life depended on it.

Why was it so important to him to hide these connections? Because he was acting on the edge of the law. Technically, he didn't violate any laws of the Criminal or Civil Codes, but if all this came to light, it would be easy to accuse him of abuse of power. And from there was only a path straight to the bottom. That's why he involved only 100% certain people into his game. Others, if they had a lead, he probably got rid of. He was capable of it, I had no doubt about that. Did it really scare Mabel so much that she dared to run away, which went so against her opportunistic nature?

So many questions now pressed against my lips, I could hardly remain silent. I preferred to not share my thoughts, especially since I felt like a trapped mouse. I began to really feel terrified. I was aware that for Hakat and Number One, organizing an 'accident' for me would not be a logistical problem. And after the fact, they certainly wouldn't feel more remorse than upon trampling on a nagging insect. Did they even have any conscience? At this point, I was beginning to doubt it. In relation to ordinary people, they must have felt like some Olympic gods, whose actions no one would ever account for. When playing their game, you had to take extreme care and hope that – self-righteous with their intelligence – they would not treat someone of my level as a serious threat.

All these thoughts flashed through my mind as I stared at Number One – a handsome, elegant woman with carefully combed dark hair – and Citizen Hakat in uniform standing by her side.

"I think that... we should go," I broke the silence at last, turning to Scott. "We have no business here. There have been no crimes committed. The man is on his own property, what would we accuse him of? That he secured it from intruders, or that he's still alive? Let's be logical, there's nobody for us to arrest here, and there must be dozens of people waiting back at the police station."

"Wise choice, my child," the Chief of Arms praised me with a bit of haughtiness and what I would call 'tender contempt'. "You should never forget that making sure the law is followed is not the only duty of a good police officer. You also have to know where you shouldn't stick your nose in. One example is politics."

"Don't provoke me," Scott growled through his teeth.

I could see he was holding back his emotions with difficulty. His sense of justice was contradicting with being Hakat's puppet. I understood it well, though unlike my boss – thanks to Cynthia Lara's upbringing – I was more flexible. I never tried to pierce the wall with my head, and when something overwhelmed me, I adjusted gently, like water, to what was around me. I believed it was the best I could do. It wasn't until I met Scott Cavanaugh that I realized I wasn't necessarily right, though the attitude Cynthia instilled in me was sometimes a better option than immediately standing up in protest.

"I don't need to remind you that you are bound to complete secrecy," the Chief of Arms continued. "Not only in my affairs or the affairs of the honorable president, but also in the affairs of Leon Beavis Hampton. Don't ask any more questions, and best just pretend that such a person does not exist. Is that clear?"

We both nodded without enthusiasm. Whatever we could say, he had us in the palm of his hand, and it would be foolish to ignore that fact.

*****

We returned to the headquarters in silence. Even Yamato didn't speak a word, still going over the fact that he let someone take him by surprise on duty. He had a reason to feel frustrated. As someone 'raised in the police', that is, the son of an officer who died in duty, he prepared for the profession from childhood. The two of us didn't have any complaints for him. Members of the global government have always been surrounded by the most trained people, unmatched security. They could easily approach someone much better than our driver, a great boy, who, however, did not show-off exceptional intelligence and was nicknamed 'Bear' for a reason. That is what he looked like – like a good, but clumsy bear. It's another thing that more than one criminal could already experience it, since Yamato possessed extraordinary physical strength and, if not for his innate gentleness, he could have become a formidable opponent.

Feri Kunch met us at the police station.

"Good thing you're finally back. We have a new case: a murder in the Naked House. Regular customers, everyone knows each other, the janitress swears that there was no one new or strange that day, but the corpse remains a fact."

"A naked fact," Hallie finished.

She sat on Kunch's desk, swinging her beautiful legs in the air and chewing gum, completely unafraid of the fact that the boss was back.

"Are any of ours there?" asked Cavanaugh, trying to ignore her. The impudent girl annoyed him more than once with her carelessness, but due to personnel problems in Lunnar, he could not afford to lose a messenger. Also, although he never admitted it, he really did like her.

"Chekov and Jones," Feri replied. "Hallie, would you take these materials and get them to the storeroom already?! And don't put them in the wrong binders, or I'll tear your legs off."

The girl stuck out her tongue at him, jumped off the table and, grabbing a large box lying on top of it, went to the evidence storeroom.

"Forgive me, inspector, you know how this one can be. Our new photographer is also on the spot, what's her name…"

"Connie Benedict," I helped him.

He nodded.

"She's doing the documentation."

"Well, no choice," Scott sighed, "we have to get there, too. We'll need to interrogate the visitors of this establishment."

"Maybe they'll at least put some clothes on for the occasion," I muttered in disgust.

"Wouldn't count on it. Where is Kelly?" he turned to Kunz.

"In the hospital, near Maru."

"Call him."

"I've tried already. His communicator and pager are both turned off."

"Then send Hallie to get him! Damn it, am I the only one here who can think?!"

Feri hurriedly went away from the desk, instinctively saluted and ran to the warehouse to get away from Scott's eyes... or rather, his visors. As usual, when our boss raised his voice, everyone hid in the corners. I may have been the only one he didn't terrify. Knowing about my own implants, I didn't feel any fear at the sight of his nightmarish prostheses, as if living their own lives. And maybe I knew him too well to be afraid of his shouting. I followed him in silence when he turned sharply towards the door.

The cultural phenomenon called 'Naked House' has always puzzled me. I couldn't understand the inner need to walk naked in the presence of other people, often ones who don't even know each other. It used to be called 'naturism', and beaches for people who didn't like tanners were everywhere. Then, when the ecological disaster became a reality, for a long time everyone had to wear clothes that covered almost the entire body, and relaxing by the water became something of an extreme sport. Even now, individual beaches are separated from the sea by a high fence, and no one goes there to sunbathe. That's what tanning beds are for. And so, naturism died a natural death.

The 'Naked Houses' were a bit more fortunate. Apparently, their origins are actually several hundred years old and once acted as perverse entertainment for the rich and bored. The opportunity to find themselves in a usually luxurious mansion, where all the regulars of both sexes walked around without any clothes, excited their degenerated senses. Today, when the human body is no longer considered a taboo, no one calls such preferences perversions, which doesn't mean that everyone likes them. Another thing is that no one forces anybody to go there.

Lunnar's 'Naked House' was on the side of a road, not far from the commercial area. Outwardly, nothing about it stood out. It didn't even have any markings on it, and if we didn't have the exact address, I doubt we would have found it. However, on the inside it didn't resemble anything that I had seen in person before. And not only because the entrance was an absurdly high room by the Moon's standards. It made me stop in place in surprise.

The wallpaper and upholstery alone must have cost a fortune. Purple, deep green, violet, navy blue and a large amount of gliding made me think of the National Museum, specifically the 'old traditions' sections – or more precisely, a section on the history of debauchery. Whoever decorated these rooms must have either had awful taste or was inspired by the late Middle Ages. I looked around, stunned, as Scott walked over to Chekov and Officer Jones. They were sitting against the wall, watching over the janitress – a pretty middle-aged woman. All she wore was an elaborate haircut and make-up smeared from tears.

"Where's the body?" he asked.

"First floor, room ten," Chekov replied. "I forbade anything to be moved, of course. I've locked the people in the dining room, Nat Fillert is watching over them. Benedict is going around the place with the cameras, taking pictures, but she knows what she shouldn't touch. Where's Kell?"

"He'll be here soon with the technicians, else I'll tear off his head, and both his legs before that," growled Scott. "Where are the stairs?"

The staircase was behind a masked door. Someone really wanted any unwanted guests to see only the entry room. The doors leading inside the building, of which there were four, were hidden behind wall coverings, so well disguised that no one would ever see them with the naked eye. Either way, they opened only after entering a code into a nearly invisible sensory panel on an opaque pane, so even an accidental discovery of the doors wouldn't be of much use.

"Holy smokes, it's looking like some damn brothel in here," I muttered as we climbed the colorfully carpeted stairs, bounded on both sides by carved and gilded balustrades. The hallway was as high as the entrance, and I realized that every room in this place must be this way.

"What's a brothel? A wolf breeding ground?" Cavanaugh asked.

"Well, how should I put it..." hesitated, because in this moment I had a certain superiority over my superior. As a librarian, I had access to books that the general public had never even seen, so I knew more about history of traditions than the general curriculum allowed. "In a time when sexuality was considered embarrassing, there were no Dating Centers, and there was a rule of faithfulness in marriage. As a rule, it applied mainly to wives, husbands had more freedom. Many men then paid women they didn't know to have a one-time opportunity to have casual sex with them."

"Nonsense!" Scott stopped and looked at me in amazement.

"No, it's the truth. Those were some dark times. Some women treated such activities simply as a profession, as paid work. Others were forced by ruthless criminals to earn money for them this way. That's the kind of people who created the brothels, these buildings where they kept the prostitutes, as they were called. Such places, the more expensive ones of course, often looked just like this. I've seen photos and engravings."

"That's sick."

"Yes, but it was very common, even in countries where such practices were prohibited by law. Now it's not because we have Dating Centers."

"And floresses," he mused. "Aren't they actually...?"

I denied it vehemently, offended by such an idea. After all, Mabel, my closest friend, was one, and I didn't want her to be compared to the harlots of the old days.

"It's true that today, when someone wants to hire a woman for company, they go to one of the Social Life Agency branches," I said, "but a girl hired there is not required to have sex with the person, even if sometimes people think of them that way. A floress must be educated, cultured, well-groomed, and taught etiquette appropriate to each group. You pay for her company for a limited period of time, not for matters in the bed. A prostitute wasn't allowed to protest, she had to serve as many customers as were brought to her. She was often beaten, suffering from drug addiction and, in case of disobedience, maimed or killed."

Scott flinched slightly. I understood how he must have felt on the mere thought of such a world. I felt the same way myself when I first learned of it. But well, it's a known fact that people were not always as enlightened and civilized as they are today, and now that was clear to me. It wasn't the right time or place, however, to start explaining it all to Scott.

First, we checked the dining area – a large room with a very long table and many chairs on both sides. Of course, it was adorned with the same senseless splendor as the rest of the house. On the chairs sat people of various ages, men and women, naked like newborns, all of them extremely nervous. Only Chekhov and Jones were fully clothed.

Seeing us, one of the naked people, a dark-haired, thin man, about two meters tall, got up and came up to us.

"The rules of this place prohibit anyone from wearing clothes," he said quietly but firmly, "you must respect our customs."

I was speechless.

"One more word and you'll be arrested for insulting an officer on duty," Scott replied coldly. "Please sit down and wait. You will all be interrogated and hopefully released, but first we need to see the crime scene."

He was cold and calm, as professional as always when he was doing business. He looked at the people gathered in the room as if there wasn't anything about them that stood out and they were dressed as normally as anyone. I, on the other hand, didn't know where to look, even though from early childhood I was taught, like everyone else, that the human body is not a reason for shame. Speaking of the body...

The corpse to which we were lead to lay in the room with the pool table, twisted in an unnatural position on a fluffy rug. The man's graying hair was drenched in blood, and his hands were cut and bruised. The murder weapon lay next to him – a long boat hook used to straighten the curtains. The heavy curtains hanging from the decorative cornices were meant to give the impression that there were large windows behind them, rather than the small armored glass portholes typical of lunar architecture. To move them apart by hand, one would have to climb on a ladder.

Connie Benedict was photographing the corner of the room with a Polaroid. She stopped at the sight of us and straightened up, greeting us impartially. Her boyish figure in a poorly fitted uniform was decorated with all kinds of cameras hanging on her like on a Christmas tree. In her hand she held several cardboard photographs – despite the undeniable superiority of digital technology in forensic science, the old technologies were still in use. They had their merits.

I answered with a vague murmur. I still didn't know her well, and thus far she didn't arouse my sympathy. Short and thin as a board, she had a flat face with an unpleasant expression, framed by tangled strands of hair. When it comes to her appearance, she was an even bigger slob than Sue Hereforth. As for her mind, none us of could even begin to guess so far. Nobody wanted to, and she didn't make it very encouraging. The eternally silent introvert didn't reveal her thoughts to anyone. In fact, she was extremely unsociable and most of all loved solitude. Although her talent for photography was undeniable, and she wasn't intimidated by neither the crime scenes nor by the corpses in various stages of decomposition.

"I'll be done soon, Inspector," she said in a bland tone. "I've documented the other rooms earlier."

"Why didn't you start from this room?" I asked.

"I was helping Officer Jones find any missing people," she explained. "Chekov was guarding this room, so I knew that outsiders wouldn't enter. I had time."

Cavanaugh leaned over the deceased and looked at him carefully. His implants popped out. He moved them around the deformed head of the corpse and its bloody face. As he straightened was silent for a moment. Then he grunted in a way that signaled both great confusion and a bit of amazement.

"This is attorney Cable," he said.

I flinched. Of all the people it could possibly be, the Attorney General of Lunnar, who was also the president of the city, is the last person I'd expect in such a place. On the other hand, he's a human being just like anyone else, so why shouldn't he be entitled to his own quirks? I also had to admit that Nick Cable didn't have a very good reputation anyway. Some said he drank often, or that he was seen at one of Lunnar's fly-aways. Well, a so-called immaculate person would probably not be found in such a place. However, he did quite a good job governing and performed the duties of a prosecutor with dignity.

Now he lay on the carpet of this richly decorated and incredibly tasteless room, dead as a stump and naked like a Turkish saint. I felt strange. Raised in respect of the law, from childhood I looked at the representatives of the legal profession with respect, considering them to be impeccable people and absolutely untouchable. There was something to that, because extremely strict regulations regarding the safety of government officials – police, military, and the judiciary – made attacks very rare. They simply weren't worth it.

However, attorney Cable was murdered, without any doubt. His skull was shattered, and the murder weapon lay next to him. Someone dared to commit an act unprecedented in the last century. Who? And why exactly? Cable was not the object of universal enmity, as was the case with some officials. I remembered well the cassus of the president of Chicago when I was ten years old. A man named Adrian Jesse turned out to be so inept, but at the same time arrogant and corrupt that in the end the townspeople wrote to the government to remove him from office. Due to a belated response, one day the whole of Chicago disobeyed the mayor's office. This had dramatic consequences. It turned out that an audit and the introduction of a state of emergency in the city and its environs for several weeks was necessary.

Of course, nothing like this ever happened in Lunnar. Nick Cable was considered a good manager and, at the same time, an attorney who didn't abuse his influence. Of course, not everyone liked him. If they had a guilty conscience, they simply couldn't. Overall, however, he was considered the right person in the right place. What happened was probably not a political issue but private retaliation. But whose? And for what reason?

I was standing there, trying to remember if anyone had threatened Cable and if there was any mention of his enemies in the police file when Dr. McCave appeared, accompanied by two technicians carrying all the necessary equipment to secure the traces.

"Oh, so you've finally decided to come," Scott snorted sarcastically. After a while, he softened his tone. "How is Constable Maru?"

"Better. She still has delusions sometimes, but she's better. Doctors say that she should be discharged from the hospital in about a week." Kelly ran his fingers through his hair and looked at the corpse. "Well, well, they sure took care of him. Modern criminals have no grace. All right, spread out and do what you have to... I mean, get testimony from whoever it's needed. We'll do the work here, it will take some time."

"Will I be needed again?" asked Connie Benedict, eloquently patting the camera.

The doctor glanced at her briefly.

"Stay a little longer," he decided after a moment's reflection. "You and your equipment might come in handy. Just don't get in our way. And you two, get out."

"Did you take my place as the commander, or did I miss something?" Scott growled but walked away. He knew, as we all did, that when our coroner starts working, he becomes overbearing and unpleasant, and that it's best not to interfere with him.

I followed after him. The thought of having to interview all the naked people was both funny and unpleasant, but it didn't seem like I'd be able to avoid it. Scott Cavanaugh was in favor of interrogating all suspects' right where they were arrested so that they did not have time to prepare any excuses. Upon the arrest of a large group, as is the case today, it was important not to let the suspects talk to each other. This is what Chekhov and Jones were making sure of now, rather than just locking the whole group in one of the rooms and doing something more constructive.

As I suspected, our detainees firmly refused putting on clothes, as long as they were inside the Naked House. We had no choice but to interrogate each of them as they were. It wasn't fun. Many would surely be wondering why, since the naked body, as people are taught from childhood, is a work of art. However, this is not exactly the type of art that I would like to see. Most of the patrons of this establishment were neither young nor built like models, so the aesthetic impressions, I had to admit, were quite mediocre. In addition, many of them acted unnecessarily defiantly, trying to provoke us into something that could be attributed as 'behavior unworthy of an officer on duty'. Both Scotty and I had to keep ourselves in check in order to not react in a way we'd later regret.

By the time we finished, we were both exhausted and irritated, making no progress in our investigation. If our suspects were telling the truth – and according to the standard detectors we had in our inventory, they weren't lying – it couldn't have been any of them who committed the crime. And yet someone did it. Someone committed manslaughter and disappeared. The janitress didn't see him, the sensors on the doors and windows didn't register anything. There were no cameras inside, which seemed quite logical given the type of locale this was, but in this situation it made our work more difficult. Much more.

So far, we have had no reason to arrest even a single person from amongst the patrons of this outlandish place. None of them had any traces of the deceased's blood, none of them lied, which we confirmed at the police station. The specific circumstances justified the use of the scopolamine test, and everyone passed it with flying colors. The scans also ruled out the possibility of any of them being implanted with a neutralizing implant, so the likelihood that they were telling the truth was quite high.

Busy with obtaining testimony from people refusing to cooperate, and then with paper work, it was only after some delay that I realized that what happened will have much more serious consequences than it initially seemed.

It wasn't just some ordinary person who was killed, it was the chief prosecutor of Lunnar, which already seemed quite unfortunate. But that's not all. The city has also lost its president of many years, tested in difficult situations. Now we had to notify governor Khamala and, of course, Earth. All this will have serious consequences, and if we don't find the criminal quickly, we – that is, the colony's police force – will have really big problems.

After letting the last investigator go home, we were finally able to go to the lab where Dr. McCave examined Cable's body. We found our pathologist sitting on a high stool and reverently smoking a thin cigar. This is the first time since my arrival on the Moon that I have seen such a scene. Tobacco was a luxury item even on Earth, where prices for it reached dizzying heights.

Scott was amazed too, so much that his visors protruded about an inch.

"Where did you get this, Kell?" he asked.

The doctor exhaled a ball of smoke from his mouth and only then replied:

"He had it in the inner pocket of his jacket," I also examined his clothes.

"Do you realize that what you've done...?"

"...is highly unethical," he added nonchalantly. "I know, and I don't care. He no longer needs it, and I have not smoked for four years. I forgot how good it feels."

The inspector shrugged in resignation.

"Will you at least tell us what you've found?"

Kelley nodded.

"The deceased's health was so-so. He loved junk food and alcohol, so his liver was badly worn out. The heart was also in poor condition, but it wasn't anything serious. The intestines are full of fecal residues, so he was constipated. Left kidney was with onset of calyx degeneration. He probably didn't have any obvious symptoms yet, so I doubt he was aware of anything. He could still live for a while. What else... the lungs had residues typical of passionate smokers. The contents of the testicles indicated that he has been neglecting his sexual hygiene for a long time."

"He was divorced."

"That doesn't excuse him. Overall, this shows that he avoided doctors and lived the way he wanted. It had to end badly."

He inhaled the smoke again and exhaled a ball of bluish smoke through his mouth.

"He also had a sewn in implant," he added. "I still don't know what it contained. I'll figure that out."

Cavanaugh tapped his fingers on the freshly washed autopsy table for a moment.

"What killed him? Because I'm sure it wasn't his testicles...?"

"You're funny, Scotty. A denture of the parietal bone and damage to the occipital bone, an extensive cerebral hemorrhage. The angle of the impact is unusual. And that's not the only thing."

"What do you mean?"

The doctor inhaled the cigar's smoke again.

"A person capable of delivering this blow would have to have been four meters tall," he replied. "Or stand on a tall piece of furniture. There is no such thing in the pool table room."

"Any other revelations?"

"Yes. Golden rain. Mr. Cable had it in his blood and respiratory system. And he's not the only one. I checked several blood samples from our detainees. They're taking that filth too. I could bet that rest of the samples will have same results."

Scott looked surprised, but it didn't surprise me at all. It was to be expected that desiring unusual experiences, the prosecutor would probably lock himself in that place, or perhaps go 'undercover' to one of Lunnar's fly-aways. It at least guaranteed safety and immediate medical attention in case of problems. After all, anything could happen. Cable was not an idiot, he would've known that."

"What about the photographs?" I asked.

"Connie is getting the digital ones ready. I've got the polaroids in the room with the negatoscope."

One would think that small, cardboard photographs are useless in this day and age, but they weren't. Most of all, the resolution of modern cameras is so high that our ancestors, for whom Polaroids itself were a novelty, would find them unbelievable. Even the simplest camera today offers a resolution of billions of pixels, making it possible to design magnifiers without losing sharpness. With today's technical capabilities, few people liked to use these for personal purposes, but they quickly became indispensable in police work.

We spent the next hours inserting photographs into the macroscope and carefully examining the details of the pool table room. This included the photographs of the corpse and murder weapon. Only now were we able to correctly judge certain things, and one thing immediately struck us: the angle between the corpse and the bloody boat hook. There was something unnatural about it. Just like the fact it wasn't cleaned. Sure, there was probably no need to bother, it's obvious that it must have had the fingerprints of anyone who manipulated the curtains. One could ask why they were hanging there at all. There were no windows behind them. The 'Naked House' did not need them.

The curtains had a completely different purpose. They covered the adjacent rooms, where you could play cards, pool or table tennis in private. They were uncovered each time the club held a larger competition. By sliding the curtains to the sides, it was possible to create one large room for the players and the audience. That's what the boat hook was for. It was available to all members from the list, one hundred and fifty-seven people in total. There were twenty-six of them on site at the time of the incident, and we would probably find fragments of prints from all of them.

The point is that the killer's fingerprints should be superimposed on them and available in an identifiable state. Even a moderately knowledgeable person should know this and should have therefore wiped the object. Meanwhile, nothing of that sort happened. Many intersecting fingerprints were taken with the greatest possible care, obtaining also bits of cuticle, but it was difficult to get our hopes up about this. Leaving the murder weapon with such carelessness could only indicate one thing – that it wouldn't help us in the investigation.

Ahead of us was a difficult journey.

III

The sound of a cheerful conversation in the living room surprised me so much that I froze in the corridor with the remote in my hand. Sue wasn't a very social person, and since we moved in together, she hadn't invited a single person to our apartment. She didn't really talk to Monty either – while she accepted his presence in our lives, she treated him more like a piece of furniture than a rational being. She didn't get into conversations with him, and the fact that I do she treated with leniency, like a harmless quirk.

When I looked into our living room, I saw an unexpected guest. Chris was sitting in one of the armchairs, a mug of tea in his hand, joking with a cheerful Sue. Her round but usually pale cheeks flushed pink, possibly under the influence of the wine, the bottle rolling freely on the table. Monty was standing near them, his arms down, and I would swear he was watching them with an examining look.

"Hello, sister," Chris called when he saw me. "How are you?

"Hello, Chris," I kissed him heartily on his puckered cheek. "It's nice of you to visit. Has the construction started yet?"

"It will start in two months. The whole team is already deploying wherever they can. I'm working conceptually half the time, so I rented an apartment in this house, instead of getting a flat in a workers' hotel. The way to work is quite long, but the lunar high-speed capsules shorten the distance."

The so-called LFC – short for Lunnar Fast Capsules – they are been transporting workers to the largest mines since the beginning of the colony's operation. Due to the geometry of the connections, they are also known as star communication. They moved through the airless lava tunnels, in a straight line from the center of Lunnar to their destination, but people didn't like them that much. Air tunnels were more popular because they formed a network similar to terrestrial highways. You could travel through them, changing the route if necessary and, in the event of a communication disaster, survive until help arrives. A crash of the capsule could cost the lives of all who traveled in it.

Nevertheless, the LFCs were irreplaceable – very efficient, cheap, and fast as the wind. From what Chris had told me, it seems that they've already made a tunnel from the center to the place indicated under Selenoport, which meant construction was about to start. I myself was curious how the finished complex would look like. For my brother, it was an important step in his professional career. Very important.

"I'm glad that you'll live next door," I said. I found a clean cup and poured myself some tea, too. "I missed our chats."

"Me too," he smiled carelessly, winking at me as he used to when we agreed to play a prank on our friends from the neighborhood. "Thanks to the construction, we'll be living close to each other for some time: me, you, your android, and this nice lady."

Sue chuckled. She didn't even try to hide that she liked Chris. It made me happy, though, to both of our disappointments, my brother was paying more attention to Monty than to her. He was an engineer, so it wasn't surprising

"I spoke to your android a little," he said. "He is a real work of art. I would like to have a few words with his creator."

"Talk to her uncle," I pointed at Sue. "He could arrange that for you."

He suddenly became gloomy.

"No, better not. No offense, Sue, but I'd rather not deal with your uncle more than necessary."

She shook her head with a superiority, not fitting her childish face at all.

"Why are you all so afraid of him?" she looked at me. "Leeta, get another bottle out of the bar. If we're going to celebrate, let's do it right."

"No way," I objected energetically. "I can't drink right now at all, since the investigation is underway, and I don't even know what day or hour it is. Both of you have had enough, too. You can get some caffetino at best."

From the cabinet, I took out a bag of real Brazilian coffee. I received it as a birthday present from the rector of the Medical Academy and was saving it for a special occasion. And what better occasion than the fact that Chris and I will be living nearby again? Only now did I realize how much I missed him. I had a lot of questions, but I decided that there would be time for that later when he was sober and in another place. Although Sue was a friend of mine and I really liked her, we didn't grow up together and there were topics that she just didn't need to hear about.

We drank with pleasure, slowly sipping the fragrant infusion. Real coffee was now so expensive that not everyone could afford it, definitely not a librarian, not a female police officer, not even an engineer or a virtualist as good as Sue. Oddly enough, since I got to the Moon, I've been thinking more and more about how much natural food has become unavailable for ordinary citizens. Perhaps these considerations were related to the fact that the inhabitants of Lunnar didn't have the earthly system of monthly allocation 'rawness', as we called it in childhood. I remembered the small-leaved salad Cynthia used to serve with a sprinkle of vinegar and an artificial sweetener. Thinly sliced apples pitted cherries, grapes distributed among us by several berries for each. A wonderful thing.

Natural fruits and vegetables came to the Moon only in processed form, and the most expensive delicacy, meat, was marinated. Fish and shellfish were cultivated mainly on water farms. The rich couldn't order everything they wanted, even if they were on a whim. On the other hand, simple workers, due to a constant shortage of employees, earned enough to sometimes visit an exclusive restaurant. Unfortunately, they were more likely to visit fly-aways and illegal casinos. Either way, what else could they do with their pepes in such a place? Lunnar was egalitarian in its own way.

Monty didn't drink anything, of course. He just looked at us, as if observing a subject of research. I knew that this was just an illusion, but someone who didn't know this and didn't know the general theory of androids would likely feel uncomfortable. Books and films about rogue robots were very popular among young people, and I, too, once indiscriminately devoured them. Now I had more knowledge on the subject than many cybernetics experts, and all thanks to engineer Karpinsky – or should I call him a doctor? He was an engineer, but also had a PhD in neurophysiology. I didn't know what to call him.

The fundamental difference between the human mind and what is in the head of an android is motivation," he wrote to me. "People *are controlled by impulses of biochemical nature, and their behavior is conditioned by evolution. It was an evolution that taught us to look back even in a safe environment and explore everything with our senses. Androids lack the typically human characteristics, such as curiosity. If they are watching something, it is only in order to adapt. Not to learn for the sake of their own desire to have information. This is the domain of humanity. We are not only users but also data collectors, of which ninety-five percent will never be useful to us. However, we cannot stop collecting them. An android only learns what it considers useful.*

Monty's polymer eyes could have misled an outside observer. But I knew the truth. My companion was only waiting in case he is needed by us. He couldn't exist for himself. Another weakness of androids and another difference from humans. Their existence must have a specific purpose, otherwise, they stop doing anything. A human, even if they have no goals, will create one for himself. The human mind is flexible. Artificial intelligence, although it thinks independently, cannot create, it only recreates.

I won't be able to create an artist android, even though I can give it dexterous hands, sight with the highest resolution, perfect pitch, and an ultra-sensitive tone sensor. If it tries very hard, it can perfectly copy a painting by Rembrandt or Picasso, make a copy of a sculpture by Michelangelo, or play the Moonlight Sonata in imitation of any piano master. However, will not create anything unique. The clay in his hands will remain as just dirt if it does not receive a ready-made pattern. The violin will be a tool for transferring the learned sounds and not a generator of the deepest emotions. I'm unable to break from this limitation. Perhaps, my successors, one day can.

I don't know whether Monty was aware that there is something he can't compete with people in. However, I doubt that he would consider it worth paying attention to. The desire to compete was also alien to him. But he did have his own desires, and one of them was... my company. I didn't understand this, and Karpinsky couldn't explain it either, but Monty felt a connection with me. Strong enough to keep seeking my company and to see his own existence as aimless without me. If he were an ordinary robot, it wouldn't have mattered to him. However, he was a rational being. I couldn't program him to exhibit a different kind of behavior, let alone a different attitude to the world.

*****

Up until now, I've never seen the governor of the Moon's colony. There was no need for me to visit him. After all, I didn't even know the mayors of Lunwark and Lunchester in the factory districts adjacent to the Lunnar Center, voted for during the last elections. In fact, I saw prosecutor Cable for the first time at the Naked House, I have never met him before. Even more so, I didn't visit him in the town hall. Simply put, he was way over my head. And the president of the city ranks lower than Solo Khamala, the governor appointed by the earth's government.

I figured that Scott Cavanaugh had taken me to the governor's mansion with him for no particular reason, perhaps so he wouldn't have to go there with Yamato alone. Only Kelley dispelled my naive doubts. When I asked about it, he looked at me as if I was retarded.

"Woman, he is preparing you to be his deputy," he said with pity. "That's his goal."

"Are you serious?" I got scared.

"Did you really not realize that? Scott's former deputy, Ted Levesque, had died in the line of duty before you joined us. He hasn't had any since then, but it looks like he has found a candidate for this position. Congratulations."

"Me?! That's absurd," the very thought was so nonsensical that it made me dizzy.

"Maybe for you. Seriously, Scotty knows a lot about people and always knows exactly which horse to bet on."

Seeing that I was not convinced at all, he added:

"Maybe you can't see your advantages, but he sees them. Trust him."

Even if he knew what he was saying, it didn't bring me any comfort at all. I didn't feel strong enough to fulfill some higher role and was terrified that I'm failing Scott's trust. I decided to talk to him about it as soon as I could.

For now, it wasn't time for these discussions. We had to visit the governor at his personal request – and be very careful about what we say. Solo Khamala was known to be tough, uncompromising who was not easily daunted by others. There was a lot that depended on him, and while Citizen Hakat could naturally sweep him away with one move of his hand, he did take his position into account. He didn't care at all about having to replace the most important person on the Moon, so we had to be careful that Khamala did not unknowingly endanger the interests of the Chief of Arms. We would all be in trouble then.

The governor's residence was located on the south side Lunnar. I have only seen it from afar before. Surrounded by a number of security measures, guarded by the army and internal guards, it was closed to outsiders. Sometimes elite representatives were invited to a party or a private meeting in this small but well-fortified fortress. But no one knew if Khamala himself ever leaves its walls. He certainly wasn't doing it officially. He only attended any necessary meetings through a video link. From what I've heard, he would sometimes go on a trip like the second Harun Al Rashid, dressed as a worker or clerk, and he would go around among ordinary people watching the city life. At least that's what the rumors said, nobody knew the truth.

Yamato dropped us off at the residence. After that, we had to rely on the governor's guard. We were scanned, our weapons were deposited, and then we were invited further. We had to pass two more guard lines, at each of which, again we were probed with detectors with equal care as if the earlier ones might have neglected their duty. Only after all that were we able to ring the doorbell of a low building, built from armored plates.

A beautiful Japanese woman in a long dress, stylized as an antique kimono, opened the door for us. I've never seen a similar material or pattern. I could have sworn that the embroidery – orchid flowers rendered with striking accuracy – was applied by hand, something no one has done in ages. I've heard that there are still families out there, cultivating a skill that was useless in current times, passing on old techniques from generation to generation. As for the material itself, I wasn't sure how or what it was made of. If I hadn't known with certainty that silkworms are a long-extinct species, I would have sworn that it was made from natural silk.

I took my gaze off the dress with difficulty and moved it to the face of its owner, smooth, gentle, and smiling. Her beautiful head was adorned with a *shimada*[3] haircut, which only reinforced the feeling that I was facing an aristocrat from Edo[4].

"Come in, honored guests," she said politely, "the governor and I have been expecting you."

Scotty bowed and I followed.

---

[3] A type of female hairstyle in Japan of the samurai era.

[4] The capital of former Japan.

"Hello, Mrs. Khamala."

"I do not carry this honorary name, I am only a contracted friend of the governor. Please call me Raiha. And come in, let's not stand in the doorway."

I've read that in the countries of the East, the institution of a friend by contract is regarded as an official cohabitation, almost like a marriage. The only difference is that with such 'friends' you can have more than one. Therefore, I was not surprised when, entering the house, I saw two more girls in the spacious living room. They were kneeling in front of a low, wide table stacked with oriental snacks. They looked very young, probably still underage, pretty, smiling, and dressed with the same refined elegance as Raiha. My attention was immediately drawn to the makeup on their faces, which made the teenagers look like twin dolls and was indeed too strong for their age. They both stood up and bowed to us almost simultaneously.

"Hello, ladies..." Scott stopped in the doorway, hastily removing his shoes.

I did the same. Now that we were entering a clearly oriental-style house, it was time to adapt.

"This is Megumi and Miniko Ichisawa," Raiha said, gracefully pointing at the girls, "the governor's nieces who have lived in this house since childhood and treat him like their father."

I involuntarily blushed thinking about what kind of stupidity I could have done if I made an inappropriate remark.

At the same time, I began to sense a certain tone of falseness in this scene, or rather, of staging. I couldn't imagine anyone these days seriously living in a Japanese style from a long-gone era. I smelled a discreet aroma of incense. In the corners were openwork screens made of rice paper, on the floor was a woven rug, on the walls engravings of the old masters along with hand fans. Chrysanthemums in decorative vases. It felt more like a show for guests, a way to charm and intimidate them. I looked at Scott. His face was completely blank and expressionless. I already knew him well enough to know that he, like me, was now doubly alert.

According to tradition, we both thoroughly washed our hands and faces in a tiny sink behind a screen in the corner of the living room. After washing up, we knelt down in places indicated for us, or should I say, sat down in a Japanese style. At this very moment, at an almost theatrically perfect moment, a door in one of the walls slid open and the governor entered the living room.

Judging by his appearance, he didn't look Japanese. He looked more like a Filipino or Javanese phenotype – a bit corpulent, with a square face and very dark skin, black hair curled in old-fashioned dreadlocks. Unlike the women, he has dressed with artificials nonchalance. Shorts, sandals, a Hawaiian floral shirt. He looked as if he had just returned from a pool or a tennis court.

"Welcome to my home," he said with false cordiality as he sat down at the head of the table, "before we get to more serious matters, I'd like to invite you to a humbly dinner."

I looked at the table. It was rather the opposite of modest. Although the quantity of each dish was rather symbolic, the quality took my breath away. Hardly anyone could afford such an exquisite feast. The snacks themselves must have cost a fortune, while the fruit reigning in the center of the table were cut into small triangles melon, mango and papaya, black grapes, greenhouse raspberries, inside of each piece or berry was a wooden skewer. In some diplomatic banquet, such a luxury would make sense, but for the sake of two simple police officers? Something here didn't seem right.

The 'humble dinner' lasted an eternity. In keeping with the Eastern tradition, we ate slowly, savoring and delivering neutral comments about the weather, fashion trends, and the city's development prospects. This was only the second time that I've had the opportunity to use chopsticks while eating, but luckily I managed. Khamala's nieces did not eat. They entertained us with talking, reading poetry, and playing the shamisen, which was very old and definitely did not come from mass production. It took me a while before I finally remembered the term for women, of whose role they were playing for us: geishas. I felt more and more confused. I sat motionless on my heels and tried not to disrespect the etiquettes. Thankfully, at least I knew about it from the old books.

At last, the blessed time came when, after drinking the customary cup of sake, Khamala got up and invited us to his office. I was relieved to see that it is arranged in a completely normal manner and could be found in any municipal office. There was even a simple rug on the floor, and photographs of important people adorned the walls. Next to the heavy table were soft chairs with folded backs.

"Sit down," the governor said, pointing to the chairs.

Upon crossing the office's threshold, he left behind the tone of a worldly man and of the sybarite which he took on when talking to us at the table, and he now began speaking normally. We sat down. Khamala himself sat down on a chair on the other side of the table.

"Well, tell me everything now. How is the investigation into the death of Nick Cable progressing?"

I looked at Scott. He shifted in his chair.

"We are doing our best," he replied vaguely, "it's a difficult case."

"That much I know. Do you already have a suspect selected? "

"No," Cavanaugh said reluctantly. "For some time we were even inclined to classify this death as an unfortunate accident."

"Maybe it was so?" Khamala asked hopefully. At the thought, his narrow eyes flashed.

"No, it was not. Certain clues pointed towards it, but the accident theory quickly fell apart. Believe me that is not in our favor either."

I thought about the hours I spent in the laboratory. Together with Connie and the doctor, we went through hundreds of photographs, endlessly analyzing every square inch of the resulting image. All because of McCave's unexpected judgments.

"After reexamining the body and the murder weapon," he said, "I'm sure that boat hook wasn't dropped on Cable's head by the force of a human arm, but fell by inertia. Plus-minus from under the ceiling."

Initially, we found he was fantasizing. After all, boat hooks do not fly around. After looking at the entire pool table room inch by inch and drawing about a dozen blood splatter drawings, which took us two days of work, we agreed with him. At first, we felt relief (that the case could be closed, being an accident, not a murder), but it was short-lived. After interrogating the Naked House receptionist again, we found out that the tool always hung from the ceiling, as we thought, but it was held by a clamping mechanism, closed on a metal hook. To unlock it, you had to pick up the boat hook and slide it left and right twice. Otherwise, it would not be possible to take it off. The boat hook couldn't fall down by itself.

"We looked at the crime scene again," Scotty said. "Our pathologist's opinion was clear, but the testimony of the receptionist and the club guests seemed to contradict it. After examining the ceiling cornice, on which the boat hook hung, we discovered something unusual. The empty places were literally packed with electronics. There were cameras and a remote control system. The locking mechanism was released when Cable's head was at the right angle. Someone was observing him, and then in just the right time... bang!"

Khamala rubbed his soft, thick lips with his finger.

"Someone came up with a pretty elaborate plan," he muttered.

"Exactly. Governor, we need your permission to search prosecutor Cable's home. If we're going to catch the killer, we'll need all the clues we can get, and there might be something in there."

The governor was silent for a long time.

"I liked Cable," he said finally. "He was smart and overall a good man. We were almost friends. But he was struggling with something that drove him from Earth. If I forbid you to rummage through his things, you will never catch the killer. And if I let you, you could find something that... shouldn't be leaked to the media."

"What could that be?" I blurted out. Scott stepped on my foot significantly.

Khamala was not looking at me. His eyes were fixed on the desktop while his fingers drummed on top of it. It was obvious that he was gathering up to say something that he didn't want to say.

"It's not so simple," he said finally. "Nick once turned to me for help. You must understand that in a legal sense he didn't do anything wrong. But by chance, his... rather unusual preferences came to light."

"How unusual?" Scotty asked sharply. His vigilance increased immediately, and I sensed it without much effort.

"Nick was perfectly normal in every way. Except for one thing. He was only sexually attracted to little girls."

I shuddered. Scotty stiffened.

"He never hurt any of them," the governor continued. "He knew he had a problem, and as a civilized man, he knew how to control it. He was treated chemically, visited a psychologist, and even tried to start a normal family. Nobody in the immediate vicinity knew about anything until a fire broke out in his house. While extinguishing it, the firefighters came across, well, inappropriate pictures and videos. A week later, Nick was on the Moon."

"Well, there aren't any little girls here, and never have been," Cavanaugh muttered.

"As I understand it, you're trying to say that we should hide any potential findings of this type from outsiders?" I asked coldly.

"Yes. That's exactly right," he got up and began pacing nervously around the office. "It's not just about Nick's memory, because that's silly. Cheap sentimentality. The dead have no feelings to hurt, and the family has long since disowned him. It's more important not to undermine the citizens' trust in power. It would have bad repercussions to expose such inclinations to someone who was the local palestra representative and city president. And there could be various things on his computer... irrelevant to the investigation, but compromising nonetheless. Better that they don't fall into the wrong hands."

There was silence. I didn't know what to say, Scott considered what he heard.

"We can't promise anything, Governor," He said finally, "if our finds really are irrelevant to the investigation, they won't see the light of day either way. But if they are..."

The understatement was all too understandable. Khamala paused, turned his eyes to my boss, and for a moment their gazes crossed in the air like swords in battle.

"What connection could they possibly have?" he asked finally in a low, almost growling voice.

I understood immediately what was going on. Years in the office made Khamala unable to bear opposition, especially from people who, in his opinion, were as insignificant as we were. Since he said that these things were not important, we should nod and treat it like the undeniable truth. Especially if he was kind enough to welcome them like diplomats or prominent entrepreneurs, which he intended to be proof of outright generosity. Such thinking proved that he never had the chance to meet Scott Cavanaugh before.

"I don't draw conclusions before seeing the evidence," my boss said coldly, "so don't expect me to do so this time. I asked for an audience mainly out of courtesy, because you must be aware that I could have used my special rights. However, I prefer to take the traditional route, as long as I have a choice."

The governor was silent for a long moment, clearly trying to control himself. The opposition of the Lunnar police chief was the last thing he expected. Certain that the elegant takeover would dazzle and intimidate us both, he went with it, with no plan B at hand. He could only stand and stare at Scott with a murderous gaze.

The silence went on for a few seconds, then Khamala took a deep breath in an attempt to control himself

"I understand, inspector," he said. "I don't expect you to break procedures, I only ask for some caution in selecting the evidence which is disclosed to the public."

Scotty got up.

"Don't worry, Governor. I usually don't reveal anything to the media unless I have to. Thank you for the nice welcome party, but I and Agent Ankes have a lot of work."

I stood up too, obeying the gaze of his visors. The audience apparently ended, even if it had turned out differently than the initiator had intended. I knew there was nothing the governor could do to us now, but I felt a little apprehensive nonetheless. I didn't like something about all this, and Scott – as far as I could tell – didn't either.

Khamala restrained his emotions forcibly and an almost sincere smile appeared on his broad lips.

"I hope that you didn't misunderstand my words," he said with forced joviality, "and that we will still be on good terms."

"Of course. As long as you stand on the side of the law," Scott replied. "Does that mean we'll receive permission to search the deceased's apartment?"

"You'll have it in a moment. I never said I wouldn't do it."

He took an official computer foil from the drawer and quickly wrote out the document we needed, confirming it with an electronic stamp of the office and his own, worn on the finger in the form of a signet. We looked at him distrustfully, prepared for any surprises, although everything indicated that he wasn't going to do anything.

"Thank you," Scott took the piece of foil handed to him "I assure you that we will not exceed the powers of the police, and I will personally make sure that no unauthorized person has access to the collected evidence."

"That's all I'm hoping for."

We left the house on soft legs. We were expecting a shot in the back or a blow to the head the whole time, and even though we didn't talk to each other, we sensed our mutual thoughts and fears. But nothing happened. We were driven in a melex to the gate, where Yamato, biting his nails with nervousness, was waiting.

"And?" he asked when he saw us, distrustfully measuring the eyes of the guards walking us away.

"Shit," Scotty grumbled. "Easy with the curiosity, you'll hurt your stomach. Get in, Leeta, what are you standing there for?"

Only when we moved away from the governor's house did we dare to breathe.

"What do you think about that guy?" Scott asked, looking at me.

"That he's slippery like a fish straight from the water," I replied angrily. "The whole time we were there, I felt shivers down my back. I feel sorry for those women who live with him."

He threw up his arms.

"Can't be that bad, otherwise they'd leave him. Although... there is definitely something I don't like about him. That whole party, the setting, it all felt fake."

I looked at him questioningly.

"Do you think Khamala is hiding something?"

"That's nothing surprising. Every politician has something hidden behind their ears. But there is definitely something here that stinks, and it stinks really badly," he took a deep breath. "We have to do our usual police work, that's all."

"Did you get permission to search? " Interrupted Yamato.

"Yes, we did..." said Scotty thoughtfully and suddenly offered: "You know what, Ted? Take us straight to Cable's house."

"Right now?!"

"Yes, right now. What do we have to wait for?"

I understood what he meant.

"We have no equipment."

"Ted will pick it up. And Benedict too. We may need her. Did you hear me, Yamato? Destination: Union of Nations Avenue."

IV

Prosecutor Cable's apartment was in one of the several exclusive homes occupied by the corporate leaderships and other VIPs of the Moon. It made an enclosed residential area with their own guards. The ordinary inhabitants of Lunnar were not allowed there, of course, but that didn't affect the army or the police, of course. I haven't been here before, I only heard that there really are no special amenities there. Hah, maybe there aren't, but I had to admit that the manor was furnished with taste.

The houses were built on the plan of an oval. The square in the middle served as a recreational area. It was surrounded with synthetic trees of such high quality that they could fool anyone but an expert – and they sure fooled me. I had to touch the bark and leaves to make sure they weren't living plants. A videoart imitation of a fountain gushed in the center. A camouflaged closed-loop sprayer constantly spread real water onto a wide, flat pool, the bottom of which returned precious liquid back to the pump. The entire square was paved with polished granite – it may not be an extreme rarity on the Moon, but it was enough to be extravagant.

One of the guards looked at our IDs, then examined the Governor's papers. Only after making sure that they were genuine, he took us to the prosecutor's office, to which he had a copy of the access card. I had a feeling that he still thought letting us in was like breaking some sacred rules, but he wasn't stupid enough to say it out loud.

"We seem rather unwelcome here," I muttered as he left.

"Well, the agreement was clear. When they built the estate, it was established that the investigation of disputes should be conducted by the internal security, and in criminal cases they conduct searches and give evidence to the police. Of course, a crime like this was not foreseen," Scott surveyed the apartment, less impressive than expected, but still extensive.

It was made partly as an office, which was understandable given Nick Cable's social function. The living area looked surprisingly modest, the office area consisted mostly of computers and folders. On the walls hung diplomas with IQ test scores and 'conferment' – written evidence of Cable's appointment to subsequent positions. He must have been very proud of them. We had to review everything and document our every step so that nothing could be challenged in court.

"You know what, Leeta?" Scott opened the drawer of a heavy desk and began to methodically scan its contents. "I'm starting to make some connections."

"What kind?" I started one of the computers and started cracking the password. Sue's teachings turned me into a real hacker, and in many cases, I could do it without her help.

"It's too early to talk about it. But if I'm right, we're going to have an earthquake... or rather, a moonquake. My brother-in-law will be shocked," he chuckled as if the prospect had lifted his spirits.

From the drawer, he took a small vial of dark plastic, the so-called 'nostril', because the shape of its neck was adapted to the shape of a typical human nostril.

"What is that?"

"I have no idea. Some dust. We'll have to analyze it, but even without that I have a bad feeling about it."

I had to agree with him. Even if this gadget was evidence in some cases, the prosecutor should not have kept it in his home.

"Now the question: has your floress friend recovered yet?" Scott stowed the vial away and continued rummaging through the drawers.

"Mabel? I think so. The last time I spoke to her, she was calmer. Why?"

"I have to talk to her, too. I should have done this a long time ago, but you know how it is."

I turned away from the computer.

"She won't testify against Hakat if that's what you mean."

He shook his head and smiled wryly.

"That's not what I want. Much braver than that girl would refuse to confess or disrespect the Chief of Arms. I just want to talk."

"What for?"

"Oh, you know, you'll find out in due time. What do you have there?"

"Nothing yet."

I went back to work reluctantly. The computer I was examining was for private use, and as such, it interested me the most. There must have been files of Cable's cases on his official machines, but it was in the private one that he probably kept something for which he got killed. There must have been something like that. And to find it, I had to search through the entire hard drive. Sue would probably have handled it better and faster than I could, except that she could not participate in the search without law enforcement authorization. Whether I liked it or not, I had only myself to break the successive access codes with which the prosecutor protected his private files.

It was immediately obvious that he did not use the help of an expert virtualist, and did everything himself. The codes were good but not extraordinary. Although I was far from being a data hacker, I was slowly breaking through it and opening access at all levels. Meanwhile, Scott was rummaging around the apartment and at one point came across a standard wall safe.

"Oh, this might be interesting," he said, looking at it.

"We'll have to call the electronics engineers," I said.

"No need," from his watch's strap, he took a keyring, which he always had with him. He said it was 'for good luck' just an ordinary little thing in the shape of a huddled monkey. You can buy one at any souvenir shop.

He adjoined the smoothly sanded bottom part of the keyring to the control panel reader.

"What are you doing?" I asked in surprise, stopping my work.

"Opening the safe," he said. "It's an electrical pulse emitter. They automatically adapt to the rhythm that opens the device."

I was speechless.

"Is that legal?"

"Of course not. Are you going to rat me out?"

I shook my head disapprovingly. This was not the first time Scott had used an illegal gadget, and he saw nothing wrong with it.

The safe played a little melody and the door opened. Scotty opened it full width and whistled in amazement.

"What do we have here?"

He began to take out the contents and put them on the chair.

"Allocation cards with different names, mortgage receipts, and that's... quite a stock."

The box taken out of the safe contained miniature closed foil bags and probably several dozens of those 'nostrils'.

"I bet it is golden rain. The lab will confirm. What else..."

The few next very strange objects: heavy crowbars, knives, pieces of glass, and metal, each protected with foil.

"Do you understand what all this is?" I asked, confused.

"Seems like a small evidence repository. Nothing of the kind, of course, should be in a private apartment."

"What would he need all this for?"

"We'll find out when the technicians investigate."

I went back to the computer, which had just accepted the encryption program I had entered. Another moment and its contents were revealed to me. In the end, I realized that what Scott did with the safe wasn't much different from what I did here. We both used means which contradicted the law. I sighed and focused on browsing its contents. It was obvious that most of the files were photos and videos. Remembering Khamala's words, I didn't really want to open them, but I had to do it.

Some of it was related to Cable's cases. It seemed that they were not included in the official files, but were stashed away by the prosecutor for some purpose known only to him. It was quite unexpected to find amongst these things the tapes of Hermine Arango, the killer of my first investigation. He worked for the Horus Corporation, although he was also vaguely associated with the Romain Corporation... and with Harry Johnson, Cable's deputy. In all this chaos, I completely forgot about him, only after seeing this was I reminded.

From the recordings, it indicated that Johnson met with Arango while we were looking for him, and his boss was well informed about it. And this was not an isolated incident. At one point, I also found a transcript of an interview with Marceline Munro, as well as photographs of George Torres, an agent who died shortly after my arrival on the Moon. I could link some of the other records to what I knew, others would be clear to Scott for sure. Either way, I looked through everything. All of these files had to be carefully copied and analyzed on professional equipment. I had a feeling that they would shed new light on more than one of our investigations.

Without going deep into the content of the files, I started comparing their size and quality. I suspected that some of them might contain more than secret records of meetings or material exposing the Moon's celebrities. I have come across this method of storing valuable files before, and have sometimes used it myself when sending sensitive data to Earth. Sue was a good teacher. Before the flight to the Moon, I had no idea about the techniques of virtualism, she taught me everything.

The method of attaching one file to another by 'oyster', as virtualists call it, has been known for a long time and was both primitive and effective. It was considered quite safe – a minor operation is enough for the attached file to be automatically deleted when the attachment is downloaded by an unauthorized person. And few people could create really well, hard to detect 'oysters', many were content with the rough idea, which was relatively easy to discover. Sue taught me not only to create real gems but also to discover them, both of which were just as useful.

I found the first 'oyster' quite easily and started looking through it. At some point, my breath became stuck in my throat. The attached file didn't concern criminal cases. There were such disgusting videos and photos that it was even difficult to believe they even existed. I must have groaned unconsciously because Scott left what he was doing and walked over to me. He stared at the computer screen for a while, swiping his finger across the screen to open other files, then tapped me reassuringly on the shoulder.

"Now do you understand why Khamala invited us over?"

"What is all this? How is it possible for a person of sane mind...?"

"Don't be so shocked. Once upon a time, making such a film required live actors, which would be truly outrageous, but now the process of making them is impersonal. They're just holograms and advanced computer graphics."

"I know, but who could watch stuff like this? And with children in the lead role?! I mean, I know they are just holograms, but still..."

I couldn't understand how anyone could watch something like this for entertainment. Nowadays, the sphere of sexuality has ceased to be a taboo subject, and subjecting it to top-down control has eliminated the most dangerous disorders. However, there were still some deviations from generally accepted standards, and our prosecutor was probably one of them. In an instant, Cable ceased to be a victim of crime for me and became trash that someone cleared away. I stopped caring about finding the killer, especially since in light of these findings he could've had real reasons. I preferred not to even think what kind, because it made me sick.

"Are we collecting all this too?" I asked, just to say anything.

"Of course. These recordings must be carefully examined. You know yourself that these could just be 'oysters' again. Earlier, I saw real "multi-story", up to a dozen camouflaged sub-folders. I don't suspect Cable of such finesse, but who the hell knows..."

He was interrupted by the ping of the opening door. Connie Benedict strode into the suite, carrying her cameras. Without asking anything, she went straight to work.

A long time passed by the time we finished. We drove Benedict to her apartment, then we ran into the police station to leave the collected materials there.

"I have a request to you," Scotty said as we drove to my place. "When you report for duty tomorrow, take the android with you."

"Monty? What for?" I was surprised.

"I have an idea, but I need to talk to him first."

"TALK?" my amazement was limitless. Scott had treated Monty a bit like a barrel organ so far. He found him useful in certain situations, but it would never occur to him to talk to him about anything.

He didn't answer right away. He stepped out of the service car and opened the door for me. I got out, still staring at him questioningly.

"Yes," he murmured finally, "I think it's time to change my attitude towards artificial intelligence. Karpinsky swears this model can be trusted, and he must be right. He was already helping us."

"You want him to join the police?"

"No, I wouldn't go that far. However, I would have a task for him. Take him with you."

It sounded very mysterious. Due to exhaustion, I didn't want to pursue it further and decided to wait until tomorrow. All I thought about now was getting to my bed.

Sue was still awake. She wandered around our apartment in a tracksuit, her hair tied in ponytails, singing to herself and cleaning. I was almost amazed. For as long as I knew her, she would hardly ever picked anything up off the floor, and the pinnacle of her ability was tossing a box after instant food into the shredder.

"Are you high?" I asked, hanging my door buzzer on the hook.

She looked at me with glistening eyes.

"Chris is going to come over tomorrow. He promised to show me the graphics of how Selenoport is going to look like. He describes it in such a way that you could listen to him for hours."

I raised my eyebrows. This was completely unlike my friend, and it piqued my interest.

"You like him, don't you?"

She smiled in a dreamy pink that told me more than entire volumes.

"Oh, Sue... you fell in love with him!"

She sat down on the chair.

"You think? I've never been in love before, but if this is... oh, it's a wonderful feeling..." she looked at me with sudden suspicion. "Are you not jealous?"

I had to laugh.

"Come on, honey! Chris is my little brother. I love him, but not like that."

"You're only social siblings."

I pulled up a second chair. We had never spoken so honestly before, I felt that there was an even longer meeting ahead of me.

"So what? I really could never think of him as a potential partner. Neither could he about me. I bathed him, taught him to use the potty, I was helping him to pee, and was wiping his nose when he first started living with us. He was less than two and I was nine, but I was, shall we say, mentally more mature than my other brothers and sisters. I was very caring, and I think that I needed to convey to someone the need for the care and affection that I carried in me."

"You immediately became attached to him?" she asked. She was eager to hear all about Chris – another sign of falling in love. I was almost jealous of her now. I've never experienced that feeling before.

I returned to those times in my mind. I had no living relatives, at least according to the law. Adoption was unlikely as my parents died when I was seven years old, and according to the rules, the maximum age was five. After spending several months in the shelter, and after they took care of all the necessary documents, I ended up in Lara's family. At that time, apart from me, there was only the oldest kid, Brasco Defoe, a fifteen-year-old boy. He had already been sentenced to juvenile prison twice, once for a series of petty thefts, and once for beating and attempting to intimidate a colleague who reported him. When I first met him, his head was still shaved bald from his second stay. He would probably have been taken away from the Lara family if someone else decided to take care of such a problematic teenager.

Despite everything, Brasco was not a bad kid. He was simply exploding with energy and a desire for freedom. Over time, I came to the conclusion that Lara loved him more than all of us. Maybe because he was their first social son, or maybe because he needed them the most. Over time, when new kids appeared – Willbur, Ivan, May, Chris, and, finally, Milla, our dear little devil – it became more and more noticeable. Either way, the rebellious boy grew up to be quite a decent person. He joined the Academy of Social Structures and is today one of New York's most respected family curators.

Chris appeared when I was a teenager and maybe that's why he stole my heart right away. I became his 'little mother' so much that I reacted with anger and stomping when Cynthia Lara wanted to change him or measure his temperature. He, a sweet little boy with blond curls, from the very first moment snuggled up to me with full trust and love and listened to me much more than his social parents. It was unlikely that either of us would treat the other as an object of sexual desire.

I told all this to Sue and she listened with wide eyes, absorbing every word.

"I've always thought that social families were as strict as the military," she finally said when I finished.

"Maybe some are. Not in ours, and all the ones I came across were rather relaxed. After all, it should be a family, not a penitentiary company. Where is Monty?"

"He's at the computer. I made an educational program for him. You know, Karpinsky said that he should study, and I am of the same opinion. He assimilates knowledge and can process it like a person. I would even say that he needs it."

I felt guilty. I've recently been neglecting my android, immersed in a job that was taking more and more of my life. This was not a problem from a social point of view – people with no or limited private life were valued. Only doctors wrinkled their noses at them because sooner or later they cause trouble. As for me, I have lived for my work from the beginning of my professional career, which was all the easier for me, because I did not have a family to occupy my attention in my free time. Sid didn't ask for much, cats are introverts and sleep most of the time. But now I had Monty, and I had to take care of him, at least a few hours a day.

"I really don't know," Sue was clearly still thinking about Chris. "Your brother thinks that Monty is equal to people, maybe Scott got the same idea."

I laughed.

"You're kidding?"

It seemed unlikely. Although, on the other hand... I didn't know my boss as well as I would've liked to. Who knew what was on his mind.

I was too tired to think about it. I said goodnight to Sue, changed into my pajamas, and went to bed with relief. I was half asleep when I felt Monty settle down next to me. I put my arms around his neck and fell deeply asleep.

I slept so hard that I didn't hear the alarm clock. Sue had to wake me up and I made it to work with difficult. When I entered the headquarters, I noticed a few surprised looks. Nobody expected me to take an android with me, and I usually wouldn't. Many people felt uncomfortable around 'artificialities', even the simplistic ones known as TA – technical androids that help in factories and on interplanetary ships. The mere thought that they think independently bemused and even frightened. And how much more when the AI has such a deceptively human shell as my Monty.

Only Scotty smiled when he saw us.

"Glad you brought him," he said happily. "Come to my office after the briefing."

I was very curious about what he had come up with, and I was sitting on high heels throughout the briefing. As soon as it finished, I went straight to the inspector's office.

Scott walked in a few minutes after me.

"Can I talk to your android directly?" he asked, sitting on the edge of the desk.

My eyes widened in astonishment.

"Of course. What questions do you have?"

"Nothing out of the ordinary. You're in the role of the... well, I don't know... owner, guardian? Either way, you are the first instance."

I looked at Monty, standing still beside the chair I had occupied. I didn't feel like his owner or guardian. I felt more like he looked after me.

"Feel free," I sighed. "Should I leave?"

"No need for that." Scott turned to Monty, "Do you remember when Leeta shielded you from the gunfire?"

"Yes. I do."

"I want your opinion. Was that necessary?"

"It was not. My body is very resistant."

Scott nodded.

"I know how resistant. I also spoke to engineer Karpinsky and I know the technical specifications of your shell. Rather, you should be the one protecting Leeta from danger. I want you to get self-defense training and become something like a bodyguard for Leeta."

I felt my eyes get even rounder.

"Bodyguard? Do I really need one?"

Scott pursed his lips lightly.

"I'm not sure," he replied after a moment, "but I will feel a lot better if someone you have someone trustworthy with you."

I got up. Suddenly I felt very uncomfortable and had to react somehow.

"If you mean our relationship..."

"Leeta, honey," he interrupted, "you are the most capable intern I have worked with within in the last twenty years. Nowadays, people from class C or D are the ones who go to the police, someone from class B is rare. Don't get me wrong. I'm not a classist... this job is all about commitment and honesty... but when it comes to staffing the management, IQ is important. I was looking for a long time for someone who could be my successor in case of misfortune."

I was still standing staring at him. I remembered the doctor's words and it chilled me. It made no sense.

"Scott, I'm not fit for..."

"Let me judge that," he interrupted me again. "That will take time, of course. You're going to be my assistant for now. This means that you can become a potential target of an attack."

I sat down as if someone had cut off my legs. I was beginning to see what was happening.

"You nearly died twice already," he continued. "You were shot and then an explosive was planted in your apartment. It was a great relief for me to relocate you and Herefort to the police headquarters for a while, but you insisted on renting something bigger. Fine, I mean, you're not a slave, and you have the right to privacy. But it can be dangerous. I don't want anything to happen to you, and it's not just because you're... so personally important to me. From the perspective of the Lunnar main police headquarters, I cannot lose such good material for a deputy. I wouldn't find another one for a while. That's why I want Monty to learn how to defend you."

It was like a surreal dream.

I shook my head in disbelief. I couldn't find the words and didn't even know what to say.

"Who would train him?" I finally gasped out.

"Who else? The same instructor as you. I've already talked to him."

"And he agreed?"

"He was a bit surprised, but yes, he agreed. He is ready to take on this challenge."

I looked at Monty. At this point, I really wanted to know what he really was thinking. And even his creator didn't know that, because the android thinks independently, completely independently. In what language do I formulate my thoughts? What terms does he use in the depths of his consciousness?

"Monty... do you want to learn how to defend me?"

"Yes, I do," he replied immediately.

"Are you aware of what this means and what it requires?"

"No. That is something I will be taught."

He stared at me with shining eyes with some primal innocence peculiar to androids who are alien to all falsehood and generally typically human vices. Again, the basic question was – do I have the right to take advantage of that?

"You could die," I objected weakly.

Scott opened his computer and searched for the appropriate file.

"Not easily," he said. "Look, this is the tech spec that Karpinsky sent me."

He showed me a document bristling with numbers, formulas, and chemical formulas that I couldn't understand. I must have had an extremely stupid expression because he rushed to explain.

"The outer shell is made of high-class cyberskin, resistant to high temperatures and corrosive agents, but with poor resistance to mechanical damage. Same as the artificial muscles. If I'm talking about mediocre durability, it means, of course, that they are as plastic is. However, they can regenerate to some extent. Maybe not for extensive damage, but to a satisfactory degree. Such as other self-repairing items, tires, shoe soles, etc."

He explained it all to me like to a child, and I absorbed all his words. So far, Karpinsky has refused to reveal any technical details to me, on the grounds that I would not understand them anyway. Scotty was apparently more convincing.

"All this is a trifle," he continued, "but the skeleton is made of pure tungsten, and the shields covering the internal mechanisms are a tin alloy with barium titanate. Of course, tin sounds... soft, but I can assure you that its alloy with barium titanate is a great achievement of scientists of the twenty-first century, so far highly valued. I know what you're thinking now, but you are wrong. Just because something was invented ages ago doesn't mean it's antiquated... like concrete, which is, after all, an invention of the ancient Romans."

"Go on, it's very interesting," I encouraged him. With the eyes of my soul, I saw what kind of expression Chris would make when I told him about all this.

"I'll put it briefly, these shields are impenetrable, unbreakable. The alloy developed in the twenty-first century has been improved by our engineers. Maybe a decent quality bomb could destroy it, but not for certain. One weak point, as Karpinsky said, was the camera covers – his eyes. After many attempts, he finally used a new material, called 'liquid diamond'. I don't know its specifics, but I've heard of it before Karpinsky told me. One gram of this miracle costs as much as twenty kilos of pure platinum."

It had never occurred to me that Monty was looking at me with something so precious. Anyway, Scott said that there was no price for him at all.

"Other androids were produced in a cheaper way," Scott picked up the topic after a moment. "Yes, we know some of them to serve Hampton. But there are others, and we can't find them, as you well know. Yours is Karpinsky's most perfect creation, but we have a lot to teach him if he is to protect you."

I wiped the sweat from my forehead. I didn't know what to say myself. It seemed that the desperate act that resulted in me taking the gunfire aimed at my android was unnecessary and pathetic. I felt ridiculed.

"Hold on!" I called out. "So the man who shot Monty knew nothing about the details of his construction! Whoever sent him couldn't have known about it either. So it couldn't be Brel!"

"Where did this conclusion come from?" Scott was clearly surprised. His visors slid slightly out of the frames.

I was just now beginning to understand it, so I waited a moment before starting to speak.

"Brel is a clone of Hampton. He matured in the F lab. We don't know what he had access to and what his perception was back then, but I think he knows a lot more about androids than 'The ABCs of artificial intelligence'. So, he probably wouldn't have sent a thug with a liquid nitrogen rifle on the android. The man wasn't aiming at me, the ballistics analysis ruled that out. I was absolutely sure of it from the beginning. This means that not only was our bomber not familiar with the construction of androids... but also that Monty was one of them!"

I looked at Scott.

"You're right," he said in amazement, "Brel knew him. Monty initially worked with him. And that means..."

"And that means we're back at the starting point," I added in a low voice, "we still don't know who was behind the attack and what role Brel is playing. And whether Hampton was honest with us."

The inspector shook his head.

"I wouldn't build any conclusions around that," he said. "Monty, close the door, please. On the other side. I mean, leave us alone."

As the android left the office, Scott turned to me again.

"The very fact that Hampton is supported by my brother-in-law should give us a red light. He is capable of anything just to achieve his goal. And Hampton himself... I know that his current condition arouses sympathy, especially from you, because you have a good heart. However, the mere fact of being disabled does not make anyone an angel. A mutilated man is exactly the same man as before, a decent person, or a villain and a crook. That doesn't change. In my experience, people rarely change at all. In other words, you won't make silk out of rags."

"But silk can become rags as well," I remembered the story of my childhood friend who joined into a gang of cheating in casinos and ended up on death row for the murder of a croupier.

"No," said Scott. "Not exactly, anyway. If someone is spoiled, so to speak, it means that the rot was inside from the beginning. It might have been carefully wrapped in good manners and barriers imposed by inculcated ideals, but it was there. And it was only waiting to reveal itself."

I fell silent, not knowing what to say. Compared to Inspector Cavanaugh, a veteran of the law enforcement struggle and a police legend, I knew almost nothing. I was like a chick learning to fly. No wonder he was worried about me.

"So, our enemy could be Leon Beavis Hampton," I mumbled.

"Maybe," he nodded, "although not necessarily. He's a businessman. He runs economic games, there is no doubt about that. However, I don't think he gets involved in politics. He doesn't care who is in charge, as long as they don't interfere with the trade."

He got up from the desk and walked slowly around the office. He always did that while thinking about something. He couldn't think while sitting.

"I'm concerned about the presence of Number One on the Moon," he said finally, stopping beside me. "The game must go deeper than we thought. That's all the more reason for you to have a bodyguard. Monty needs to start training today."

V

The large board in my room certainly didn't match the decor. It was sent to me from an earthly mail-order store that usually supplied kindergartens and elementary schools. I picked up the parcel a few days ago, along with a bonus pack of electronic markers. I needed these ancient items for my concept work. Even in the age of holo screens and other fancy gadgets, such a simple board was always useful. Scott had one in his private room at his headquarters, too, and he used it in every case.

There were thoughts written by me on the white plastic.

1. Who shot at Monty?

2. Where is Brel?

3. What is Brel doing now and what is his goal?

4. What was his relationship with prosecutor Cable?

5. Does it have anything to do with his death?

That was a very good question. Brel appeared on a few recordings found on the prosecutor's computer, including the more personal ones. It was hard to distinguish him from Cable's replacement, Johnson, but it was possible after careful analysis.

6. Who murdered Silvana Evans and her husband and why?

7. What did Silvana learn?

8. Did she attempt to put pressure on someone by herself?

9. If so, on whom?

We still didn't know that. All evidence lead to nowhere. Well, maybe not exactly, because we made several arrests thanks to Silvana's notes, but none of them were linked to her death. There must have been data we haven't found yet. Unless the one who sentenced my friend to death got to it first, then the matter was hopeless.

10. SOLO KHAMALA

The last one I underlined with a double line. The figure of the governor of Lunnar seemed more and more mysterious to me. I looked for information about him, of course for those not publicly available. Sue helped me, delighted to browsing on the net using police lines, faster than the public and much cleaner. As she told me, breaking through the 'electronic trash bin' sometimes takes half the time allocated for data collection.

What we both found was surprisingly sparse. Solo Khamala was born in the Philippines, grew up in Honduras, and graduated in Japan. Then the trail broke off. His character once again made his mark on the data network only two years before he was appointed as the governor of the colony.

He appeared as an apprentice, deputy to the newly appointed minister of the food economy, and immediately made himself known as an exceptionally efficient politician.

As I was aware already, such positions are allocated by the main selection computer, based on IQ tests, education, and post-graduate work performance. The Selection Center has the results of tests, learning, and life path of all those who are registered in the central file. People are grouped into sections and subsections. The main one is divided by IQ score. Then come education and professional achievements. Politicians are selected only from the last subsection, grouping the most intelligent who, in addition, we're able to properly use this intelligence. The mere privilege of being included in this small group was a huge distinction, available only for A1 and A0.

Solo Khamala was chosen the traditional way, so he had to have all the qualities needed to hold political office. Only that there was little we could find in support of that. Almost nothing, some one-sentence mentions in the reports of the ballot counting committees of several larger companies. The documents of the university were richer, but even there we didn't find anything special either. An exemplary student, showing respect to lecturers, systematic in learning. Good relations with colleagues, not tolerating anarchist slogans, no compromising habits were noticed, a candidate for wife approved by the genetic selection committee.

"He's married?" that information surprised me while analyzing the contents with Scott.

"He was, at least. They divorced before he was appointed governor. He told me that she didn't want to move to Lunnar, at least that's the official story."

"And the unofficial one?"

"I'm not sure. According to rumors, she took it as an opportunity because their marriage was not going well."

He flipped through several files.

"This *obasan*[5], Riha, came from Tokyo. She's a performer at the Museum of Japanese History. She participated in custom visualizations for tourists and this is how she met Khamala. She flew here with him, officially as an assistant. Both of the other girls too. They must have been nine and eleven then and will be back on Earth in two weeks. They didn't return, as we can see."

"Are they really his nieces?"

"That's the case according to the documents. The sister's family died in a natural disaster... according to the records, during the tsunami of the century. But I can't find any documentation on the transfer of care..."

---

[5] The name *obasan*, or Aunt, is the name of the caretaker of geishas and apprentices who live with them in the *okiya*, or geisha house. The owner of the *okiya* is *okesan*. The term *mamasan*, which means the owner of a brothel, is often misused.

I could tell that he was gloomy. He didn't like any of this. I didn't either. The documents we were looking for were simply not in the available data space. This made no sense. Social control 'loses' two girls and no one is looking for them? How did Khamala achieve that? How did it happen that they grew up in his house on the Moon and no one, not a single soul, asked any questions?

"I think Cable has something to do with this," I finally said.

"That's possible. We have to watch ourselves and take extreme care of what we say. We're stepping on thin ice. The Governor cannot figure out that we're suspecting him or know that we looked through him."

"Don't worry about that," I said, "Sue is a master in covering tracks."

The office door opened and Dr. McCave entered.

"What do you have for us, Kell?" Scott asked, turning away from the computer.

"I just got the results from the lab." the doctor tossed the stack of printouts onto the table.

He sat down on one of the chairs and poured himself a gin from the decanter that was always at hand here. He drank with clear pleasure.

"I thought I've seen everything," he continued after a moment, "but the late Nick Cable's collection exceeded my expectations. This person shouldn't have slipped through psychological tests, and I will never understand how he did it. The only explanation would be a special type of psychopathy that allowed him to hide almost everything from people and deceive the most modern polygraph. He also secured himself before possible chemical interrogation. That implant I mentioned, neutralized substances such as scopolamine."

"How nice," Scott muttered, frowning in disgust.

"If you only knew."

I remembered the nostrils and the bags of powder in the safe.

"Were there any drugs?" I asked.

He looked at me. He had deep circles under his eyes as if he had not slept in days.

"Yes, but it's not 'golden rain'. Inside the 'nostrils' there was a mixture of hermezine and H5, and in the sachets synthcaine... not a drug, but a powerful stimulant. The artificially produced equivalent of cocaine. Technicians are now working on the signatures of both substances to identify the lab they came from."

He took a deep breath.

"I had to analyze his files to create a psychological profile," after a while he brought up the topic. "I haven't seen such filth since university. It was once called pornography and it was somewhere within the boundaries of the law. It was very popular at a time when even ordinary sex was considered indecent. People solved their tensions with the help of such videos."

"Whatever someone's into," Scott muttered.

"Yes, but keep in mind that back then real people were involved, often stuffed with all kinds of nasty things, to have sex for as long as possible. Now, so to speak, no one is getting hurt...

but what I saw in Cable's collection, in my opinion, should still be banned. Kids in such..." he shook his head.

The inspector opened the desk's drawer and took out a box of cigars confiscated during the search of the prosecutor's apartment.

"Here," he said almost heartily, "you could use some after that experience. As you said yourself, he no longer needs them."

"But that's evidence."

"Irrelevant to the case. Take it."

"What about the weird stuff we found in the safe?" I asked, silently deciding that I didn't see or hear anything.

McCave lit one of the cigars so solemnly as if he was celebrating Sunday service.

"Ah, that gets even more interesting," he replied. "Each has fingerprints and biological material. We can easily identify who they belong to. The technicians are working on it. So far, they've identified four people. And get this, none of them were involved in any criminal activity. None. So why would there be potentially dangerous items with their identification in the general prosecutor's safe?"

The conclusion was self-evident, although it was difficult to draw in relation to the general prosecutor and seemed absurd. Something unprecedented has been happening during the last few decades.

"Blackmail? A priori?" I took a guess.

Scott looked through the printouts with an unreadable expression.

"The people identified are ranked highly in the management of companies. Looks like Cable was collecting evidence on them in connection with some planned operation. We have to check if we've locked up someone in recent years based on these kinds of traces on the murder weapon, with no other evidence."

"I'll take care of that," I offered and ran out of the commandant's office.

My head was bursting at the seams both from too much thought and the smell of cigar smoke. Not that it smelled particularly bad, but it gave me a headache right away. There must have been something nasty in it, and I wondered how our doctor could so delightfully draw it into his lungs. I have had contact with smokers before and I always recognized them by smell right away, although there weren't many of them. Nowadays, natural tobacco was very expensive, and flavored substitutes for some reason have not been adopted on a large scale. Vaporizers loaded with liquids containing a synthetic nicotine solution are already in greater demand. Luckily, they don't produce nasty-smelling smoke.

I took a seat behind my desk and rummaged through the police database. This is the most boring and exhausting part of police work. Working in the field may require greater dexterity, engages physical strength, and can be truly dangerous, but during that your adrenaline kicks in. When you sit behind your desk and spend hours shuffling through files on your computer, soon your whole body starts hurting, especially your neck and eyes. And you can't stop unless you are already unconscious from fatigue.

Taking into account the size of the archive, such rummages would of course be unimaginable if it were not for the possibility of data filtering. But even the best filters weren't perfect. The final stage of the search had to be done 'on foot', as Sue liked to call it. And it was usually a long road.

By the evening, I had isolated sixteen files and began to analyze them thoroughly. After an hour, I rejected three. The evidence in them was richer. The rest was exactly what I was looking for. I drank another caffetino, adding a few drops of stimulant to it. I rarely used it. The doctor was skeptical about stimulants, any highly commercialized substances, such as the popular 'Fatigue Killer' syrup, and similar wonders of chemical engineering. Not only did he not recommend them, he even advised against them. Even so, in the headquarters, there was always a set at hand which we called 'hammer aid'. Sometimes it was indispensable during police work.

The thirteen files concerned thirteen different cases. Convictions were passed in eight of them, and in five defendants acquitted. In all of them, the only hard evidence was the biological material on the tools or at the crime scene. The other ones were circumstantial and it was up to the judge to accept or reject them. Now it was necessary to look at the convicts and their connections. And I had to be the one to do it. Sue would probably help me if I asked, but ever since she agreed to work for the police, her hands have always been full. After all, she had kept most of her old contracts, and that meant she was covered with work to the top of her head. I couldn't add mine to hers right now.

By the time midnight hit, I looked through over half of the documents and picked out two persons from them. Then, despite the stimulant, I fell asleep, with my head resting on the desk. I didn't even feel Monty picking me up and, in the simplicity of an electronic spirit, carrying me to Inspector Cavanaugh's apartment.

"I froze in shock when he carried you into my bed like it was nothing," Scott was telling me about it later, amused like never before. "He was acting like it was normal. I was lying under the blanket, naked, you know, completely, I'm reading a book, and then suddenly the door opens and your android comes barging in. My eyes widen, and he takes off your shoes, pants, and blouse, and in underwear alone places you right next to me, covers both of us with a blanket, and leaves. And you don't even wake up, just keep snoring, like under your mommy's blanket. So what was I supposed to do? I turned off the light and went to sleep, too."

"I have no idea what got into his head," I groaned.

Monty's behavior has confused me more than once, ever since the day he rescued me. He was as unpredictable as a human, or even more so. After all, even without knowing what a human may do, one could predict the likely course of events, meanwhile, the android's behavior eluded even these patterns. It had an inner logic, but one that made sense only to him. So how could I trust him with my life?

And yet I had to. He was the best choice for a personal guard.

"I've never had a student like this before," Meesh, a police instructor, told me. "He doesn't need to practice at all. All I have to do is show him once and he'll repeat without the slightest mistake, as many times as necessary."

Yes, that's something I could believe. And I had no intention of informing Meesh that the android's defensive utility could collapse in a situation requiring improvisation.

Scott patted my shoulder.

"Come on, go clean yourself up and I'll make you some breakfast."

I showered in the disinfecting mist, then took my clothes out of the freshener. I didn't like these kinds of devices. In the long run, they destroy materials, poorly positioned can burn through the dirty area like acid, but from time to time you had to use them. Right now was one of those times.

Combing my hair into a small bun and carefully twisting the curls at my temples, I left the bathroom. There was a plate of biscuits smeared with artificial jam on the table and a cup of Pure Taste tea. Initially, it was only available in a single, quite exclusive chain of stores. Recently, in the form of soluble grains, it made a sensation in mail-order sales, and in this form, a few weeks ago, it hit the Moon. From the beginning, experts claimed that despite the sensationally low price, it has almost the same taste as a natural semi-fermented one with lemongrass.

I didn't know whether that was the truth, I have not had the opportunity to try tea from the natural leaves of Chinese camellia. It was too expensive for me. Lemongrass was different, I knew it and even kept it in a pot myself so that I would always have a fresh addition to my drinks. Pure Taste must have contained it. It was much tastier than cheap substitutes made of herbs that were easier to grow. This new blend had a rich, bitter taste and was just as well hot or cold.

I ate my breakfast quickly and made it for briefing. Then I immediately sat down at the computer to finish what I had started yesterday. By noon, I had managed to establish a short, but indisputable list of five people who had been convicted solely on the basis of biological evidence. In the files I found, Nick Cable wrote all requests for legal action personally, just as with these five. No additional evidence appeared on them, and the convicts claimed to the very end that they were innocent. Three of them had negative scopolamine tests, while the other two such measures could not be used because of allergies.

"Why is the truth serum still used, if it has already been known for a while that such measures are not reliable?" I asked Neil Slavik when he showed up at the headquarters. This question bothered me.

Our lawyer stopped and looked at me through his dark glasses. He suffered from some kind of photosensitivity and had to wear dark glasses even indoors. It gave him a certain feeling of mystery, chic, and even charm. He was successful with women, and it didn't surprise me.

"It's not unreliable," he replied, "it's just that it could go either way. If it comes out positive, you've got proof. And if negative, you just have to keep digging. Did something happen? Anything I can do to help?"

I shook my head.

"No, I don't think so. If I have trouble, I'll report to you."

"I hope so, princess."

He tugged playfully on the curl at my right temple and continued walking.

I went back to the file. The general prosecutor is not involved in writing conclusions, which is done by his deputies. In this case, it should have been Harry Johnson, so why didn't he? Something was starting to dawn on me.

I opened the Lunnar Prosecution files and began looking through them. As I delved into them, my suspicions crystallized into more and more precise shapes.

Finally, I was certain.

"Scott, I found something," I called, storming into the commandant's office, "remember the Johnson case?"

He looked at me in amazement, stopped the ham sandwich before it reached his mouth. He always ate while he was working, without interrupting what he was doing.

"What about it? It's closed, the guy is behind bars."

"Unjustly!" I fired back. "Cable set him up, just like the others!"

He put the sandwich on the paper plate.

"It would make sense," he murmured thoughtfully, "he found the perfect scapegoat and thought he got away. Well, I suppose he was right because if he hadn't been murdered, many things would never have come out. He'd still be a prosecutor, doing whatever he wants... What exactly did you find? Tell me. From the beginning, don't leave anything out."

I pulled up a chair and sat down.

"I checked a couple of things. Primarily, Cable used Brel as an informer in Romain Corporation. He tried to obtain evidence that would allow its management to be prosecuted. He already did the same with Horus, Big Zealand, and Nippon corporations. The file shows that for these three he obtained evidence but didn't use it. They remained in files, and no official indictments were brought forward."

"Interesting... so what were they for?" Cavanaugh decided that he couldn't think on an empty stomach and picked up his sandwich again. "What was he trying to achieve? Power? He already had it. Money?"

"Those assignment cards," I remembered, "he had a lot of them. If they're counterfeit, then that's genius. With such an amount of pepes you could go wild.

Even though food rations were calculated according to the same pattern for all citizens, regardless of class or social status, and it was not possible to shift points from the industrial card to the food card, there was a catch. I found out about it myself recently and it surprised me more than it angered me. You see, in the locales of extra classes, you could pay for meals from the 'top shelf' with the industrial card. In other words, the very rich since a long time ago have been avoiding the allocation system when they ordered the most expensive meals from the elegant clubs. The introduction of this option was abuse, but not a breach of the law. I understood very well why it was hidden from the public. The authorities wanted to avoid an outbreak of social discontent while maintaining the status quo of the top-earning class."

Scott waved his hand dismissively.

"That's for minor expenses. I think our deceased was aiming for something much bigger. The safe in his apartment is a trifle. He must have had an extra hiding place somewhere, and we need to find it."

"There's something else," I continued, "all the traces seem to lead to Hampton. Johnson is his close relative, and he was probably the one who controlled Brel. That would mean that, at least at first, he was going hand in hand with Cable. Then they had some disagreement since Cable blew his cover."

Scotty kept chewing for a while, thinking intensively.

"From what you're telling me, I'm getting to a different conclusion," he finally said. "Hampton didn't seem to know about the prosecutor's cases. He would've told us something. It seems that his half-brother didn't care about him and was fine with taking over his trust. Did he manage to convince Brel to go with his plan, or was he manipulating him? What do you think?"

"He manipulated him," I said firmly. "Before Brel deactivated the implant, Hampton could see and hear everything he did. Johnson couldn't act openly, and Brel didn't break the law. What happened afterward, we have to unfortunately guess."

"Yeah... I'm starting to get a really bad feeling about this," he opened one of the files on his computer screen. "Before you came here, I received a report from Ostronos. He's sniffing around in the Naked House. Spoke to the sidewalk cleaner... those guys like to talk to random hobos since they themselves aren't of a much higher status. It's their last stop before eventually rolling out of the game."

I knew what he was talking about. Lunnar was a special place. In order to save energy, it sometimes happens that jobs, which on Earth are performed by semi-automatic machines or robots, are entrusted to people who have not retained their professional position. Clerks, engineers, and specialists in various fields become cleaners. After an addiction, whether it be drugs, alcohol, or gambling, they reach the bottom. One could ask: Why aren't they returning back to Earth? That I don't know. They probably can't bring themselves to make such a decision and vegetate from day to day, hoping for a miracle.

"According to Ostronos, this supposedly exclusive club wasn't really that inaccessible," the inspector continued. "It's not just registered members that frequented the place. Anyone who received an invitation from a nude guy with a club ID could take part in the so-called 'open nights'. And the night of the murder was one of those 'open nights'."

"Why didn't anyone tell us?"

"Because it's illegal. Houses of this type operate according to the rules of extreme entertainment clubs. One of the legal requirements is the obligation to have an identity card and no access for persons not registered in the register of participants."

This opened up completely new possibilities and, unfortunately, added more work for us. It could take a long time to figure out who it was on that ill-fated night at the Naked House since we weren't going to delude ourselves that anyone would voluntarily admit to being there. Fortunately, we were able to secure the city monitoring records, even though we were assured that they would prove useless. Now we had to analyze them with extreme care. This meant looking at the screen and checking every shadow that passed. Considering that the cameras of the local monitoring systems are generally of rather low quality, there are some rough days ahead of us.

Neither Scott nor I took into consideration the old saying that 'in war, the situation can change at any moment". In the afternoon, as I was returning from dinner, at my desk was a strange man about forty years old with a distinctly Asian appearance and a kind smile.

"Officer Juliette Ankes?" he politely asked. "Allow me to introduce myself. Elton McNamara, WBI. Here is my ID. We're taking over the investigation into prosecutor Cable's death. My manager looks forward to your full cooperation."

"Yes, of course," I muttered, stunned.

The World Bureau of Investigation had the right to take over our activities. That was more than clear. They have the authority to take over local police affairs anywhere – on Earth, on the Moon, in orbital cities, and anywhere else we may be in the future. Such as a Martian colony, let's say if that ever becomes a reality. However, we didn't expect such a quick response.

We deliberately postponed the delivery of our discoveries to Earth, hoping that we would be able to solve the problem ourselves. We knew that they would send a new prosecutor to look around and, perhaps, decide what to do next. Meanwhile, the new prosecutor has not arrived yet, and the WBI has already appeared. Someone was working behind our backs. Someone gave a signal to Earth that we're stuck looking for the killer. At first, I thought about the governor, but then I rejected this possibility. Khamala sought to hide Cable's dirty secrets. The transfer of the case to WBI staff meant that nothing could remain hidden. No, I can clear Khamala from the list.

"Could you wait one moment?" I said.

"Of course, Officer Ankes."

I ran to Scott's office. I caught him furiously throwing bits of computer foil from drawers into a box.

"Here," he hissed through clenched teeth towards a beautiful woman in a navy blue trouser suit. "These are my notes concerning the case. You can download all the files from the main server. Take what you want and get out of here. You can take over the case, but not my police station. I'm in charge here until I'm officially fired."

The woman watched him calmly, her arms crossed over her chest. She was one of those types of people who are very difficult to bring out of balance, and the more difficult it is, the more a person gets angry with them.

"Calm down, Inspector," she said after a moment, "no one questions the competence of you and your people. Simply put, the case is too serious to be left in the hands of the local police. The assassination of the attorney general..."

"Blah blah blah," he interrupted her. His visors nearly fell out of their sockets, he must have been really furious. "I know these arguments by heart. Take my notes and leave my headquarters. You can stay wherever you want, but not here."

The woman took the box shoved into her arms as calmly as if it had been handed to her with complete courtesy.

"Inspector, you play a very important role on the Moon," she said, "but prosecutor Cable's case is a matter of politics. You can help, but you cannot do it alone. As soon as you calm down, you will understand that yourself."

When she left, I saw Scott sink helplessly into a chair.

"I've never been so humiliated before," he whispered. "Nobody has ever taken over my case."

There were shock and disbelief in his voice. I began to gently massage his neck and shoulders, as Mabel once taught me.

"Calm down, Scotty," I said softly. "You can't do anything about it. Let them do it if they want to. At least Khamala won't bother us when something leaks into the media. And any failures will be on the WBI, not on us. It's always something."

For a while he was silent, giving himself up to my massage.

"And just between you and me, I'll tell you something," I continued. "After what I learned, my sympathy is more on the killer's side. Let's take this opportunity to do something else. For example, Silvana's case. We still don't know who killed her and Milton. Or why."

I felt his tense muscles relax slightly.

"I would also advise you to warn Khamala immediately," I added. "He has to believe that we are on his side, especially if you are going to investigate him further."

"I understand," he said dryly, almost reproachingly. "You're right about that. But remember once and for all that the police are not supposed to morally judge the victim and the murderer. That is the prerogative of the court. Our only job is to catch the culprit and secure material evidence. That's what we're there for. However, you are absolutely correct. We have other things to do. Your fingers really work wonders," he added after a moment, quite reassured. His visors were finally back in the frames. "Where did you learn that?"

"That's my secret. And if you're nice to me, someday I'll show you what they are really capable of," I promised with a laugh. "I promise that you'll be surprised. I have to go. A hotshot from the WBI is waiting at my desk. I don't want him to write in the report that I obstructed his investigation."

VI

The construction site left a huge impression on me. When you're on the Moon, everything seems enormous, since these are spaces devoid of the diversity typical of the Earth. It just seems so... empty. The so-called 'seas' and 'lakes' were simply huge basalt fields, eruptions of magma from the distant volcanic past of our natural satellite. But this site really had an impressive size. It filled almost all of Lacus Timoris, the closest to Lunnar, relatively flat 'lake'. The basalt covering this area has been described by selenologists as extremely stable and extremely dense for volcanic rock. They could build on it without having to fear that the ground beneath would suddenly collapse. The only difficulty was that instead of digging the foundation, it had to be cut with a laser cutter. We saw them do it from the terrace surrounding the administration building.

"Our ancestors wouldn't be able to handle this," Chris said as he showed me and Sue around the construction site this morning. "Their Achilles' heel was the lack of energy. They had no way of storing it, except in very small amounts. Now we have the appropriate batteries, powerful enough for one of them to power a medium-sized city for several weeks. We also already know how to extract energy from the sun without losing most of it and how to use solar wind to power the batteries of ships. All the more we can power the construction lasers without worrying about the supplies from Earth"

Even in a protective builder suit and a helmet on his head, he looked like a representative of a higher class. This was not the first time I wondered who his parents could have been. Cynthia and Sean never told us about the personal affairs of the family we created. This was one of the basic rules of social families. The children knew only what they remembered themselves. They didn't receive any information that could change the perception of their relatives in their minds. They also didn't have access to files even at a later age. It might have been for the better, but... probably not always.

I knew my parents, albeit not very well. Brasco, who became an orphan at the age of eleven, was also one of the privileged. Mila remembered her family home, but, in her memories, it was hell, from which the social commission pulled her out. They acted late, but sometimes it's hard to figure out the intelligent psychopaths posing as the model family. Willbur, Ivan, and Mae knew nothing. They came to Lara from other social families, disbanded for various reasons. Because sometimes they were liquidated from the top-down as a result of formal flaws, accusations of incompetence or abuse of the system, family breakdown due to divorce, or the death of one of the guardians.

Chris found himself in a different situation. He was from a foreign country, and no one ever told us which one. The only thing we knew was that all of his relatives were killed by intruders who broke into their house. At this time boy was then in the hospital under observation after a minor accident, so he was able to escape death. His parents, his grandmother, and two aunts died. The police never found the criminals. He was included in the witness protection program not because he could identify any of the assailants, but because the criminals in that country didn't play around. Chris was placed with the Laras for his own protection. At the time he didn't know any of us, and not even a word of English. But he made up for it quickly.

From the beginning, it looked like he would grow up to be handsome. But unlike many strikingly handsome men, he was not a narcissist or an empty mannequin. Even as a child, he loved exploring the world and learning about it. Sometimes I wondered on what basis he, same as me, was given the B3 classification. Even at a glance, it was clear that he was much better than that. The academic results showed this from the very beginning. There was something wrong. I thought that in my free time I should finally check who my social brother is.

"It's going to be a beautiful place," Sue said without conviction, looking back over Lacus Timoris, full of construction equipment.

At the moment it looked like... a quarry or a giant excavation. It was hard to imagine a great entertainment town here, almost the second Las Vegas.

"Let me show you the mock-up. It's inside, in the conference room."

We entered the building. The mock-up really did look great. It occupied four large tables pushed together and, as far as I could tell, was still being worked on. In a small room behind the conference room, someone was hunched over an electronic drawing board. A woman.

"This is the chief architect Nora Yonescu," Chris introduced her to us.

She got up to greet us. She was short, slender, with graying hair tied up in a small knot at the back of her head. At first glance, it was obvious that she didn't really take care of herself, being busy twenty-four hours a day. I would also bet she doesn't take antiage pills. Among conceptual workers, there was a conviction that they are bad for cognition and concentration, but I didn't even know how accurate that was. We introduced ourselves to Mrs. Yonescu, taking turns shaking her small hand, slender like a wicker bunch. Then she went back to work as if we weren't there at all.

"When are you planning the grand opening?" I asked.

Chris pulled the helmet to the back of his head. We wore similar ones. Entry to the construction site without personal protection equipment was prohibited.

"I don't know," he admitted. "I'm lacking specialists. Not workers, we have this in abundance. Some are volunteers from

Earth, and there's plenty of locals, too. Many derailed people are seizing the opportunity to become useful again and earn something for themselves legally. But I need engineers, electricians, metallurgists..."

I thought of Sven Thorvald. Judging by the symbol on his forehead, he is an A3. I didn't know whether he would be interested in working for Chris, but it was worth a try.

"I might be able to give you an expert on electronic scrap," I said. "There is one in Lunwark. He's running a scrapyard and a workshop in the hall of a closed factory. He's not just anybody, although he must have a reason for being stuck in that stinking workshop and not sticking his nose out of it."

"That doesn't matter. Will you take me to him?"

I had some doubts about revealing Mabel's hiding place to Chris, but in the end I decided that I needed to trust him. I doubt that he would betray me for the benefits that Hakat would offer. One of them was the ability to manage the construction. Were there others? I considered it clear-headed, calmly. It was a long time ago already that I stopped being the trusting, naive girl, who, against her will, became involved in high-level political games. I learned to be suspicious and analyze everything at least twice. I've known Chris since childhood, but people change. I had to assume that he was not as I imagine him to be. Although, if it turned out that he is, I would be pleasantly surprised.

"I'll talk to him myself first, brother. I don't know whether he would want to work for the government, he is a peculiar person."

He nodded with some displeasure. He must have realized that I didn't trust him the way I used to, and that must have hurt him. But I knew he would understand. We always got along well.

"Stay here, Susan," I told my friend, whose eyes almost flashed with joy at these words. She dreamed of nothing but spending a few hours alone with Chris. "I know that you would like to look at everything carefully. I have to go back anyway. I have night shift today and I need to prepare for it."

I didn't really have a night shift. Scott gave me 24-hour leave to sort out my personal affairs, including visiting my brother at the Selenoport construction site. Although Chris lived in the same building as Sue and I, we rarely saw each other. He mostly stayed here, slept in the break room of an office building, and watched over the construction all day. That was his life, his passion. He was ready to sacrifice everything for this construction. This is why I had to approach him with limited trust.

I had a sincere intention to spend more time with him, but while we were watching the shares together, I received a message from Sven Thorvald on my communicator. It was short and to the point: *We'd like to remind you to pay the service fee on time.* After reading it, I almost dropped my communicator. It was a password. The agreed upon password which meant that Mabel's hiding location has been discovered. I had to act without wasting a minute.

One of the supply drivers dropped me off at the city center. While there, I rented a slider and moved through Lunwark into the distant suburbs. I didn't fear driving anymore. Scott forced me to get a basic driver's license and learn different maneuvers that could help during a police chase. This allowed me to move freely, and the police ID gave me access to anywhere I needed to go. Although, naturally, I chose to not use that unless there was a real need for it, but having it was at least reassuring.

Monty was sitting next to me, stiff and dignified in his new uniform, which had just been sent from the warehouse. There was a whole argument concerning this uniform. Scott insisted that he should wear it, but he couldn't make the decision himself. Only after several consultations with the headquarters, who initially called him an idiot, was it possible to come to a consensus. We received a special brochure in which it was written that an android serving in the police has the right to wear a uniform without stripes, with a badge that says: 'Assist'. So that's what Monty was wearing.

The only ones who knew what his true role at my side was were Scott and I. For everyone else, the android really was an assistant, whose job was to carry my bags, hand me whatever items I require, and do what I tell him in general. Like a secretary and an errand boy rolled into one. Nobody was too surprised. From time to time, it happened that a uniformed detective would take on a police student or messenger like our Hallie instead a full-fledged. That happened because of the rules forbidding officers from going out in the field on their own. This was most often done in pairs, but lately we haven't had enough members in our ranks.

After the tragic deaths of Silvana and Milton, the number of recruits willing to join Lunnar's security forces dropped nearly to zero. Even if someone wanted to wear a uniform and enforce the law, they would rather join the security of industrial plants or homes. A quieter job with a much better pay. And so, the headquarters had to do whatever it could to fill the outposts, which sometimes proved difficult. That's why even people with ancient views, who opposed the presence of artificial intelligence in public space on principle, turned a blind eye to the fact that an android was my partner. Admittedly, it wasn't really a 'partnership', but at least I didn't move around town alone. Monty, trained by Misha, became my protector, and I believed that in the hour of need he would not fail.

The road to Sven's electronic scrapyard was long and seemed even longer when I was at the helm of the rover. Maybe because I had no one to talk to. Monty didn't know how to do small talk. After all, talking to him was like talking to a computer. He answered briefly and to the point, without any embellishment, he said as much as he needed, and never more. Sometimes he asked questions, but that was rare. When he didn't know something, he would rather search for that information in the net. He didn't do anything to 'kill boredom' because he didn't feel such things in the first place. This feeling was closely related to the perception of the passage of time, and how androids perceive time hasn't been made clear so far.

That topic was an unresolved enigma, although Dr. Karpinsky suggested that their so-called 'sense of time' was related to the actions they take and that they could manipulate it at will. In support of this thesis, he wrote an entire dissertation. He sent it to me, but I got stuck after the first paragraphs, it was full of scientific jargon and book references that I didn't know. I couldn't comprehend a thing from it. Although it's true that I was moved to the A3 classification, since that's what the prestige of the agency subordinate to Hakat required, but it's not like that fact alone added to my intelligence. Some things were still too difficult for me to understand.

Even though at first I would attempt to engage Monty in a casual conversation, now I stopped any such attempts. They were meaningless, and Monty clearly didn't understand what exactly I was trying to get from him. I had to come to terms with the fact that he was not a perfect copy of a human being, but another being entirely. I couldn't ask too much of him.

Even the longest road had an end somewhere, and we ended up on the site of a factory closed for years. I immediately noticed that something was different. It looked like as if someone was renovating the warehouse and production halls. There were fresh stains on the walls in places of damage, irregularities were covered up with a sealant and leveled. Someone was working here recently – was that what alarmed Sven? It's entirely possible. I didn't notice anyone while driving through the factory grounds, but it was obvious that since someone started a renovation, they were going to finish it. Where, then, would Sven go along with his small business?

I put these thoughts aside for later. I could most definitely find another location for Sven's scrapyard, but for now the priority was to get Mabel out of there. She was in danger. Although... was she the only one? I was reminded of my own doubts about him. What was someone of his class doing in this dirty hole so far from all inhabited places? If something had happened to him, the ambulance would probably not arrive on time. Even if the driver didn't get lost in the first place. Why did he decide to lead such a lonely life? I should have checked this long ago, but I neglected it. I ignored him. Hopefully that doesn't come back to haunt me.

The office was open, but when we crossed the door, red dots appeared on our uniforms. I froze.

"Sven"! I shouted. "It's me, Juliette! Where are you?"

Something blinked, then the red dots disappeared. The door to the office swung open, and Engineer Torvald looked out. He examined the office and the space behind us carefully before deciding to get out. Behind him, my friend slipped out of the back room in a suit that was too big for her, shrouded in grease and oil.

She really looked miserable, like she was another person entirely – smeared with dust and oil, her nails black with grease, and her hair, coarse with dirt, gathered in greasy pods. Yet her eyes, large and bright, surprised me with their determination. I felt like I was looking at a brand-new Mabel, and the clothes or hairstyle (or rather its absence) had nothing to do with it.

"They were here," Sven said without a preamble. "They were pretending to be tax control. I immediately realized that their documents were forged, but I didn't react. They rummaged though everything."

"How did they not find her?" I asked, stunned, not taking my eyes off Mabel. She was silent, as if she had lost her tongue somewhere, which was usually circling around like a windmill.

"I used a security password. She managed to hide in a cell under the floor. It's hidden, someone who doesn't know about it wouldn't be able to see the flap."

So, they came up with a security password. Maybe even more than one. Sven really had a good head on his shoulders, and I, on the other hand, also had a flash of genius when I entrusted him with the safety of my friend. No one would've been able to take better care of her... even though, looking at how she looks right now, one could doubt that statement.

"Close the stall," I ordered in a voice that wouldn't accept any objection "and pack yourselves, both of you, as quickly as you can. I'm taking you out of here."

"Well, I sure came out of that nicely. It's my only source of income, I'll have to go live under a heat and power plant or go to the wastewater treatment plant," Torvald muttered grimly.

"Not under any circumstances. You will have a job until you come back here. A fully legal and well paid one. And if those looking to rebuild the factory decide to kick you out, I'll make sure they pay more than your entire scrapyard is worth."

He looked at me, then at Mabel and shifted uncertainly from foot to foot.

"Go ahead," he said. "I'll join you in a moment."

I realized that he probably didn't want anyone to see his methods of protecting the inventory. It must have been an original idea, perhaps even his own production.

"Of course," I agreed.

I took Mabel to the slider, where Monty was waiting for us.

"How are you feeling?" I asked stereotypically, just to say something.

It's strange, but I felt like I was talking to a stranger and did not quite understand how to approach her.

She looked at me with her beautiful eyes, shining on her dirty face like jewels in the dirt.

"Better than ever," she said. "You won't understand, but I can finally just be myself. I don't have to pretend to be anybody."

"You're right, I don't understand," I admitted.

When it came to Mabel she always seemed like someone who does exactly what she wants, without bothering with conventions. Ever since we were kids, she had a very strong personality and character that drove our teachers to the pits of despair. Certainly, nobody could force her to do anything.

She looked down.

"My parents always said that I have to reach high. That this alone determines the value of a person. I was always told: Half of success is a complete failure. You almost succeeded, which means that you've failed completely. I had to be in the first place in any competitions I took part in. Get the best grades in any subject. But at one point even this stopped being enough. In order to fully satisfy my parents, I had to break out of my class and enter higher society. The job of a floress was to make this possible."

"And it did," I replied.

She looked me in the eyes again.

"It wasn't worth it," she said emphatically and got into the rover. Monty, without asking, arranged for her to sit next to him in the back seat. I guess I'll have to properly clean the slider before returning it to the rental.

Torvald joined us a few minutes later and sat down next to the driver's seat.

"You're going to be driving?" he asked with open skepticism. He must have remembered that no matter how many times I visited him, someone else was behind the steering wheel every time.

"I trained myself," I solemnly assured him and started the engine.

We left the factory premises to the communications tunnel. Almost immediately, two elongated shapes broke away from the group of sheds under which were standing decaying machines from the factory's past, and began following us like two ghostly shadows.

"We have a tail," Sven remarked dryly.

"I can see that. I'm surprised you didn't spot them earlier."

"They are good, that's all."

I had to admit that he was right. But something didn't feel right.

"This isn't Citizen Hakat's style," I said. "He wouldn't sneak around, he would burst in your place with his thugs and find everything, including that hideout. His equipment is so high-level that it would blow you off your feet. He can't be behind all this."

I looked at Mabel. She was sitting in a chair with her hands folded on her lap.

"What?" she grumbled. "You're right, it probably isn't him."

"Then who?"

"I'm not sure."

"Leave her alone," Sven said. "Now is not the time for interrogations. You'll talk when we get out of here alive."

That's right. I had no idea how I was going to do that. I only knew of one way to this shithole, the one that I came here through. And it was wide enough that the vehicles following us could overtake the skimmer and block us before we got to the main road. There we could probably count on some help. Here, probably not.

"Turn left," Sven told me, clearly thinking the same thing. "Where you see that narrow passage. They won't catch us on that road."

"Where does that lead?" I asked, nervously maneuvering the steering wheel.

"To the military training ground. I don't know if anyone is there right now, but I know they often hold exercises there, and the whole territory is guarded. If we're lucky, they won't dare to follow us. If they take the risk, we'll still turn on the alarm that will send patrol down. And of the two bad things, we are probably better off getting grabbed by the soldiers than those guys, whoever they are."

It was hard to disagree. Although I didn't know the identity of those who were after us, their behavior was, to put it mildly, unsettling. They approached slowly but inexorably. In the rearview mirror, I saw that both cars had a 'PER' badge on the bonnet, denoting an improved short series model. If their drivers wanted to, they could've outran us already. I looked at Mabel again, but she just pressed her lips and looked down. This behavior was really not like her, and I felt uneasy.

Thorvald grabbed my elbow.

"Turn it," he hissed. "We have no choice."

I had to admit that he was right. We really don't. I turned and stepped on the gas. The slider immediately started getting thrown from side to side. These types of vehicles do not perform well on unpaved roads and the detour Thorvald indicated was not well maintained. The police maneuvering area wasn't any better, but there I at least didn't feel the breath of the strangers following me. And I didn't have the certainty that I won't be able to count on any help.

Sure, I could've called for help with the police radio. From nearly any location. However, this area was a telecommunications 'hole'. Nothing here worked, only the cable devices Sven used. When inside a vehicle, you were cut off until you drove into an area in the range of transmitters. On one hand, it was very unfortunate, on the other, I felt some relief that I didn't have to explain why I didn't ask for help. If Mabel really had something on her conscience, and I could say with certainty that her behavior was at the very least strange, it was better not to immediately put her into the hands of the law. I preferred to talk to her first.

In the rearview mirror, I noticed that our pursuers were getting closer and closer. They must have sped up. I pulled the turbo lever and then grabbed the shuttle with both hands to keep the slider on course. The only consolation was that the vehicle in the rearview mirror also wobbled dangerously. This meant that they were also adapted to even surfaces and here they lost the advantage over us. Even the 'perfects' weren't really that ideal. Fortunately.

We drove at full speed, passing by warning signs with yellow and red lights flashing against a black background with the words NO ENTRY, NO CROSSING, and MILITARY ZONE. Then the thing that could kind of be described as a road suddenly stopped without warning. Our car fell into a flat spin, that is, it spun sharply like a carousel, and then crashed sideways into a concrete post supporting the fence mesh. Fortunately, the shock absorbers worked flawlessly, covering each of us with airbags, but the engine stalled and stopped responding to the switches.

The airbag release button worked. I pressed it down and the flexible balloons collapsed into their frames again.

"Are you in charge here? Are we fighting or negotiating?" Sven asked dryly.

"We'll negotiate first," I said.

I opened a cache in which I hid an additional weapon. I had on my side a service stunner for electric missiles. Just in case, I also took a gun with me. I handed Sven one of the pistols and gave the other to Mabel.

Monty was already armed with a handheld paralizer and a telescopic baton, and that had to be enough for him. During the training, we decided that this would be the best option. Android shouldn't take aggressive actions against people, only defensive ones. Otherwise, legal misunderstandings could arise, and none of us wanted that.

We got out of the car. The cars that followed us stopped nearby. Four heavily built men in suits and one woman came out of them. All of them wore large WBI badges on their lapels, visible even from afar.

"What now?" Mabel asked softly, hiding behind Monty.

"Now we'll find out what you did and what they want from you," I said sharply. "Don't forget to not shoot without my order. Attacking the 'worldlies' is a felony, for which there are twice as many penalty points as for robbery with a dangerous weapon. Regardless of the circumstances.

This was something I was taught even back on Earth. The World Bureau of Investigation was under the same protection as the uniformed duty officers, but in the event of proven mutual aggression, the 'worldies' were in a better position. Even the worst kind of criminal would think twice before attacking someone with a 'WBI' badge. In short, one had to be extremely careful. Which didn't mean that we should just give ourselves to them like lambs.

When they got close, I pointed my service weapon at them, while shouting the standard formula with my name and service number, and held up an official copy of my ID with my left hand. The original was kept in a safe at the police station, as were the IDs of my colleagues. The rules allowed carrying only a copy, tied to a special chip with the owner's cardiovascular and respiratory rhythm. This eliminated the possibility of impersonating an officer.

The woman in the suit stopped.

"Let's not do anything rash," she said, raising her hands slightly. "Allow me to introduce myself. Diana Foxx, written with two x's, WBI. We're on the same side."

"If that's the case, why did you chase us?" I asked, trying to speak as calmly as possible.

"We were not chasing you, Officer Ankes. We received information that a wanted anarchist was hiding in the area. We have reason to believe that you have just retrieved that same person from Sven Thorvald's workshop. Please hand her back to us and we will part in peace."

"I'm not protecting any anarchists. I don't even know any," I said firmly, although a storm of thoughts flashed through my head. Anarchist? Mabel? Although, it would explain a lot. Quite a lot.

"Her name is Clare Fortenberger. The one behind your friend."

I looked back instinctively.

"But that's not... stay back! I raised the pistol higher as Diana Fox used my second of inattention to get closer to me.

"I can see, Officer Ankes, which you don't even know whom you are protecting."

"Please, stay back!" I shouted, seeing that the agent again took a step forward, and the men follow behind her.

Monty moved to the front, partially covering me. In his hand he held a stun gun, and his pose clearly showed quite decisive intentions.

"Calm down," Diana Fox stopped, slightly surprised. "Attacking a WBI employee is a sure ticket to a long prison sentence."

"Self-defense is not an attack," Monty said. His gentle voice seemed out of place in this situation, more suitable for quiet conversation while chatting in front of the TV. He never changed the tone of his voice, and that gave him away. Even a person with a superficial knowledge of androids would know who they are dealing with. Fortunately, no one here was paying attention to it, and Monty was nearly forced to demonstrate what he is capable of. I wasn't planning on stopping him. Luckily, I didn't have to.

Before the situation became dangerous, we were surrounded by soldiers – most of them armed with live ammunition.

"What's going on here?" an imperious voice sounded. "By what right are you invading military territory?"

Lois Ann Sirtis walked between her subordinates and stood between us and our pursuers. She looked impressive, and not only because of her height and muscles, which were really uncommon for a woman. She simply had that 'something'.

"We're on business here," Fox said. "We want to interview this one..."

She nodded to Mabel.

"This one?" the colonel repeated ironically. "And on what basis do you want interrogate 'this one'?"

"There are reasonable suspicions that she belongs to the anarchist organization Black September.

"Suspicions, all right... what about evidence? Any at all? I mean, any I could see with my own eyes?"

I loved watching a WBI official lose credibility under Sirtis's scornful gaze.

"We have clues. Very strong ones."

"Oh, clues... and how do you know that this is the woman you're looking for?"

"We received a tip..."

"A tip? What kind?"

"That the wanted Clara Fortenberger is hiding in Sven Torvald's junkyard!" Diana Foxx blurted angrily. She was clearly losing her composure...

"And of course, you've got an arrest warrant, issued *lege artis*[6], with you?" Lois Ann continued.

"When we're dealing with such an unusual situation..." Foxx began, but the colonel interrupted her, turning her head towards us.

"Hey there! What is your name?"

I also looked at my friend.

"Ma..." she stuttered, "Mabel Rochester."

Sirtis raised her eyebrows.

"So, not Clara Forten-something?"

---

[6] Done according to the rules of the art, in this case – the juridical (latin).

Diana Fox plucked a folded hologram card from an inside jacket pocket.

"We were given this photo at the headquarters!"

The colonel took the card and unfolded it. A three-dimensional figure in a soapy blue evening dress and gold high-heeled shoes appeared in the air. Mabel. In this image, she was neatly combed with an intricate secular hairstyle, and her slender neck and ears were adorned with jewelry, probably bought for the equivalent of my annual earnings. She looked so stunning that I began staring myself.

Lois Ann looked around and looked at the grubby girl in dirty rags curled up next to me. The colonel's face twisted into a sardonic smile.

"Ah, you're right, she's basically a perfect match," she said with such cold irony that it almost froze in the air.

"If you just washed her..."

"If, if, if," Sirtis folded the holograph and pressed it firmly into Diana's hand. "To summarize: you have no warrant. You are not sure about the name. You don't even know if you're chasing the right person, because you can shove that picture up your ass. A good hundred models of major fashion houses in Detroit alone look exactly the same, not counting the holograms. But, despite this, you violate the civil rights of these people and the boundaries of the military zone. Not bad, for a member of the WBI."

Fox turned pale and pursed her lips.

"Our mandate allows us to conduct preventive detention," she said, struggling to contain the anger that was constantly rising and escaping.

"And I'll allow you to drive you out of here," Lois Ann continued. "The military does not obey civilians. Not under any circumstances. So, what will it be? Are you going to get out of here on your own, or do you need our help?"

The soldiers crowded menacingly around us and their commander, tightly gripping their weapons. The 'worldies' hesitate, then let go and backed away to their vehicles.

"I'll write a complaint about you," Diana Fox said as a goodbye. She clearly wanted to save face.

"Go ahead!" she heard in response. "Sirtis, Lois Ann, colonel, service number 883005780. Veteran of the Cartel War, awarded the Silver Star twice, the Purple Heart three times, and one Medal of Honor. Currently assigned to Lunnaria, main force, commander."

She didn't add anything else, since the vehicles marked 'PER' left and disappeared as quickly as possible.

"Thank you," I sighed from the bottom of my heart, instinctively grabbing Lois Ann's hand.

She looked at me and I, embarrassed, let go of her as quick as possible.

"No need," she replied. "I'm always happy to chase away a worldly cat. They're bloated, nasty assholes. But they have power. I invite you all to the barracks. To my office."

The barracks were located behind the training ground. Low, ugly, rather primitive, but they weren't meant to be a five-star hotel. The colonel's office didn't look very luxurious either.

"Sit down," Lois Ann growled as we closed the door behind us. She took a dark bottle from the closet and poured us all some artificial whiskey.

"How did you know they had no warrant?" I asked, out of politeness dipping my mouth into the vile liquid. Sven drank with pleasure, Mabel didn't even touch it.

"They rarely do," Sirtis sat down at the table and casually put her feet on the counter. "They are so used to the fact that they can get away with anything that they don't even bother with the paperwork. Of course, in this particular case, they could've had one, but I took the chance. But I won't always be here like I was today, so why not tell me what's going on here? And who knows, maybe I can help?"

I looked at Mabel. She was sitting on a rough chair, hunched over, her hands folded in her lap. Only she could explain anything here, and we all knew that.

"I'm not an anarchist," she said quietly.

"That's what I thought," Sirtis nodded. "At my age and with my experience, you can recognize certain things at first sight. But why are you suspected of it?"

"That's what I want to know as well," I muttered.

My friend looked first at me, then at Lois Ann.

"You can trust her," I said, "just like me or Scott."

"Okay, I'll tell you," she finally decided. "I guess it's about time. And I can't live like this anymore. Whatever comes next, so be it."

"Well, we're listening," the Colonel poured himself another whiskey. We didn't refuse some more either, although it tasted awful.

"Citizen Hakat, that is, the current Chief of Arms, has long suspected a conspiracy at the highest level. Someone is trying not so much to seize power as to gain unlimited influence over it. For this they are using, among other things, Black September. They are indeed anarchists. Their goal is to block the migration from Earth program."

"Does one even exist?" I blurted out.

"Yes. As a last-resort in case of extreme danger. But you know, you can't just leave our solar system, as if you were taking a walk in the forest. It requires preparations, testing and enormous financial support. Black September thinks this is a waste and that someone wants to take the planet away from the people... which is sheer nonsense, since not everyone could fly to the stars, after all. Only the selected group. But as you know, conspiracy theorists are easily manipulated. And somebody is doing just that."

"Who?" Lois Ann asked, then added. "You don't have to tell me if it's a secret."

"I don't know. As Clara Fortenberger, I infiltrated Black September and found some information that I passed on to Hakat. It was encrypted, but he knew what it meant. He turned pale and advised me to immediately run as far as possible, as if I feared the worst. And to not trust anyone I've met since he hired me for our first night. Not even him."

This really was surprising, and at first, I had no idea what to think about it. Then it dawned on me, something so monstrous and incredible that it was hard to believe.

Sirtis frowned slightly.

"Not even him," she repeated. "And that's why you escaped all the way here?"

"Yes. Leeta was the only person that came to my mind who I could trust. Initially, I was going to just hide with my family, but..."

I noticed that Sven squeezed her hand lightly, as if to encourage her. They must have become friends during all the months she was hiding in his workshop – maybe even more so than I thought.

"But what?" Sirtis encouraged her.

Mabel drank her drink with one breath to the bottom.

"On the way, I stopped to visit an ex-boyfriend," she admitted. "I didn't plan on it. It was an impulse. I figured that everything would be fine if I arrived at my parent's house a few hours later. But something did happen. Thanks to that, I survived. Can I have some more?"

Lois Ann refilled her glass.

"As I understand, someone was in your parents' house before you?" she asked.

My friend nodded.

"When I arrived, it was full of police and firefighters. I heard from the rescuers that they came too late to save anyone. I turned around and caught the first auto-walk I could find to the ferry landing site. I managed to do this before the official autopsy of the victims was carried out, and they found out that I was not even at home at the time."

I didn't know what to say. Now I understand why she decided to go on such a difficult path, why she was hiding from everyone, why she was in such a terrible state. It's hard to forget such a terrible experience. It's probably not possible at all.

"Not everything is clear here, but you must be telling the truth," the colonel said after a while. "And if that's the case, then you are in extreme danger."

"No way, really?!"

"Sarcasm won't help. You have to hide so that the WBI isn't able to get to you."

"That much we know too," I remarked. "But how? I'm out of ideas."

Finally, Sirtis took her feet off the table and stood up. She walked over to Mabel, examined her critically from head to toe, and thought for a moment.

"Actually, I don't have an orderly," she finally said. "Can you handle military discipline? Be aware that it's no picnic."

"I did some training in survival techniques... back at the agency. Citizen Hakat demanded me to do so when he decided that I would be one of his people."

I suddenly realized that I didn't understand why my childhood friend, so in love with luxury and fun, decided to accept the Chief of Arms' offer. After all, she was only his 'companion' at first, a mascot who was taken to social meetings and making his free time more enjoyable. This is what the role of the floress comes down to, any way you think about it. She liked living this kind of life, where she was only required to maintain good manners and impeccable appearance. What changed?

"Survival techniques," the colonel repeated. "It'll have to do for a start. Life in the army is not easy or romantic, but it's still life. We are a closed system and are loyal to each other. We are subject only to military courts and the High Command, so we don't need to explain ourselves to anyone who's not wearing a uniform with higher distinctions than we do. We could protect you much more effectively than the Chief of Arms could, who, no offense, has nothing to say in our affairs. Of course, the question of price remains. You will become, as it were, the property of the army, and this has its consequences."

It's true. The Chief of Arms had complete authority over the police and all forms of uniformed security. However, the military obeyed exclusively the generals and did not even obey the First. The high command addressed the entire government as equals. In disputes, they could come to a consensus, but the civilian authorities could not order the army. The separation of powers was strictly obeyed. Only one professional group could command both civilians and the army – the medics. The fourth power.

Legislative, executive, judicial and medical. Four-leaf clover on the crest of the United Earth.

Mabel stood up as well. Without several-inches high heels, which were usually inseparable from her attire, she seemed rather inconspicuous, and compared to Sirtis, tall and built like a man, she looked even smaller still. However, determination and conviction radiated from her character. Despite the fact that she was dirty beyond imagination, her clothes covered with mud, she looked respectable. Her innate dignity could break through anything. However, she was no longer the girl I knew. I was looking at a stranger.

"I accept," she said quietly but clearly. "I want to be a professional soldier under your command."

VII

Corpses were never a pleasant thing to look at. Dr. McCave was the only one used to them and was even able to eat in the police morgue. He drank caffetino in between taking out the liver and weighing the contents of the intestines and stomach. He ate a sandwich next to the table on which rested a dismembered body without even changing the bloodied apron. Everyone was shocked at this sight at first, but they got used to it later. Detectives, in particular, had to build a certain degree of resistance to such things, as they spent a lot of time in the morgue. When it comes to them, at the moment there were only four in the whole Lunnar – Scott, me, Feri Kunch and his apprentice partner, Kathy Jouvenaux, a volunteer sent from Earth last month.

Then there was Kevin Razor Winslet, 'private cop', as we called him, still the only one on the Moon, but he helped in the economic department, led by Lieutenant Rosanda Merrick. Criminal cases were left for us to deal with. One would think that four investigators for the whole colony is not enough, but it had to be in this case. The other officers did everything they could to support us. Bit by bit, every police officer on the Moon became a detective, and it saved us. Otherwise, we would never have tamed this cage full of squirrels.

"Another victim of the golden rain," the doctor said as we entered the morgue. He was just looking at a patch of brain tissue under a microscope. The screen, combined with the enlargement system, showed a complex network of dendrites and branched synapses. Even I, someone not specializing in this field, could see the damage done in there. "How can people take this filth... but that's not what killed him. He was stabbed in the heart."

"Who is it?" Scott asked.

"A miner of the AMOS Company. A foreman from one of the far mines. He used hard during the past few months."

"Maybe he couldn't bear the accommodation in a working-class hotel on the outskirts?" Scott suggested.

Some mines were so far from Lunnar that it doesn't pay off to deliver the workers to the site every day. A certain two-shift system is then used. For two weeks, one shift works sixteen hours a day, with an eight-hour break to sleep in a container hotel next to the mine, and of course meal breaks. Then the second team goes in, rested after a two-week vacation in the city. So every two weeks we have our hands full, because on the first day of their freedom the miners usually get drunk and cause problems. They have to cope somehow.

There are always a few cases that go to court even though the police try to be understanding. More serious crimes are rare these days. Usually it comes down to disturbance of peace, fights and, ultimately, acts of vandalism. This time someone clearly went too far. That didn't surprsise us. In fact, it may have been more surprising that heavy crime among the 'long shifters' was so rare. Work in such a system is extremely exhausting physically and requires iron nerves. Not to mention that it is in clear contradiction with the Labor Code.

So why do people agree to do it? Because they earn some good money, much better than with traditional systems, and the food provided to them at the mine is always of the highest quality. It pays off for the companies to offer this group of miners more money and privileges than others, for a very simple reason. These companies also include shops, bars and entertainment venues where miners spend all their income during long breaks. It is created a closed financial scheme, much to the satisfaction of the chairman.

The man lying on the autopsy table was very young, maybe twenty years old. Judging by his hands, he only recently started working in the mine.

"One of these types of kids, lured by a vision of good wages and premature self-reliance," muttered Scott. He looked at me. "Did he have any papers with him? His family must be notified."

"The data in his documents is 'officially fresh', I've checked already. They were registered under the name Thomas Sanderson.

Nothing strange, I suppose. Many people acquire new documents when moving to Lunnar. If they don't have a criminal record, no one makes a big deal out of it."

"Right," he scratched himself thoughtfully next to his left visor. "You will need to take a DNA sample and ask for a central database for identification. No point in trying at the police one, if he was given documents in a new name, there's not a chance he'll be there. They will probably send a response in a month at best."

"I'd still try the police one," I said. "Some counterfeiters can be very smart. The documents look authentic, but I wouldn't trust them."

He nodded slightly.

"Let's go to my office. I don't think we'll learn anything else here."

The commander's office had the only connection, with full access to the police information database, including destroyed data deleted for various reasons. Only the inspector had the right to use it, and no one, not even the doctor or me, would dare to fire it up on their own.

"Scotty, can I ask you something?" I said, closing the door behind me.

"Of course," he looked at me as he turned on the computer.

I sat in the corner.

"Colonel Sirtis recalled during our conversation that she was awarded during the 'cartel wars'."

"Yeah, what are you confused about?"

"That's the first time I've heard about such wars. To tell you the truth, of any wars. After all, there are no more armed conflicts between states on Earth... I searched the net, but I couldn't find anything there. What's the big idea?"

He smiled with a slight pity, as he always did when I was uninformed on some important issue.

"Not everything can be found online. You could try Sue, if you'd asked her, she'd probably have pulled that information. They are well disguised, but this girl managed with more complex things."

"So?"

He looked at the screen where the network accessibility icon flickered.

"Cartel wars began when we were both young, even before you were born, and lasted two years. They were associated with the destruction of criminal bastions in Eastern Europe in areas affected by environmental disaster. The criminal cartels had enough money to get there and do their business from there. Lois Ann then volunteered for an operation to free the world from organized crime. Though of course, information about the war and its course was blocked. The general public couldn't find out about it because it would undermine humanity's sense of security. It couldn't have been allowed to happen. Officially, the military was sent to the second hemisphere to help clear the area after the disaster. All in all, I guess that's technically what happened."

"The colonel must be very brave to volunteer to go there," I said, when he paused, probably looking for the right words.

"That, too… but mostly wanted to prove her usefulness in the army. You see, before the disaster there was another civilization… we came from it, but we have different priorities. Back then, when a boy wanted to become a girl, it was treated as having a different 'mental gender', and no one was really that surprised about it. They even helped undergoing such changes. The approach to homosexuality was also very tolerant, but I guess that's not surprising."

"I know," I recalled the students' history books that I read enthusiastically. "There was a nightmarish overpopulation back then, so the issue of fertility was an unregulated problem. Then, after the disaster, when more than half of humanity died, it became difficult to access food, and the number of healthy children decreased dramatically, so the approach changed. Deliberately mutilating your body to achieve self-served comfort has become something overly undesirable."

"And euthanasia was introduced for those who were completely useless," Scott added. "It was a drastic decision, but we cannot judge the decisions of the authorities at that time from our point of view. Anyway, we're not much better today either. We can't afford to be."

I nodded. The well-being of society requires sacrifice, it's taught to children from when they're little. It's not possible to please everyone and at the same time support the sociostasis.

Society is like a machine. When we allow inefficient parts to exist in it, we weaken the whole which eventually leads to disaster.

"I don't understand, however, what problem is it to anybody that someone surgically changes their sex," I muttered.

"You haven't figured that out yet? After all, from the point of view of biology, a person after such a surgery is neither a man, nor a woman, or even a hermaphrodite. They become completely useless when it comes to reproduction, whereas before surgery they could've had healthy, fertile genitalia. Wastefulness, child. Something we're been fighting against for decades."

Ah, yes. They fought against it more strongly back then, because the Earth was being depopulated at an alarming rate. Therefore, transgender people began to be treated for psychiatric and neurological conditions in order to maintain the gender balance necessary for procreation. Once the nutrition problem was brought under control, a healthy reproductive cell became as precious as gold, because in principle every newborn consumer will eventually become a manufacturer. Someone had to develop the goods of common use.

"But automation..." I began.

"Even in an era of automation and robotics, you're going to have a hard time without people in the industry. That's why, for example, homosexual people began to be treated as reactionaries. Their way of life, previously accepted and even subject to legal protection, has become a threat, something disgustingly antisocial. I'm not saying at all that it was fear, but that's just how it was reasoned back then. And it took a long time after the disaster before non-heterosexual stopped being persecuted and were allowed to live peacefully. Although they are still treated like freaks when they don't agree on treatment. As you know, a simple neurological procedure is enough to change someone's orientation nowadays, but not everyone is willing to do it."

I understood that. I also learned in school about the post-disaster period, called the Great Despair, when it was unclear whether humanity would go extinct or not. All students listen to lectures in schools on how this has affected all sectors of the economy. Although now only the most recent history is taught, so as not to put young people under a historical ballast, you had to know a little bit about it to understand the modern world.

"So what does this have to do with Colonel Sirtis?" I asked. "We no longer have these problems, on the contrary, since we even need genetic control."

"Not exactly. Genetic control is to give birth to healthy babies, not to just let any and all be born, as many as possible, no matter how they turn out. And we still have a problem of under-population. However, people like Lois Ann are seen today simply as freaks who don't want to be treated, and ones like that are not eagerly accepted into the military. And so, her journey really wasn't an easy one. At first, she fought to be allowed to change her body, and then to join the army as she is. As you can see, she managed both. She earned the respect of colleagues and superiors, she was even promoted. Hardly anyone in her place would achieve such success.

It was hard to disagree. I didn't know anyone who would change their gender before, but I've heard of them. They were classified as 'incurable' and eventually had surgery allowed, but it was difficult for them. They had to change not only the gender, but also the person and place of residence to avoid not so much social ostracism but more a misunderstanding. People just didn't know how to react to them. Families were usually rather relieved to forget about their existence. They had to build their own life and their own little world from scratch.

Colonel Sirtis was lucky. She found her place in the army and probably didn't need anything else. I was just wondering how a floress used to a comfortable life would find herself in that place. I couldn't imagine it, despite my best wishes.

"All right," I sighed. "Input the data of the killed one, let's see what we get."

We both leaned over the computer.

"Hmm, interesting," Scott said a short time later. "It looks like we have something, just not in the section we expected."

On the screen we saw a folder marked with the letter T. We both knew what it meant – Top Secret. Cavanaugh quickly entered the code sequences, but had to enter a special access password. For this part of the operation, he told me to turn around, and I did so without objection. Working in the police, one becomes accustomed to the fact that there are things that cannot be betrayed even to someone who is trusted unconditionally.

"Interesting... It seems that our deceased didn't find himself here for no reason."

A photo and a short data bar appeared on the screen – Jose Martin Sanchez, born in Sao Bernardo, graduate of the Political Academy, registered two years ago as an apprentice at the Department of Economic Control. So, he was older than he looked, and he certainly wasn't just a simple worker. I looked at Scott.

"You have to go to Merrick with this. That's one of hers."

"It looks like it. But if so, how did someone like him become addicted to 'golden rain'?"

"He didn't," our doctor's voice sounded from the door. He must have been standing there for a while.

"What do you mean?"

"I think that he wasn't aware about consuming the drug," McCave came up to us and looked at the screen. "I checked the intensity of drugs in his hair with a spectrograph. It's a fairly accurate way of testing for poisons, because hair grows at a certain rate, four yoctometers[7] per femtosecond[8] which means, about a centimeter a month. And chemical compounds are deposited in them like tree rings in a tree trunk so it's easy to determine when someone began receiving a drug or a poisonous element... "

"So?" he was interrupted by Scott, who didn't like such lectures.

The doctor threw him a wry glance. His blue eyes, which, with his black hair and slightly intriguing skin, seemed even brighter, glowed with irony.

"So, our deceased received very large doses of 'golden rain' in a relatively short time, about five weeks. Someone intentionally poisoned him in a way that looked like a 'natural' overdose. And they probably would have qualified his death as that in the hospital morgue if he hadn't been stabbed and sent to us. They just wouldn't do any extra tests then, because what for?"

---

[7] yoctometer, submultiple of a meter, equal to 10^{-24} m.

[8] femtosecond, one billiard of a second.

"Five weeks, you say?" Scott went back to the computer and started typing. "Interesting. According to the official records, Thomas Sanderson started working at AMOS two months ago. They figured him out quickly... don't you think that's weird? That it's way too early?"

McCave shrugged. He took the nicotine chewing gum out of his pocket and threw it in his mouth. He was saving the cigar given to him by the inspector like the biggest cheepskate would his pepes, knowing very well that obtaining another box was unlikely for the next few years.

"In this cursed by all the legendary gods and modern people colony, nothing will surprise me," he said. "But that's not my business. I only provide results of tests, you're the ones looking for culprits. Let everyone do their job, and the world will go on spinning."

He was always caustic, ironic, but now I felt that there was something else bothering him. I asked him directly. He looked at me, surprised.

"And I thought I was controlling my facial expressions well," he said after a while. "Maybe you're better than I initially thought. Yes, I'm worried about something."

"About what? Kelly, you can trust me, you know that."

He forced a smile.

"Kendra wants to become a detective, he said. "She's been going on about it for weeks, so it's not just a whim. Do you think she has a chance?"

I wasn't very surprised. Officer Maru wore a C1 sign on her forehead, but she didn't lack ambition and stubbornness. She may not have had a very high intelligence ratio, but she made up for it with incredible diligence. I could have guessed that sooner or later she would want a promotion.

I felt embarrassed. It wasn't just Kelly, but the rest of my colleagues have also been treating me for some time as if it was only a matter of time before I was officially declared the deputy. Sometimes they came up to me with cases that had to be approved by the inspector or disputes that had to be resolved from above, and I didn't know what to say to them. Instead of being proud of myself, I felt like a concubine, promoted through... the bed. It was very embarrassing for me, especially since Scotty himself saw nothing wrong with it and even encouraged me to make decisions that I haven't grown up to make yet.

"You know, I think she would manage, actually," I finally replied. "Of course, not just like that... such work requires training. And the commander would have to agree to it..."

"I don't see why not," Scott said. He must have known about this already, but he didn't say anything out of habit."

McCave sighed heavily.

"And now there's a second problem."

"What's that now?"

"I'm worried about her. Up until now, she mostly worked with papers, or she was a driver like Yamato. As a detective, she will put herself into the very middle of the local swamp. I don't want her to end like Evans."

Scott looked at me.

"Yes, that's a valid point," he said. "But I believe we should leave that decision to officer Maru. Talk to her, Kell. Tell her that I agree. If she persists in this idea, let her write an official aplication and bring it to my office.

"All right," the doctor sighed again, and stood up. "I'll go back to the morgue. If you need me, you know where to find me."

"We know. And you, Leeta, go to Rosanda Merrick and give her the results. She doesn't know anything yet."

I moaned silently.

"Do I have to? Maybe it wasn't her worker."

He looked at me with surprise.

"What are you talking about?"

He couldn't have known. After all, I didn't tell him about every little thing so as not to bore him. And especially because Lieutenant Merrick instilled an irrational fear in me from the beginning.

The reason was the extraordinary resemblance of this woman to my childhood teacher. Her name was Selaya Johnson. Like Merrick, she was a stout and burly African-American, with a very flat, wide nose, short-cut graying hair and small, mischievous eyes. I was terrified of her because I feel that she missed her calling and, despite her role, she couldn't stand children. Of course, she didn't harm us in any physical way, but for all the disciples she referred in the same cold, desolate, subtly sarcastic way that worked better than any old-school whip. We all trembled in front of her, and I did so more than anyone. Bad memories came back to me when I first saw Lieutenant Merrick.

Fortunately, we didn't have much in common with each other. The economic police made life a little easier for us, we were able to deal with strictly criminal cases, but sometimes our spheres of activity became closer, and we had to cooperate. It just so happened that I was the one responsible for this cooperation from the beginning. Merrick must have seen that I was afraid of her since she literally took pleasure from it. Her character was also similar to Mrs. Johnson.

This time, however, she didn't feel like teasing me. When I put the results from the morgue in front of her, she went noticeably pale and her lips were trembling. For the first time, I felt a little sympathy for her.

"How could this happen?" she whispered, looking at the results of the autopsy.

"We don't know," I said honestly. "The investigation has only just begun. I know that economic issues are your department, but this time I think we should cooperate."

She turned her eyes to me, for the first time without a sadistic flash in her eyes.

"You're probably right, sergeant. We've started working in this area rather recently," she looked again at the pictures. "I'll have to notify his parents. How am I going tell them about this? He was their only child."

"Police officers sometimes die on duty. I know those in the economic department are less likely to do so, but it still happens,"

I said coldly, but not out of my dislike of Merrick. I also hated notifying the families. There are few things that are equally depressing. "Allow me to return to Inspector Cavanaugh. As soon as we have a plan, we'll let you know."

She nodded slightly. I left her with her worry and walked out.

I was beginning to see a certain plan. The miners were a rather airtight environment. So airtight that even in the case of a serious crime, they were silent in solidarity. We had serious suspicions that they had something like their own courts which issued punishments, but by agreement of the city authorities with corporations, we did not try to penetrate through that. All companies maintained their own security units to maintain order in factories, processing plants and mines. Normally that was enough. Probably not this time, though.

There was a murder – not in the location owned by AMOS, but in public area. So the case was handed to us. We had to investigate it and solve it as best we could. And this may turn out to be impossible without infiltrating the miners' community. There was no doubt, this was where we should look for the killer. And yet we had only a vague idea of how their community worked. The Vice President of AMOS, Jennifer Testa, promised us all the help she could give, but we didn't count on that.

"We need to have a plug," Scotti said. "Otherwise we won't learn anything. All we have right now is a dead body, we don't even know who could've killed him. No one saw anything, no one heard anything. A typical knife, one you could buy anywhere. There are no fingerprints or foreign DNA. The deceased's connections, sympathies, enemies, all this remains a mystery, because the miners don't want to talk. We don't have a starting point, and overall we can go screw ourselfs."

It was hard to not agree with him.

"That's right," I said. "I fear that we'll have a hard time getting someone inside. Our people tend to be pretty well known, easy to expose. Professional undercovers like Ostronos have their places and have worked hard to earn their trust, so we can't send any of them to the mines just like that."

He raised his eyebrows a little.

"You're right, child. We have very few of them, and the cover of each of them is priceless. What do you suggest?"

I think he was starting to figure it out. I saw the way he looked at him, putting his hands on his stomach.

"Monty spent a lot of time in the mines of Romain Corporation. He knows the job, he knows the professional jargon, and I think he can impersonate a miner. Until now, probably no one knows his true identity, and there are probably no rumors about an artificial man at the headquarters. More likely than not, no one will suspect anything."

He nodded.

"Well, all right. We send him to the mine, and then what? You know very well that an android is not suitable for a conspirator."

"I know," I confessed. "My plan assumes something else. Monty would only listen and remember. Nothing else. And that's what he knows how to do. We give him, say, a month. Then we enter AMOS and pre-emptively arrest all the miners. We'll have forty-eight hours to find the killer among them."

"And you believe Monty will be able to pin point who that is?"

"I don't know. But I think that he will have the information we need, and thanks to that we're going to find out who killed the guy. And why."

For a moment he pondered what he had heard. I saw that he was looking for weaknesses in this regard and considered any potential dangers.

"There's one problem," he finally said. "Monty is very poor at imitating. Androids don't have spontaneity or imagination. They're simple. And... don't function like humans. They don't eat, they don't drink, and they don't go to the bathroom. How is he going to fool the miners? They can easily notice that something is wrong."

"Yes," I confessed. "That's why Monty won't be pretending to be human, but a robot."

"What?"

"A robot. In the mines they use TAs, technical androids. They only roughly resemble people and are not particularly smart, but have a large compartment of personal freedom. It's necessary because they're doing the most dangerous job, they're going where they're afraid to send people to. Monty can be presented to the miners as an improved model. No one is going to be surprised."

Scott's visors pulled a little out of the fixtures and his mouth puckered. He was beginning to like the plan.

"That Jennifer... I think she's sincere," he said after a while. "Just in case, I'll look through her data and see if there's anything suspicious in them. I think we can trust her. We should let her introduce Monty into the team of miners, as a, I don't know... a robot-sapper? You said yourself that he knows about explosives. However, I have a question. Don't you worry about him?"

He hit the nail on the head. I was afraid, and very much so. However, the stakes were high. An important point of police training is the 'elementary community awareness', as the official guidebook calls this part of the lectures. It can be described by the old saying: One for all, and all for one. Like the miners, they were a consolidated environment. I myself went through the One of Us ritual when I was put on the official list. Only that back then I didn't understand what it all meant.

When one of us dies, the rest will not rest until they find the perpetrator and put them to justice – or kill them, which also happens. I haven't yet witnessed such an execution, but I've heard of them. The justice system lets it pass, and the police – I had to admit – did not abuse this privilege. The loudest of such cases was the shooting of the son of the Governor of California by the police, who lured two officers into a deadly trap. But even then, they allowed the police to walk free.

"We have to take a chance," I finally said. "We have no choice. Otherwise, we will never get to the bottom of this. The miners have their own code of honor, none will testify against the other. Meanwhile, one of ours is dead. We must do our best to make the offender pay for it."

"You're starting to sound like a real police officer. We have to talk to your android, call him, he's probably with Mustache."

When Monty wasn't working as my personal bodyguard, he mostly sat on duty or in the archives. Running around with business affairs, Hallie always exchanged a few words with him when they saw each other. It didn't bother her that the interlocutor was artificial, on the contrary, I even had the impression that she likes Monty and was trying to coquette him – rather amusing, because androids, despite having fully functional genitalia, do not feel any libido. They are not capable of that, just like of any typical human emotions.

"People are visuals," said Kelley McCave when I asked him what he thinks about it. "Monty looks like a human being, speaks like a human being, even behaves like a human being, so we subconsciously attribute other human traits to him as well. Which is nonsense. Independent intelligence does not mean emotional life in our understanding. But don't expect Hallie Trent to understand that."

I didn't expect it. Although, like the rest of us, I liked her and treated her like 'the youngest child in the family', I had no illusions about her intelligence. Our messenger was a typical C3, although otherwise there was nothing to complain about... all right, maybe there was, but we didn't nonetheless. Ever since she appeared at the command with an official administration, certified by the local employment office, we've all grown to love her.

Originally from Hawaii, she had lovely light-tone complexion, reaching to her butt shiny black hair and an incredibly cheerful, heartfelt disposition. As she told us all on the first day, she had dreamed of living on the Moon since she was a child and fled home on the day she reached the age of majority to buy a ferry ticket for money earned by a juvenile employment agency. In the future, she intended to become a policewoman. Although she previously thought she was too low-qualified, when she met Kendra Maru, she found that category C didn't interfere with this kind of career.

Monty referred to her as he did to others, in a 'cold, but friendly' kind of way, as the doctor called it. He was interested in my android as he was in any typical patient, he was interested in his psychology, as well as our intimacy and the fact that sometimes we have sex. He had nothing against sexbots. As he said, it is a healthy and safe form of discharge of tension, preventing mental deviance. However, Monty, as a creature endowed with an independent mind, was not a sexbot, an erotic gadget in a nice package. McCave didn't know how to treat him.

I went to the archives, where the android was helping Winston Tchernience, our archiver, to describe new material evidence. Winston, who we called Mustache, was very pleased with this, especially since, thanks to his photographic memory, Monty always knew where everything was and knew how to be helpful. No one ordered him to do so. He just wanted to be useful. I've noticed this many times. I didn't understand this feature of his, but even Karpinsky couldn't explain it

"Come with me," I said. "The old man wants to see you."

He obediently left what he was describing and followed me.

"Hello, Monty," Scott pointed him to the chair. "Sit down. We need to talk. Leeta, lock the door so that no one bursts in here."

Inviting the interlocutor to sit down is due to the fact that people get tired of standing. Androids don't have that. But when Scott wanted to emphasize that he was treating Monty as an equal, he always told him to sit down. I don't know if Monty understood it properly, but it's possible that he did, since he never sat in the presence of a human being without prior invitation.

"We want to send you to a mine owned by AMOS," Scott said as I locked the door of his office. "To the one where the murdered man, Thomas Sanderson, worked. Your task will be to listen, look at and record everything possible, according to the filter that we will develop for you. You know what I mean, we'll need to single out the messages that can help us find the killer."

"I understand," Monty said.

Scott looked at him carefully, as if judging his capabilities.

"As I understand it, you know how to work in the mines?"

"Yes. I was sent where it was a threat to human life, especially from explosives. I know the procedures, the structure of employment and the vocabulary used by the workers of mining level."

"Good," Scott nodded. "Now listen carefully. We know that you can't lie or act. Still, you will have to. You will go into the mine as a new-generation android, only externally resembling a human. For everyone, you will only be a machine. Answer all the questions they ask you as briefly as possible, and questions that aren't related to mining best don't answer at all. Simply say:

'Incorrect question', or 'No data'. No one can know that you think for yourself. Understand?"

"I understand. Why?"

"This question you are also not allowed to ask. Don't ask anything at all, there at the bottom. And that's because there's a murderer hiding among this team, and possibly more than one," Scott paused for a while and turned to me. "That's right. The one who poisoned Sanchez with 'golden rain' is unlikely to be the one who stabbed him in the heart. Don't you think?"

"Yes, that's probably true," I admitted. "I mean, he could have used the knife, impatient with waiting too long for the effects of the drug, but not necessarily. It can actually be two different people. Or more."

"Exactly. Monty, be very careful. Don't let anyone know that you're thinking for yourself," Scott's visors twitched, as they always did when he was thinking deeply about something. "Leeta, he must have a transmitter. Anything that he could use to let us know when something's not going right."

That was a very fair remark. No matter how much we think about it, we would never be able to predict every possible complication. Monty must have some sort of a 'security button'. The Lunnar police had some real arsenal and a rather skillful gadget specialist, but at the moment it was Sven Thorvald who came to my mind. Although he was currently working at the construction of Selenoport, in my brother's team, I was hoping he would not deny me this minor favor.

"Can I have another question?" Monty said.

We looked at him with some surprise.

"Ask."

"Who will protect Leeta, while I am in the mine?"

I was speechless.

"Scotty, did you hear that?" I let out after a moment. "And you're telling me that he's not a person?"

"Ah, let's not quarrel about semantic issues," the inspector was also surprised. "He can think very independently, clearly. But either way, don't worry about that. I will assign officer Maru as Leeta's apprentice. If she wants to be a detective, let her learn. "

I had the impression that the android was not convinced, but didn't say anything anymore.

"Leeta, take care of the transmitter," Scotty turned to me. "I'll bring Jennifer Testa. Without her help, the case is lost either way. And not a word to anyone. Monty, that goes to you, too. You must not repeat to anyone what we've talked about here."

"I understand, Inspector Cavanaugh."

Someone knocked violently on the door of the office. The bell has been broken for several days and our mechanic has not yet fixed it. Sometimes you could get the impression that he felt created for higher purposes, and he certainly worked in his own rhythm and nothing could change that. We all spoiled him, but unfortunately, we had no choice

"Inspector!" we heard Hallie's excited voice. "Someone's here to see you, open the door please!"

I unlocked the door and our messenger almost fell inside.

"Inspector, you won't believe this!" she said triumphantly.

"Won't believe what?"

A tall, slim man in an elegant suit pushed Hallie aside and walked inside. He threw documents at Scott's desk and took off his dark glasses.

"My name is Brel," he said calmly. "I am here to turn myself in."

VIII

If lightning had suddenly struck through the middle of the office, it certainly wouldn't have caused a bigger stupor. We stared speechless at our guest, while Hallie jumped up and down behind his back from excitement.

Scott was the first one to get back to reality. He looked at the documents, looked at the warrant of capture displayed on the electronic board, and then stood up.

"You are under arrest," he said. "Anything you say may be used against you. You have the right to remain silent. You have the right to be examined by a sworn doctor. You have the right to a lawyer assigned from the court during question. If you wish to pay an independent lawyer, the court may not agree to his participation in the hearings, provided that the opinion on his professionalism raises doubts."

This was the standard formula. Brel listened to it with a barely noticeable disregard. He seemed very determined, although he did not look desperate. I couldn't guess what he was thinking.

"I know my rights," he said as soon as the inspector finished speaking. "Although, on the other hand, I am not at all convinced that I am entitled to them, and I think you know why."

"We'll talk about it later," Scott finally stood up, walked up to Brel and grabbed him under the arm. "For now, you will be taken into custody. You will wait there until we complete our current work, which, unfortunately, is rather urgent."

This whole time Monty didn't even twitch. He remained seated, turned with his back to Brel, and stared at the wall. He had no typical human reflex to turn around when someone entered the room or stood behind him. Right now, I was very happy about that. Brel knew him. I preferred that he didn't know what his current role was, just in case. It was better to play it safe.

I took Monty, and together went to the Selenoport construction site. Due to great distance from the center, we didn't go there with a police vehicle, but via an LFC capsule. At this time of day, they were running only on special requests, their timetable included regular courses only during shift hours, that is, when the crews in the mines and near-mine sites changed places. To conserve energy, they were combined together. Although energy banks were charged by the sun, not fossil fuels, with the

Lunnar's enormous needs, every kilowatt counted. When taking them beyond shift hours, you had to pay, and quite a lot at that.

We arrived at the construction site during the lunch break, which is what I was aiming for. The cafeteria in the administrative part was already full, the smell of various dishes floated in the air. Out of curiosity, I looked at the menu board – today they served lentil soup, soy meatballs in tomato-onion sauce with groats, baked pasta with smoked meat and substitute cheese, baked beans with protein sausage and four types of salads. As a sweet dessert there was carrot cake, jelly with soy cream or caramel pudding. A rather decent selection. Portions were also plentiful, not faked.

I didn't have an employee card, but after a brief conversation with the canteen staff, they made an exception and allowed me to purchase a plate of meatballs, a salad and pudding. They didn't even charge me that much. With my meal, I sat down at the table at which I spotted Sven Thorvald, enjoying the taste without haste. Chris was also sitting at the table, discussing something with him, but at my sight they immediately stopped the conversation.

"Hello, sister!" Chris called out warmly. "Did you come to visit me?"

"Not you this time," I replied, grabbing a chair. "I have business with Sven."

Thorvald looked at me, raising his eyebrows slightly. He looked completely different from the last time we saw each other. First of all, he was now clean and well shaved. There was a dress-code on the construction site, so instead of his usual rags, stiff from lubricants and oils, he wore a Selenoport engineering uniform – khaki pants and a dark gray sweatshirt with the project logo printed on it, that is, the image of the Moon with a face, with a cylindrical object in its right eye. From what I remember, this object was a very old imagining of a space vehicle, and the graphic itself must have came from the early twentieth century.

"What is it?" the engineer asked.

I explained to him in short what we needed, not saying, of course, what we need it for.

"Can be done," he said. "I can have it ready tomorrow. It would've been faster, but if you need a signal strong enough to get to the center from the edge, or even from under the surface, I need more time. You need to fine-tune the parameters."

"Sounds good," I agreed. "I'll come by tomorrow and pick it up, around the same time. You have a good menu, it's worth every point."

The meatballs tasted really good, as did the salad, even though I knew it was synthetic, I appreciated the work of nutrition technicians. On the Moon, fresh fruits and vegetables were not available, but the synthesized ones were improved with additional flavors. They also worked on their appearance, and eventually, as the chefs liked to say, your eyes are bigger than your belly. A non-appetizing mess, despite good taste, will not encourage consumption. It's completely different when it takes the form of nicely colored crunchy leaves

"How are you doing here?" I asked between one bite and the other.

"Not bad," he said restrainedly. "It could be worse. I'll manage."

Chris let out a laugh.

"He'll manage... my dear, I have never worked with such a talented technician! He's brilliant. I'll do everything I can to keep him on my team."

"Plato said: Unfortunate! You will have what you desire," Sven muttered into his plate.

"You know Plato?" I asked, surprised. Nowadays, the writings of ancient philosophers were, well, maybe not banned, but nearly inaccessible to the average reader. This has to do with the prevailing view that knowledge of history, apart from one that is recent, serves no purpose and does not lead to anything. I mean, how will it help us today to know that some king long ago had his head cut off, or that another's army murdered half of Europe? Will we resurrect the dead thanks to it? Will we fix anything? No, we will only cultivate animosity between countries and social groups, leading to further misfortunes.

He nodded.

"I've had a lot of free time," he explained reluctantly. "I once received some old storage devices to dispose of and, for entertainment, started reading their contents. It's always some kind of entertainment."

I could understand that. He was sitting in that cut-off area for so long, having only contact with customers delivering scraps, and with inspectors. He must have been terribly bored. Actually, why did he even choose such a life? It would be the easiest to just ask him, but I never liked to pry into somebody's affairs. I preferred to wait for someone to tell me about it out of their own choice. However, all indications were that in Thorvald's case, it would take a long time. He didn't seem like he was prone to confessions.

I'd love to stay with Chris a little longer, but he's had his hands full with work, and so did I. It was time to go back to the headquarters.

The transmitter was ready on time. It was in the form of a narrow, metallic collar with a round medallion, which bore the letters RT, usually placed on robots helping in the mines. We should be free of all suspicions. Jennifer Testa looked at Monty in awe and took him with her, which unexpectedly caused me strange psychological discomfort. I felt abandoned, like I just lost a piece of myself.

"He'll be back," Scott, who could sense everything as flawlessly as usual, put his arm around me. "He'll be fine. He's resilient."

"I know," I swallowed any unnecessary tears with effort and hugged him back. "I'll still miss him terribly. And I'll worry either way."

"It may sound strange, but I will, too," he looked at me with a comforting smile. "Come on, now. Let's get to work, we'll have time off later. A man is waiting for us in custody, who has a lot to explain."

We went down to the cellar, where our temporary detention place was located. As usual, there were quite a few 'residents' in there. This part of the station was constantly expanded, mainly so we don't have to send back to Earth those who received a just few or a few dozen days of arrest. It was better economically to leave them here, though there were some problems, of course, related to the guards, the organization of all the infrastructure, and so on.

Brel was sitting in Block A, which was for custody, not temporary or criminal arrests, which were located a little further away. The rooms of the forensic arrest were simple, strict, without comfort, but Brel seemed okay with that. He was lying in a narrow bunk bed, with his hands under his head, and stared indifferently at the ceiling. His resemblance to Johnson was obvious, and as for Hampton – I couldn't tell, because I've only seen the owner of Romain Corporation in the state of a dried-up mummy, unlike anything or anyone.

"Mr. Brel," Scott said, opening the cell door. "I'm sorry to keep you waiting, but we can finally talk. I'd like you to come with me."

The detainee stood up and, without a word, went to the interrogation room behind us.

"Would you like anything?" I asked, trying to be as professional and experienced as possible, although in the presence of this man, for understandable reasons, I felt severe discomfort. "A caffetino, a sandwich, some tea?"

"Some water will enough," he replied, taking a seat behind the table. "First of all, I want to make a statement."

"We're listening," Scotty poured three cups of synthetic tea drink from the vending machine and put one in front of each of us. Then he turned on the recorder. Without it, we were unable to start the interrogation.

Brel intertwined his fingers and stared at the table. After a while, he raised his head.

"First of all, I had nothing to do with the attack on Julliette Ankes."

"Officer Aneks now."

"If you say so. I am also not responsible for the deaths of officers Silvana Evans and Milton Reeves. I also didn't kill Marceline Munroe and I did not try to assassinate Scott Cavanaugh and Ankes during their vacation at Colchid. I know that you've put the blame of it all on me, as well as a few other minor issues. One more thing, I never used the name Fernando Lopez."

Scott nodded and took a sip of tea.

"Let's assume that we believe you. How do you explain the convergence of DNA traces at the crime scene, not to mention the recordings?"

The detainee smiled bitterly.

"Your first mistake was assuming that I was the only clone of Mr. Hampton," he said. "Fernando is my, so to speak, twin... as far as I know, the other ones were not successful, but we two met all the expectations of our creators. Only that I was superior. Fernando showed some propensity for neurological disorders, his DNA was not thoroughly cleaned of errors. So they decided to eliminate him."

"That's murder!" I let out.

"You're joking. We are talking about a man who, by law, never existed. Dr. Oenas even used the term 'holoman' to describe us, meaning that we are basically air, nothing. An experiment. And if one is unsuccessful, you destroy it."

"But he was not destroyed."

"Not quite. Although, technically he was," Brel untangled his fingers and immediately intertwined them again. I noticed that they were trembling slightly. "We were operated on. I was implanted with a communications chip, and Fernando was deprived of his own will. He became a living robot, a blind executor of orders."

"Whose?"

"I don't know that anymore. Oenas sold him to someone for a good price."

"On someone's command?"

"Probably not, more likely out of her own free will... Hampton claimed that he didn't know anything about it, even though I wouldn't fully believe that."

I furrowed my brows. The owner of Romain Corporation did not seem to me capable of such cynicism, although... what did I actually know about him? Compassion often tells us to attribute good qualities to people simply because they are somehow disabled. But that's not how it works. Anyone who has bad qualities before an accident or illness will still have them. They could even turn out to become worse, since they will have more opportunities to manipulate people.

"How do you know what Leon Hampton said about this?" I asked.

Brel looked at me with his colorless, very calm eyes.

"I talked to him," he said. "Before I came to you."

At the angle of my eye, I noticed that Scott's jaw had dropped.

"How did you know where to look for him?"

"How do you think, Officer Ankes? This cursed chip works both ways. You just have to be able to take advantage of it."

Suddenly I realized what horrible lawlessness had affected this man. No matter whose clone he was or how he was made. He had an independent mind, from the point of view of biology and psychology he was a person, even if the law did not recognize it. If I recognized Monty's right to respect and dignified treatment, then all the more someone like Brel deserved that. Meanwhile, he was used as a carrier so that Hampton could have a substitute for freedom of movement. Complete dehumanization. No wonder he rebelled. Still, not everything was clear.

"Then who could've shot at me? Why did Silvana and her husband die?"

He shrugged.

"Look through their records. You will definitely find an anchor point. They didn't die for nothing, they must've gotten under someone's skin. And it's easy to do that in this place, believe me."

"All right, then," Scott said. "Let's say I buy this whole talk about the bad twin brother and so on, even though it seems like a generic cliché. And I don't really know how we could check that now. The question remains: why did you come here? For what purpose? What prompted you to do so?"

Our detainee smiled again. His face suddenly gave off a diabolical impression.

"You're detectives, aren't you? Take a guess. Figure it out. I came to put my hand in the hands of the law, not to facilitate the work of its guardians. I've said enough. Figure out the rest yourselves. I hear you're intelligent. You won't get anything else from me. May I go back to my cell?"

"Are you so eager to go back there? And not back home?" Scott didn't allow himself to be brought out of balance.

Brel's smile disappeared.

"I don't have a home. A clone is private ownership, it cannot own any possessions."

Scott's visors moved slightly.

"I'll tell them to bring a TV to your cell," he muttered after a while. I saw that he suddenly felt embarrassed. "As soon as possible, we will move you to block B, it is better equipped. If you need something, please notify the guards."

"Thank you," Brel replied politely. "There is very little that I need. I was taught to only need what is necessary."

As we left the prison section, Scott looked as if he completely lost track of everything.

"Something doesn't feel right in all this," confessed. "Do you understand any of this?"

I shook my head.

"Not completely. I have the feeling, however, that we are dealing with something much bigger. Mabel recalled that when Hakat told her to run away, he told her not to trust anyone, including himself. And when we visited Hampton, he said that he hid Number One on the Moon, while a doppelganger was being searched for on the Central Island. Don't you think this is all connected?"

"Who knows," my boss was clearly confused. I haven't seen him like this in a long time. "I need to check something, and you start looking at Silvana and Milton's records. Get miss Herefort into it as well, she's good at those things. There has to be something that has slipped by us."

This meant that I would be able to move home with most of my work for the time being. This possibility was an expression of a special kind of trust, although on the other hand Sue worked mainly from home, like all virtualists. She received the police-issued network access, of course, although I strongly suspected that she would've done great work even without it.

I was just finishing downloading Silvana's archives onto a portable storage device, when Neil Slavik appeared in the headquarters.

"Hey, come over for a second!" I said immediately when I saw him. "I have to talk to you."

"Of course, whatever you need," our penal law expert smiled broadly and walked up to my desk. He sat nonchalantly in a seat and put his foot on top of his leg. "What's up?"

I turned on automatic download and turned towards him.

"How are the civil rights of clones?" I asked.

"What clones?" he was surprised, raising his eyebrows.

"Human clones. When someone clones someone using the FGC method... and creates a doppelganger..."

He shook his head.

"Doppelgangers are formed by other methods. FGC is too long and expensive a process to be useful in subversive, possibly espionage activities. Moreover, it is now legally prohibited as unethical."

"Why?"

"FGC were cultivated for spare parts warehouses for rich and influential people. They were said not to develop a brain as a result of genetic manipulation, but this was not true. They were simply lobotomized. Therefore, such practices were prohibited as soon as a relatively low-cost method of breeding individual organs was implemented."

"Okay," I didn't give in."And if someone now, bred such a clone? What would be its legal status?"

"None. Under the law, a clone is part of a cloned organism, like an extra finger, for example. There are no solutions to treat it differently, because cloning people is illegal. And why do you ask?"

"I'll tell you later," I promised. "I can't right now, not until I figure out certain things myself."

"As you wish, princess. If you need anything, you know where find me."

I didn't want to let Slavik in for now. I knew him well enough to know that he would immediately rush into this matter with enthusiasm, and for now it should be conducted with the utmost caution. My attitude towards it has become more and more personal. Why? Involuntary, I simply felt compassion for Brel. What if people with implantations of the same scale as mine were denied rights by considering them cyborgs? What if in some court I was considered to be the property of Citizen Hakat, given the costs incurred in the reconstruction of my insignificant person? I got goosebumps at the thought, and I understood Brel's feelings well. After all, he had his own will, not someone else's. He must have felt immeasurable bitterness about his situation.

I unplugged the drive from the computer, hid it in a sachet by my waistband, and grabbed the service weapon. When taking sensitive data from the headquarters, even if it was properly encoded, you had to be armed, even when you were taken home by one of you colleagues. Of course, there could not be any question of transporting such a thing by public transport.

Yamato drove me back home and watched me until I entered the gate. The block where I now lived in with Sue was equipped with a dual electronic security system and additionally protected by a monitoring company. In Lunnar, there were three of them – one engaged in the protection of industrial facilities, the other private, and the third of urban infrastructure. In this way, they did not get in each other's way and earned well on the services provided. They cooperated with the police willingly when necessary. The only issue we had with them was the fact that they tended to steal our employees. Private companies have always had better pay than the government ones, but there was nothing we could do about that.

Going up a few dozen steps – we settled on the first floor – I reached for the remote control to individual security settings and inputted the code. The device sounded slightly, which meant that Sue, even though she was at home, armed all the external traps for any uninvited guests. An honorable cautiousness. Having closed the door behind me, I armed it again. Just in case.

"Hey, Sue!" I called out

My friend leaned her head out of her room.

"You're back already? Did the boss give you a vacation?"

"I wish. Unfortunately, I'm coming back with a lot of work. Will you help me out?"

"Sure. I'll just finish the calculations for Horus."

I went to my room and plugged in the drive. Silvana's archive was extensive, and although I could have rejected some of the issues with filters, it was better not to do so. We had no clue what gave her a death sentence. It could have been something that was easy to overlook, something that no one ever paid attention to. It was going to be difficult. I pulled up a padded chair and adjusted it to sit as comfortable as possible. Sid immediately jumped to my knees and rolled into a ball, purring delightfully.

Sue joined me after an hour.

"Where is Monty?" She asked, looking around.

"In the mines."

"What mines now?"

I briefly explained to my friend what had happened. She didn't look thrilled.

"You're not worried about him?"

Yes, that was a good question.

"Of course I'm worried," I muttered angrily. "But what were we supposed to do? We have to get the murderer, and that may be our only chance."

She sat next to me.

"I don't like it. I'm sorry, but it was a bad idea. Someone could hurt him..."

"Don't mess with my head, girl!" I interrupted her sharply. "It's not that easy to harm him. I'm sure he'll be fine."

I wasn't really sure, but what was I supposed to say? It all depended on whether Scotty correctly assessed Jennifer Testa's credibility, or whether he was wrong about her. I wanted to believe that with such an experience he could not have been wrong. After all, he repeatedly proved that he has a police instinct of the highest level. I had to trust him

"Did you talk to Chris?" I asked to change the subject.

My friend immediately beamed, as always when the conversation was about to Chris.

"Yes, he said he'll come for lunch on Sunday. I've been thinking all morning what to serve. What does he like most?"

I almost laughed.

"My dear fool, we'll serve whatever. Chris isn't picky. And you can't cook anyway."

"Yes, I can! Since we moved in here, I've been taking an online cooking course and I'm going to take advantage of that. "

I looked at her. Indeed, she looked determined to show off her new skills, and I was curious to see what would come out of it.

"Let's deal with what's most important for now," I suggested. "We need to dig through the stacks of material, and we don't know which parts of it will be relevant at all, and what from our point of view is simply garbage."

"You're right," she agreed with me.

We both began staring at the screen, where streams of data began blinking, and for now, we stopped thinking about everything else.

IX

"Sister, don't be mad at me for saying this, but why would you get into a relationship with such an old grandpa like that inspector of yours?" Chris asked with slight reproach in his voice.

We were sitting at the table. I managed to force my younger brother to leave his beloved construction zone at least on Sundays and public holidays and have dinner with us. If I was on duty, I would get off for an hour to have a quick meal at home. Sue was infinitely grateful to me for this and was practically going crazy with happiness. Me, a little less so. Initially, I hoped that her infatuation with Chris would pass, but there was no indication of that. On the contrary, it only got worse. It worried me because I knew my brother well and I didn't think that he would reciprocate Sue's feeling.

Not that Chris was indifferent to feminine charms. But I never really noticed that he was attracted exclusively to girls of classical beauty or recognized attractiveness. He rather belonged to those men for whom the sexiest female organ was the brain, and as for purely physical traits, he was attracted rather randomly, sometimes not pretty at all. Quite the opposite of our good Doctor McCave. He himself had a very high IQ, but living feelings aroused in him mainly 'small women', childish and clumsy.

Although constable Maru, with whom he lived with for some time, was certainly not like that, but at least she didn't lack sex appeal. It was enough that he felt like a knight with her. That's what he needed – to be able to say from time to time, 'my little fool, I will take care of it'. And to feel that he is the better, stronger part of the relationship.

Sue could have been Chris's type, sure. Only that right now he was consumed by the construction of Selenoport, he could not think or talk about anything else. At this point, the only woman with whom he had anything to do was the chief architect Yonescu. I was afraid that he would eventually hurt my friend and not even be able to understand what he had done wrong. I tried to explain it to Sue, but I felt like she wasn't listening to me at all. It annoyed me, but at the same time I was a little jealous of her. I've never been in love like she was right now.

Did I love Scott? It was hard to say. For me, he was more like a pillar on which I could always lean against, regardless of the circumstances. I felt incredibly safe with him. I liked him very much, and we understood each other very well. But I didn't know, I couldn't tell if it was love. Meanwhile, Sue literally beamed, walking around with larks singing in her ears and her head in the clouds, thinking only of my brother.

I envied her a little bit. To be this much in love, even though I have felt some kind of infatuation. This is normal, especially at young age. But I've always been too serious, too careful to let my feelings take over me.

"You don't know anything about that," I finally let out, just to say something.

He didn't think much of that. He continued to eat with taste, which was a good sign of Sue's freshly acquired culinary skills. I had to admit that she had actually learned some decent cooking skills, and even though she had only simple substitutes that were available in Lunnar, most of the meals she's made have been successful.

"I know what I'm talking about," he said after a while. "He's old. You can see at first glance that he doesn't take any antiage pills. You don't know how he is with fertility. And if you want to have a child, then what? With you, as far as I know, there are no issues. And him?"

It was something I definitely didn't want to talk about with anyone. Chris was right, but not for the reasons that he thought. I recently talked to Scott about these very issues. That's how it somehow worked out.

"Officially, I am forbidden from reproducing," he confessed to me. "No, not for genetic reasons, only for legal ones. I'm one of the TS Kids."

I didn't expect that, truthfully. Top Secret Kids, abbreviated simply as TS, are children born illegally by couples who have been denied a procreation license. Sometimes – the public has no idea about such possibilities – they manage to hide such a child from officials until the removal of a toddler from a loving home can already seriously harm his proper development. So, if the child is healthy, such families in a way achieve their goal. With the fact that, of course, it has a price.

"It's none of your business," I finally dished out. "Do I ask you about your romances?"

He laughed.

"There wouldn't be much to talk about..."

He was interrupted by a trill of incoming messages from my messenger. I apologized, wiped my mouth with a napkin, and picked it up. I saw Dr. McCave's face on the miniature display. He looked very serious, not to say upset.

"Leeta, I sent Idalgo to pick you up," he said. "You are needed back at the headquarters right now. I know that Scott gave you a vacation, but you have to stop it for now."

I wanted to ask if it was absolutely necessary, but he hung up. That was very alarming, because Kelley rarely did that. He was too well-mannered for that.

"I won't be staying for dessert, my dears" I said, getting up from the table. "I have to go to work, something happened."

Sue looked anxiously at Chris. He caught her gaze and smiled reassuringly.

"I'll stay," he promised. "I will gladly spend time with someone as nice as you. We'll play chess or monopoly, listen to music... I'm free today anyway."

"Wonderful, I made some peach melba! And sangria with ice..."

I listened to them with one ear, tightening my uniform. I was glad that they got along, although I still had some concerns about what would come of it. Sue was very involved, but I wasn't sure about Chris. It worried me, but I couldn't do anything about it. Either way, it looked like I was about to have bigger problems.

Paul Idalgo knew almost nothing. He was sent to pick me up, and that's all, nothing was explained. Interestingly, the order was given to him by McCave, not Scott, whom no one had seen for two days. That already was alarming, especially when it is taken into account that the inspector literally lived at the headquarters. Something must have happened. Someone else would probably know more, but Idalgo, who at the police station was someone like a bouncer, a dogsbody and a back-up driver, probably barely classified as C3, and didn't have a very agile mind.

Kelley was waiting for me at the entrance. That was also unusual.

"Come inside," he said, before I could speak. "To the chief's office."

"But he's not there."

"That's fine. You'll know everything soon."

Until now, I have never entered the commander's office in Scott's absence. I felt strange, as if I was committing some kind of offense, or at least gross obscenity.

The doctor carefully closed the door to the inner lock and only then looked at me.

"Leeta, the situation is bad," he started. "Scott disappeared two days ago and so far has not given a sign of life. One of Ostronos' pals claims he was taken away by a vehicle with the WBI marking. I don't know how much he can be trusted, he's a homeless drug addict in the last stage of degeneration... but that doesn't mean he's lying."

"He could have been wrong... are you sure it was Scott that he saw?"

"How many old officers have visors like him? Come on, think about it."

I sat in a chair, trying to calm down and think clearly. Why would the WBI take our inspector? As far as I was aware, the investigation into the tragic death of Prosecutor Cable was still ongoing, the 'worldies' had their hands full of work and would unlikely play in some meaningless stalking. Unless Scott is someone they suspect... but of what?"

"I already notified Colonel Sirtis," Kelley continued. "If Ostronos' revelations prove to be true, we will be facing a difficult battle. It is better we have the garrison's support. Just in case."

I had to clear my throat before I started talking.

"Kell... Something strange is happening. This could have to do with Scott's abduction if it was indeed an abduction. The point is that we have discovered something... I don't know if I'm allowed to talk about it. "

"In this situation, I think you should."

Under his blue gaze, my resistance gave in. I told him about the meeting with Number One and Hakat, as well as Hampton in his bedridden state, who still runs the entire company. He listened and nodded with slight movements of his head.

"It must have gotten really dangerous on the Central Island, since the Chief of Arms decided to send Number One all the way over here," he said when I finished. "A doppelganger, you say? I wonder who was duplicated. It's a complicated process, especially when you want to fool the sensors. And you have no chance of infiltrating the government without it. DNA, fingerprints, the retina pattern must match... the latter is the most difficult, but doppling specialists can manage, somehow."

I couldn't really imagine how they were doing it, but at the moment the technical details were irrelevant. Things were complicating at the speed of light, and I didn't know what to do. McCave didn't give me time to panic. He put the code on the access panel (how did he know it?), pulled out one of the desk drawers, then took out a thin rectangle of plastic, covered with computer foil and a small box.

"Scott wanted to give this to you himself," he said. "But it looks like we can't wait for him."

"What is it?" I asked helplessly, feeling as my hands become cold as ice.

"Your appointment as deputy inspector, the document of promotion to lieutenant and the new ID card, together with the badge. They sent this to you from Earth a few days ago, but Scott didn't have time to give it to you. You're the commander here now."

"WHAT?! Kell, I'm not ready!" I was completely stunned. Promotion to lieutenant, just like that? How? I have officially pinned the senior sergeant's insignia. And now I was supposed to be a lieutenant – although there were no longer such ranks as a staff sergeant, it was still a jump by two ranks, and almost immediately after the previous promotion.

"On the frontlines, when the squad's commander dies, it happens sometimes that a simple soldier takes over the command."

"But I... who is going to listen to me?!"

He grabbed me by the shoulders and shook me hard.

"Get yourself together. We are probably facing a confrontation with the 'worldies', we can't do that without a commander. You're stronger than you think, Scott could see that in you from the very beginning. Don't let anyone see lack of faith in your own abilities."

He let me go and, before I could gather my thoughts, he fastened the new badge on my belt, not a standard, oval, worn by officers, but triangular, gold-plated. He removed the now obsolete marking from the official epaulet, and attached a wide metallic beam of the lieutenant and an inverted double croc, which is available on the Moon to the deputy inspector. He threw the old badge unceremoniously into Scott's drawer. And then he saluted, in accordance with the rules.

"In this box, you also have the code for the highest access to Scott's computer. You'll need it," he added.

There was banging on the door.

"The military has come!" Hallie yelled into the internal microphone.

Kelley looked at me. I pressed the button on the desk panel and the doors spread open. Our messenger ran inside and stopped, looking for Scott.

"What are you waiting for? Tell them to come in," I said, trying to make my voice sound as commanding as possible.

She scanned me with her eyes, stopped for a moment to look at the epaulet and the marking. Her eyes rounded and she was speechless.

"Out of my way, kid," Colonel Sirtis pushed Hallie aside and entered the cabinet as if it were her own.

She looked even more belligerent than usual. She was wearing a field uniform and a military scarf, tied as usual, high enough to hide Adam's apple. She may not have been ashamed of it, but she didn't want it to remind her of the past. Through operation you can change a person's gender even to the smallest details, but this one remains unchanged and betrays everything.

Another character in uniform followed in her footsteps. Mabel. Next to the tall and muscular Sirtis, she looked even more petite than usual, but the uniform added dignity to her, and the boots with high soles to her height. The complete lack of make-up did not take away her beauty, but made her look younger, and the short hair added a new, different kind of charm. She gave off a sense of strength and self-confidence. It was clear to see that the military service was good for her, and that she felt unexpectedly good in it. She greeted me with a short nod of her head, stood against the wall and straightened herself, putting her hands behind her back.

"Hallie, get out and close the door behind you," I recommended seeing that the curious messenger wouldn't even think of leaving the office out of her own free will.

"Should I bring some tea, or caffetino and biscuits?" she offered nicely, but when I wrinkled my eyebrows menacingly, she turned on her heel and marched into the hallway, demonstratively grumpy.

Sirtis approached me and snaped her fingers slightly on my new badge.

"Congratulations, although I do not envy you," she said. "Under different conditions, this would've been a reason for best wishes and all that, but right now it would sound ironic."

"Did you learn anything?" I asked with hope.

She pulled up a chair. I saw that she wanted to put her legs up on the desk as usual, but she stopped herself somehow.

"There was no time to do an interview. But I know Scott, and I know that he would never just disappear like that, without a word. He's a very responsible man."

"Apparently, he was abducted by the WBI."

"Well, not surprising. They took away your investigation into Cable's death and are chasing after their own tail. They have no idea what's going on here, and they're too distrustful of themselves to ask for help like normal people. What are you going to do?"

"Track him down and get him back," I replied angrily. "I know that the WBI has broad powers, but what they did is unthinkable. If they wanted to interrogate Scott, they could have sent an official summons. If they're going to behave like pirates, then so will we."

"Nice idea," she admitted restrainedly. "But there is a problem: we don't know where their headquarters are. Or do you know?"

McCave made a brief sound, something between a cough and a laugh.

"Tiger Lily, my dear, after all, they are not as clever as they think they are. Nothing remains hidden from the Lunnar vagabonds, I guess the same as with any, anywhere. We know perfectly well where our agents have made their warm nest. It was necessary for us to know what place to politely steer clear of while looking for someone or something. No one would want to spend months explaining how they only accidentally exposed the secret headquarters of those wise guys."

From the voice of our pathologist sounded clear reluctance, if not contempt. I understood him well. Dressed in expensive suits, driving in service limousines. WBI agents always put up airs and not without reasons, since their privileges really allowed them many things. The result, however, was that the police and military cooperated with them very reluctantly, and only in a state of supreme necessity. And if they could make WBI lives harder, they did so with malicious joy.

"So, it's decided, then," Sirtis said dismissively. "Let's go and take what is ours."

I've already managed to get to know her enough to know that she really is willing to do it. I myself was willing to opt for such a solution. However, the matter was not that simple. First, we had no hard evidence that the WBI were behind Scott's disappearance. When thinking about the case level-headed, it was even necessary to admit that it was unlikely. The agents of the 'World's Office' obeyed the law in an almost obsessive way. The insidious abduction of a police inspector simply wasn't like them. Something didn't seem right in all this.

"Not yet," I said. "We have to check a few things first, so that we don't make a dumb mistake. First of all, we need to talk to Ostronos. And," I paused here for a moment, "notify the governor."

"What for?" Colonel Sirtis was surprised.

Ah, of course, she had no idea about our visit to his residence and our conversation with Khamala.

"I have to tell him if we're planning to confront those buffoons," I explained reluctantly. "If the 'worldies' have actually abused their power, then the governor must issue a decision to relegate them from the colony."

Which, I suspect, he will do even too willingly, I added in my mind. I knew that the takeover of Khamala's investigation by the WBI was very inconvenient for him, and that he would happily get rid of them. The question is whether it will have a legal basis.

I pressed the intercom button.

"Constable Maru, come immediately to the commander's office," I said into the microphone.

With the second button, I unlocked and moved open the door slightly. After a few moments, Kendra Maru stood in the doorway, looking at us with some surprise. Especially at me. Behind her I saw the nosy Hallie, trying to hide from my sight. I didn't let anything show. Now was no time to rug the messenger.

"Take two guys and arrest Ostronos under any excuse," I instructed her, without giving time to digest the situation. "If possible, also grab the man who reportedly saw how the 'worldies' led the inspector away. Just make it look like a normal arrest. No unauthorized person can suspect anything. Go."

Maru visibly hesitated, then soldered precariously and made a 'backwards turn' according to the rules. Through the eyes of my imagination, I could already see Hallie running around, spreading the sensational message that 'we've got a new boss!'. Her happiness must be immeasurable, there she goes, with the BIG NEWS that she's the first to pass it on. One could only guess what she would add from her own imagination.

"Do you think that such delay of the rescue operation is the right thing to do?" Sirtis asked, raising her eyebrows.

"I think it's the right thing to be careful," I said. "The 'worldies' are unlikely to hurt Scott, they won't take such a big risk. And for us, any mistake will cost us dearly. And in the end, maybe it's not them? We need to know the facts before we act."

"Maybe. All right, you rule here now, so rule. I'm taking my people to the casino, I promised them that. Let them have some fun. They're my best team, they deserve it."

"To which casino?" I asked. "I need to know where to look for you."

"Relax," Colonel Sirtis yawned demonstratively and moved to the door. "I'm leaving you, so far still, my orderly. She knows where we'll be. Call me when you think it's time for action, and if something disrupts the connection, you'll send her to me."

Telecommunications on the Moon depended on so many factors that no one could predict when they would malfunction and for how long. Even bipers couldn't always be trusted. Among other things, that's why Lunnar companies employed messengers, we too.

I tried not to let myself know how happy I was. I will have the opportunity to talk to Mabel, whom I have not seen since that memorable day. I was really curious about how she was doing in the military and whether she felt safe there. Everything seemed that she did. For now, however, we had to postpone this conversation. The door opened before the colonel and Hallie nearly fell inside, immediately taking on the expression of a misunderstood innocent girl.

"You're eavesdropping again, Trent?" I tried to be strict, although the sight of extremely false repentance on the face of our messenger could make the dead laugh.

"I just wanted to be on hand in case you needed me," she said sweetly, fluttering her eyelashes like the heroine of an old movie. It forced a smile out of me.

"If so, bring private Rochester to the social room and make her a good caffettino. And don't let me see you here until I call for you."

Hallie bent her lips into a horseshoe like a whimsical baby and marched with dignity from the office, followed by a visibly amused Mabel. I closed the door behind them and looked at the doctor. He struggled to hold back from laughing.

"You sure started your ruling with thunder."

"What was I supposed to do?" I let out. "Give me a break, Kell, if Scotty could barely take a hold of our little circus, then I'll be defeated by the end of the week."

"Well, worst case scenario you still have this week ahead of you. That's a lot of time."

"Can you stop?"

"I cannot," the doctor became more serious. "I have the results of Brel's tests for you. I didn't have time to give them to Scott. Genome mapping takes a lot of time, but you have all the answers thanks to it."

He gave me a printout, reminiscent of an old-type computer algorithm. I must have had a stupid expression, because he rushed right away with explanations.

"He's dying, Leeta. The FCG technology is imperfect. Individual organs work perfectly, but the nervous system pays for it with accelerated maturation. "

"Which means?"

"The clone grows up in about two years, that is, during a single year he goes through ten human years, in a way. This is achieved by lowering telomere levels in cells while increasing the supply of growth hormone. After that, all you have to do is to inhibit this process and bring about endocrine normalization... in theory. The central nervous system unfortunately doesn't react well to such manipulations. The nuclei of neurons themselves disintegrate, as if they were aging at a pre-imposed rate. Synapses degenerate and the production of neurotransmitters decreases. For Brel, it started about two months ago. He probably won't live to see the end of the investigation, much less the process."

It sounded horrible, like something from a nightmare.

"Did the clone makers know about this?" I said with difficulty after a while.

"Of course. When they were mass produced for organ storage, it didn't matter. They deliberately damaged their brains anyway. Those who created Brel and Fernand probably thought they had managed to solve the problem, but if so, they made a huge mistake. They only masked the first symptoms."

"Does he know about it?" I asked quietly.

"Of course he does. That's the only thing that could explain why he suddenly came here and gave himself in."

I tried to imagine what a mentally developed, even more so, a very intelligent man, could feel when he suddenly learns the truth – not only that he is not a human being under the law, but that a factory defect condemns him to premature death and, most importantly, that no one cares.

"This already happened," I muttered vaguely. "In a book... or maybe an old movie... only that there it was pre-planned."[9]

"What?" McCave didn't understand me.

"Nevermind, it's nothing. Kell, is there really nothing you can do to help him?"

"I don't think there is. I gave him the strongest drugs for demyelinating diseases, a loading dose. I hope it will slow down the degeneration."

"I have to talk to him. Come with me," I got up quickly and rushed out the door.

He caught up with me on the stairs.

"Why?"

"You'll know why soon enough."

We took the elevator to the prison level. Brel was still in cellblock A, but it was equipped with additional equipment, a TV and a beverage distributor. I easily guessed that Scott had a hand in this.

---

[9] "Blade Runner", based on a novel by Philip K. Dick.

Brel was lying on the bunk-bed, reading something on the reader, but at our sight he put it down and sat up, directing a questioning look towards me.

"Mr. Brel, I ask for a sincere answer."

"If I'm able..."

"You came to the police station after the visit of Leon Beavis Hampton, yes?"

"That's correct."

"What did you do there? Why did you go there?"

He smiled, squinting. He looked at me for a second, and then he began to lightly, almost silently, hit his hands.

"Bravo, miss. I've been sitting here for more than two weeks, and no one has yet asked me such a fundamental question."

"Well?"

He kept looking at me.

"You figured it out, didn't you?"

"I want you to say it yourself."

I had no idea by what a miracle I was able to remain calm. I would have given everything for Scott to be with me right now, but I was alone and had to face it all by myself, devoid of the moral support of the boss.

"I killed Hampton," Brel said calmly. "I turned those stupid machines of his along with the communication. I can give you his current address, you can see for yourself.

I took a few deep breaths to calm myself down. I turned on my mobile logger.

"Give me this address, please."

"Lunwark, fourth quarter, 18th sector. Mine processing plant. The residence is at level minus two, under the warehouses. Numeric code for the opening panel is 075620," Brel recited. His voice dropped suddenly, taking on a metallic, nearly raspy tone. "Access password is Uroboros."

Something has also changed on his face. I couldn't say what because I didn't have time to think about it. The image that formed in my mind was like something out of a horror movie.

I turned around and rushed towards the elevator.

"Sergeant Chekov, to me!" I screamed, bursting into the office. "Assemble an intervention group. You should be in the hangar in two minutes. Corporal Kunch! Please write an official search warrant for a factory in Lunwark owned by Romain Corporation, including hidden rooms, and immediately send it to Judge Hollstein! Ideally, take it to him yourself and let him sign it for you as soon as possible. Code black, person in danger."

Before I ran out, I saw an expression of discontent on Kunch's face and a sky-high amazement in the sergeant's face. Poor guy, he probably didn't know what to think of all this – I doubt he even fully believed Hallie's revelations, who usually passed around every rumor indiscriminately without bothering to check its credibility. I must admit, however, that he followed the order and appeared in the hangar immediately after me, leading four guys from the assault brigade.

"You're not going to wait for the warrant... commander?" he asked.

"There's no time for that, Tony. We will make use of the 38th Amendment of the Police Code. Prepare the rover."

It's probably too late anyway, I thought to myself, though we could never be sure. Leon Bravis Hampton was now personifying the status of Schroedinger's cat, and it was up to me to open the box.

I contacted Lois Ann Sirtis from the rover. Fortunately, today the communicators worked flawlessly.

"There's no time to explain, so please listen," I said. "I'd like you to go back to the headquarters and investigate the people arrested by constable Maru. They should be there soon. You'll get the directions from them. Please get the exact address, go there with your people and free Inspector Scott. Dr. McCave will explain the rest."

"Understood," the colonel replied briefly. The advantage of professional military personnel is that they don't waste time asking things such as: how, why, what for, and so on. Unless they, for some reason, refused to perform the given orders, they immediately got to work, without unnecessary whining.

"Where are we going, boss?" Chekov asked, closing the rover's door behind us.

"Lunwark, fourth quarter, sector 18."

"Understood, ma'am."

I sighed desperately. I felt extremely uncomfortable and regretted that my promotion, if at all, took place right now.

"Tony, please... I didn't ask for the promotion. No one asked me for my opinion. I can imagine what everyone is thinking of me now and saying behind my back..."

He smiled kindly and with a little leniency.

"You don't understand anything," he replied, throwing away the formal tone. "We knew from almost the first day that if you remained with us, you would become the deputy inspector. You are the highest ranked and educated of all who are on the team, as far as I know. From the beginning you were the logical choice, the question was how you would do working as a cop. You passed that test without any issue, so we all knew what was going to happen next."

All? I myself had no idea what was happening, and no one told me. I felt even dumber. Fortunately, I was saved from the next conversation by the sound of an incoming call from the messenger.

"Leeta?" the doctor's voice sounded near my ear. The quality was very bad, I barely understood it. "There's an encrypted message that came from Earth's headquarters, for Scott. It's marked as very urgent. Will you receive it?"

"Of course. Send it over," I replied, wondering, at the same time, if the file would get to me at all with this connection. Anything could happen.

Fortunately, it came through, although the download took a few minutes. I decrypted it using the universal police key, but I still had to put my fingerprint on the screen for the text to appear.

In response to your question, we inform you that the bodies of Diana Fox and four other WBI agents were identified through genetic testing, the results of which came to headquarters twenty-four hours ago. The high degree of destruction of the corpses prevented the identification via other methods.

And the caption: *Director of office unit for the extraterrestrial area, Leslie Savopoulos*

"Something serious?" Chekov asked, looking me in the face. I had to be white as sheet, since I could even feel the blood flowing from my head.

I forcefully kept myself together. After all, I couldn't just pass out right now like some damsel in distress from an old novel.

"Very," I replied, without going into details. The situation was serious, and I wasn't yet sure how we would manage.

After thinking about it a little, I picked the shortcut for Colonel Sirtis on the keyboard. For a while I listened to the intermittent signal of lack of communication, until I finally gave up and sent a text message instead. I was hoping it would arrive as soon as the administrators of Lunnar Telecommunications restored the connection back to normal. I could still try the shortwave police radio, but from experience I knew that in Lunnar's conditions they only work at a very limited distance – that is, they are useful during actions in the field, no more than two miles apart. The Moon makes life as difficult as it can.

Tony Chekov, the oldest policeman at the headquarters, knew Lunwark well and didn't even have to look at the screen panel, on which map of the city was shown. He also faultlesly found a factory owned by Romain Corporation, where the delivered output was broken by ultrasound. Then, by using vibrating sieves, they sifted through the powder to filter out lunnites – those that still had some value for technical or jewelry purposes. The filtered grains were then converted into briquettes for fireplaces of exclusive residences, as lunnite was found in magma rocks with high carbon content.

At the entrance the corporate security tried to stop us, but at the sight of our badges immediately stepped back and called the director of the plant. A stocky, dark-skinned man with African traits appeared almost immediately, showed his ID and dryly demanded a search warrant. He looked at us like at some plebeians who dared step in front of him to ask for donations. From where I stood, I started to feel a strong dislike for him.

"Amendment thirty-eighth of the Code of Police Rights," I said coldly. "In justifiable cases, especially when human life is threatened, the police have the right to intervene without waiting for a formal warrant. Take us to your warehouses."

"Don't command me!"

"Would you prefer to be arrested for obstructing the work of officers on duty? I assure you, we have our handcuffs. Take us there, Mr... Stridal, or get out of our way."

He shrugged his shoulders and, without a word, pointed the way with his hand. We went to the basement by his lead, passed by the warehouses and not without difficulty found a disguised descent to the lower level. The director seemed visibly surprised – either he didn't know about the secret rooms, or he was a great actor, since he started looking around the brightly lit corridor with a stupefied expression, probably not knowing what to say.

At the end of the corridor was an armored door. I typed the code provided by Brel onto the panel and then the authentication password. The door clattered and opened. We were immediately struck by the stench of a corpse, and we immediately knew that it was too late for any help. We went inside, taking care not to touch anything. In a comfortably furnished room, on a quiet medical bed, lay Leon Beavis Hampton, or rather, what was left of him – a green, bloated corpse. His androids stood next to walls, motionless, with dead eyes looking into nothing. Brel must have known how to turn them off and took advantage of that knowledge, and no one stopped him.

Controlling my gag reflex, I approached the bed. I looked closely at the deactivated device and was relieved to see that one of them was a respiratory muscle stimulant. This meant that Hampton, devoid of support, simply suffocated. It's not anything pleasant, but it's much better than a slow death from hunger and thirst with a complete inability to call for help.

"Sergeant Chekov, please call in the medical team, technicians and photographer," I turned to Tony. "No one is allowed to enter this room until the technicians do their jobs."

"Who is that?" Stridal asked.

I don't think he was faking it, he was in real shock. I looked at him with compassion. If I was thinking correct, his world was just beginning to crumble.

"That's your boss," I replied.

The man stepped back and hit the wall with his back. His face took on the shade of ashes.

"Him...?"

"You didn't know him and you couldn't have known him. But yes, it was him who gave you instructions and paid you a salary."

"What will happen now?" he was barely able to speak. His whole act disappeared in an instant.

"I don't know. For now, make sure no one leaves the factory site until the police do their jobs. Please block your connection and don't contact anyone yourself. Any attempt to contact anyone from the outside will be treated as sabotage."

I looked at Tony. I had a good nose for taking him with me. He was experienced and anyone would have difficulty resisting him. The police work he literally mastered, and I could rely on him completely, without any worries.

"Sergeant Chekov, you're in charge here now," I said. "I have to get back on the team."

"Yes, boss. Are you going to take the rover or call Yamato?"

"No, I'll take a cab. It'll be faster. And it's also better that you have your own vehicle here. You can't predict what will happen."

He clicked the communicator several times.

"That's for the better, since we still have no connection. "

I cursed silently.

"All the more, please take care of everything. Priority first, permission granted for the use of sharp weapons. I'll send in support and specialists just in case."

Fortunately, there was an industrial taxi company in Lunwark that did some good business thanks to the fact that, in the entire colony, hardly anyone had a permit for a company vehicle. This luxury was afforded by literally few. You could call in a cab by selecting the call code on a panel placed on one of the many concrete pillars with the sign TAXI – one of which was in front of the factory, inviting anyone to use the service.

X

Lois Ann Sirtis was sitting in the commander's office, sipping Scott's best whiskey with a gloomy expression. Judging by the freedom which she felt in there, she had the right to do so. On the plus side, at the very least she refrained from putting her feet on the table this time. It must have been because of me, which showed that she had a certain type of sense and manners.

"How did it go?" I asked, closing and locking the door behind me.

"From one hand, good, but on the other hand, absolutely terrible," she said. "I received your message, admittedly highly distorted, but I was able to read it. We arrested the WBI cell. I don't think I need to tell you what they tried to scare us with... I hope you had basis on which to do that."

She stopped and poured herself more whiskey. She also poured a second glass, for me.

"You should have a drink with me. I insist."

I lifted the transparent vessel, controlling the shakiness of my fingers with difficulty.

"Let's speak by name," I suggested. "It'll be easier that way. Unless you're against it."

"No, not at all. Well... I pushed one of them a little bit and got the location they are currently holding Scott at."

"Where is he right now?"

"Don't panic, kid. He's at the hospital. The doctors said that his condition is critical."

I sat in the second chair and, not thinking about what I was doing, I immediately drank half the glass. The fiery liquid burned my throat so badly that I started coughing, and for a moment I couldn't catch my breath. It probably wasn't just whisky, something was added to it, and in large quantities. Probably pure spirits.

"What did they do to him?" I coughed out when I was finally able to speak.

"They don't know for sure. They probably wanted to get some information out of him. Scott has an implant which neutralizes all substances like scopolamine, and he is very resistant against waterboarding and other attempts at forced extortion, so they must have improvised. We know that he was given large doses of insulin because we found the packages. You know, if you have no blood-sugar, your will is weakened. But without an accurate toxicological profile, that's about all we can tell. Actually, how did you know?"

"What?" I asked semi-consciously.

"The fact that the WBI are playing dirty?"

I shook my head.

"I didn't. Scott was onto something and sent an encrypted message to Earth. The answer came this morning. The woman claiming to be agent Diana Fox is a doppelganger, as is probably her entire team."

Sirtis whistled through her teeth.

"That's new. Doppelgangers in WBI? And not just one, but the whole team? That's spicy."

"More than you realize. Doppelganging is getting out of control. Remember what Mabel said? Hakat told her not to trust anyone, including himself. He probably had reason to fear that he had been doppeled."

The colonel sipped on her whisky with an impenetrable expression.

"What are you going to do?" she asked after a while.

I didn't know what to say. My heart was tearing out towards the hospital and Scott, but my mind was dealing with other things. This is the first time that so much responsibility rested on my shoulders and it fell on me at the worst possible moment. I had to comprehend everything that was happening here alone and I had no one to ask for advice.

Lois Ann finished her drink and got up.

"All right, I'll be back at the barracks," she said. "If you still need garrison support, you know where to find me."

"Of course. Thank you so much for your help."

"No problem. The uniform demands it. And I like you. You have balls, so to speak, even though you don't look like you do."

She left walking nonchalantly and after a while I heard as she commanded Mabel. I realized that I had to postpone the conversation with my friend for later. I didn't even have time to dwell on that, since Slavik came to the office immediately after. He was clearly worn out.

"Miss Ankes... lieutenant Anex, I mean... ah, whatever, are you sure that arresting the WBI agents was a wise move? You know the law, I'd say they have more right to command us, not the other way around."

"Of course, Neil, but they're not agents," I replied. "We're dealing with frauds. They will probably demand a lawyer, block it as much as you can. Use all possible crows, until we have DNA test results from deep samples."

"It's that bad."

"Worse than you think. If you want to help me, get a warrant from the judge to take genetic samples."

He shuffled his feet uncertainly.

"Okay, but under what pretext?"

I gave him a printout of the news from Earth's headquarters.

"Just don't tell a word about it to anyone. It's top secret, at least for now."

He read it and whistled, just like Sirtis earlier.

"I get it now. Don't worry about a thing. I'll take care of the legal side. You do your thing. Until Scott comes back, you're in charge."

Yes, I was in charge. Having no idea about directing even the smallest team. And I couldn't make mistakes because we were playing with very high stakes. I tried really hard to get myself together, took a deep breath and called Kendra Maru into the office.

She came in, saluted, and stood in the formal stance. Her swarthy face didn't express any feelings at the moment, but I figured that she must have felt a little uncomfortable. She worked here longer than I did, she was my friend, sometimes even a mentor, and she watched from the sidelines as I progressed. It couldn't be easy for her, even though she knew about class differences and everything that comes with it.

"I have your application here," I said, trying to make it sound natural. "Inspector Cavanaugh signed it and sent the scan to Earth. The official consent of the authorities is a matter of days, maybe hours. So, I'm appointing you today as a partner to investigator Feri Kunch, bypassing the usual internship and the whole pump. We don't have time for that. You'll get the documents and the new badge later."

"Yes, ma'am," she muttered, swallowing her amazement with effort.

"Take three more guys from the intervention brigade and report back here with Kunch in five minutes," I continued.

"Yes, ma'am."

I already knew what my next step would be. If that's how my life ended up, I had to play with the cards that were shoved in my hands. And the worst thing I could do now, was the thing I wanted to do the most – hide myself in the corner and cover myself with a camouflage sheet so that no one could find me, and so that everyone would forget about me.

*****

The secret headquarters of the WBI, or rather, the frauds posing as the murdered agents, were housed in a modest building on the side of the road. It was pointed to us by Mike, Ostronos' friend. A nervous man devastated by addictions who for two bottles of the worst liquor would reveal all the secrets of the government if he only knew them.

"Are you sure this is the right place?" I asked with doubt. This building didn't look like a secret housing unit to me, but more like a bunch of warehouses.

He nodded nervously.

"Definitely there," he said, sniffing loudly after every word and stepping from foot to foot.

"Health Industries?" At first glance this didn't tell me anything, but soon it dawned on me.

At the beginning of my work on the Moon, I had made contact with this company – it ran a network of wellness rooms and gyms, and distributed suspicious pharmaceutical products, like the fortestim mentioned by Sue. We passed the obtained materials to the prosecutor's office, but what did they even do with them?

"Uhm," Mike muttered vaguely, and wiped his nose with his sleeve. "On the right wall, where the garage is, there's a nameplate, you can go check yourselves. Can I go now?"

I looked at him with compassion. He belonged to the category of people who can no longer be helped since they don't want help themselves. Their fate is a long-decided conclusion, whether we like it or not.

"Yes, you are free. If you ever decide to do therapy, please report to the police station and ask for me," I said.

I don't even know if he was paying attention to those words, he disappeared so quickly between the houses, as if he was afraid that I'd change my mind.

The door of the building was not locked, but it was sealed with military tape, so we really must have been in the right place. Taking all possible precautions, we went inside.

"Collect all the data carriers and all the documentation," I recommended. "Take samples. I'll check the garage. You," I pointed to one of the stormtroopers at random, "you're coming with me."

According to the guidelines, the search of any location had to take place in groups of at least two people, and I was not going to start with a violation of procedures.

There were three dark blue 'perfects' with WBI markings in the garage. All had barely visible rings on the headlights, closed by round flaps. This meant that the trucks were armed and designed for more serious action. I couldn't explore the interiors yet, since that was an area meant for forensic technicians. Important traces could be inside, and it was necessary to ensure that they were not lost.

I finished sealing the door of the second slider when a strange, deaf sound caught my attention.

"Did you hear something?" I turned to the stormtrooper accompanying me. He shook his head in denial, but then the sound repeated, and he heard it, too.

"I think it's coming from that vehicle," he said, pointing at the third slider.

The sound was clearly coming from the trunk. I took care of the lock with the help of a universal police lockpick and to my eyes appeared a gagged man, expertly tied up with duct tape. I immediately recognized him – he was with Diana Fixx when she chased me and Mabel around the military. This time he did not look as menacing or dignified, looking more like a homeless man after solid drinking.

With the help of the stormtrooper, I pulled the man out of the trunk and cut his ties.

"What's going on?" I asked.

"I need to go to the bathroom... right now..." he groaned.

We brought him to where he needed to go. He took care of his business immediately, not paying attention to our presence. I was worried by the sight of blood in his urine.

"You need a doctor, sir... Munroe," I read his name from his ID card.

"First, give me a drink," he said imploringly.

The bathroom was ordinary, that is, with disinfectant spray, not a water faucet, so we had to go to the kitchen. The man rushed to the water tank and started drinking greedily. Seconds later, he vomited into the kitchen sink, also with blood.

"Enough is enough," I said. "Get the ambulance right now. Sergeant Kunch!"

Ferry looked into the kitchen and raised his eyebrows in amazement.

"Who is that?"

"Not important. You're taking over this place. I expect complete professionalism. We can't afford any mistakes at the moment."

"Obviously, boss. Don't worry, I'll keep an eye on everything."

"One more thing. From now on, constable Maru is under your personal supervision. You'll be responsible for training her. Please let me know about the progress of your training and anything you think is important. I need to know if she's right for this type of work."

He smiled under the mustache, which he didn't want to shave despite our ridicules that he looked more like a cowboy from old paintings than a police officer.

"No problem. Although I can say in advance that she is."

"Sure, sure. We'll see."

An ambulance drove up to the building with a siren. Rescuers put Ray Munro on a stretcher and pressed him with belts. I was sitting next to him. The stormtrooper sat in the corner, from where he could observe the road through the viewfinder. Like all those from the intervention brigade, he didn't trust anything or anyone.

"What happened?" I asked when the ambulance began moving.

"I have been compromised," Munroe said, not very clearly since he had an oxygen mask on his face. "I knew that they're frauds, but I was afraid of reporting the matter to the chief. The whole cell could have been infiltrated. I thought I'd get the evidence on the Moon and go straight to the director of WBI, bypassing the business route. I couldn't make it."

"On the Moon... wouldn't it have been easier to do that on Earth?" I asked.

"I wanted to find my sister," he muttered. "I lost contact with her more than a year ago and could not learn anything by conventional means."

Suddenly it dawned on me. Munroe...

"Is your sister's name Marceline?"

"Yes. You know her?"

It was all coming together. He really couldn't have known anything. We kept Marceline Munroe's death a secret in the hope that it would help us find the killer. The only person who knew the truth outside the police – a guard in an office building owned by Romain Corporation – went back to Earth a few months ago, disappointed by the colony's possibilities. Of course, the killer knew the truth, too, but who even was that? Brel? Maybe Lopez? Evidence points to them, but it was better to approach this matter with caution.

"We'll talk about her later. The doctors need to take a look at you right now," I said, as we were just reaching the hospital. "Please think about your own health at the moment."

A medical team took Ray Munroe at the intensive care unit, and we were asked to leave.

"What's your name?" I asked the stormtrooper. Suddenly I was disgusted by the fact that I had to treat this man in uniform like furniture.

"Lance Darin."

"Please make sure that Munro doesn't suddenly disappear or anything like that. I'm going to go see the chief physician Shansam."

In the chief's office I found a medic unknown to me, who apparently felt at home. He looked at me questioningly, so I asked about Scott's condition."

"Inspector Cavanaugh is currently in ICU. He has suffered shock to multiple organs, extensive damage to the cerebral cortex, we still can't stabilize him," he told me, peering into the relevant file on his computer. It seemed that he had replaced the doctor I already knew in this position. I've heard before that Dirk Shansam was here with the intention of returning to Earth, and it seems like he did it. It's a shame, since what this man was saying didn't tell me anything, and I would gladly ask for further explanations. However, all the behavior of the new head physician gave me a clear message: 'I'm busy and you're bothering me', so I'd rather leave.

"How was the damage done?" I only asked. He shrugged.

"It seems that electrodes were inserted through the base of the eye implants," he said. "Direct stimulation was attempted to extract some information. And it was done poorly."

"Can I see him, Doctor Larson?" I read his name from the pin.

"You can. But only through the glass. He is still in a coma, so third-parties are not allowed to enter the isolation chamber."

I wanted to tell him that I was not a 'third-party', but I didn't bother. It wouldn't make sense now, and this guy clearly doesn't care anyway.

I went to the ICU. The nurse pointed me to the right room, not even too interested in whether I was entitled to such a visit. Like everyone in this hospital, he looked tired and resigned. I would bet that he wouldn't be working here long either, only until the end of his contract.

Scott was lying in the isolation chamber, connected to monitors, on which indicators flickered lazily, of which I didn't understand the meaning. I knocked on the glass, but he didn't react. This complete stillness was so unlike him that I could hardly believe it was him. His visors were dismantled and replaced temporarily with an eye band. Without them, he seemed terribly defenseless and alien at the same time. I felt like I was looking at someone I had never met before. This sight was painful and I turned away from the glass feeling as my hands become cold.

Because of this I was now face-to-face with a young doctor. She must have started working here recently, since she seemed to still be full of energy and somehow... taking her mission seriously. She looked at me with interest and compassion. She was short, slender and very beautiful. With some amazement, I saw a B-grade sign on her forehead, and then I remembered that the Medical Academy, where I worked as a nurse, accepted everyone who passed the exams, regardless of class.

"Is that your acquaintance?" she asked.

"My boss. Please tell me, is his condition very bad? When will he wake up and get back to work?"

Her gaze became even more compassionate.

"Were you not told anything?"

"Dr. Larsen said something, but I don't have a medical education..."

She came closer and pointed to one of the monitors.

"Do you see that?"

"Yes, what is that?"

"A graph of the brain's function."

"But... it's a straight line."

She nodded.

"Exactly. We don't even know if he's going to wake up. And even if he does, how he will be. With this kind of damage, you would definitely lose your memory, maybe all of it. He also may not be able to be rehabilitated. For now, we're waiting."

"And is he…" I swallowed my tears with effort, "can he be helped at all?"

"You know, at today's level of medicine, there's a lot that can be done. But not everything. With these injuries… but I promise you, I will not give up," she put her hand on my forearm warmly. "He is my patient, and I always fight to the end."

I wiped my eyes. A few tears, however, ran from under my eyelids and flowed down my cheeks.

"He's such a great man…"

"Don't cry. I said I'd do my best. However, you should be prepared for the fact that after waking up he may not even recognize you. He will have to be taught it all from the beginning."

"It doesn't matter, as long as he's alive," I shake her hand with gratitude. "Please keep me informed. I'll leave you my number."

"Of course. I have to go back to work, too, otherwise I would have been happy to talk to you more," she answered warmly with a handshake, which had unexpected strength for such a small woman. "If you still have any questions, or any medical issues, you can reach out to me."

"Wait a minute… what is your name?" I called as she walked down the hall. "I'm Julliette Ankes."

She looked over her shoulder and smiled slightly.

"Jeannie McCave."

*****

I didn't come back home until the evening. I fell down from exhaustion and needed a good nap in a friendly, safe environment.

"Where have you been for so long?" Sue asked, looking out of her room. Her eyes glistened, her face was radiating. She has never looked this pretty.

"At work," I said apathetically. "Where's Chris?"

"He went back," she smiled so widely that I easily guessed what happened.

"Suzie..."

"What? We played a little, then enjoyed the music with some wine... and somehow it ended up that way."

I had to smile, even though I wasn't feeling very cheerful. Today gave me a good beating.

"So you don't think that sex is overrated anymore?"

She creaked with laughter and took on an expression full of superiority.

"Don't be silly. It all depends on who and why. It's different when you have to because the doctor tells you to than when you want it yourself."

I was reminded of texts from old textbooks.

"You used to be able to buy sex."

"Buy it? Why? You can just go to a DC."

"There were no dating centers at the time. Well, I guess there were, but you had to pay for it and sometimes horrible things happened. Young women, and even little girls, were forcibly held there and tormented in different ways."

She shook her head, looking at me with disbelief. Schools didn't teach about that, it was knowledge that was available to few. I sighed. I was too tired and too frustrated to explain to her now the issues of the forgotten past.

"We'll talk another time," I promised. "I need to get some sleep and get back to work. Until the headquarters on Earth make a decision, I am the one responsible for everything."

"You? What about Scott?"

That's right, Sue didn't know anything about it yet.

"He's in the hospital," I answered apatheticly, without going into details. "I had to temporarily take over his duties, but I'm not happy about it all. Ah, just let me get some sleep. It's not the right time to talk."

"Okay," she gave in. "But congratulations. That's a quick promotion."

"There's nothing to congratulate. It's a horrible job. Good night."

I went back to my room and fell asleep almost immediately. However, I was not allowed to sleep as much as I would have liked. Shortly before three in the morning, I was woken up by a vibrating ringtone of a mobile communicator.

"I'm sorry for waking you up," said Feri Kunch, who was commanding the night shift as part of daily service. "Unfortunately, you have to come to the headquarters. In half an hour you will have a conversation with Earth on the encrypted police channel. I've already sent Yamato to pick you up."

I jumped out of bed, pushing Sid to the floor, who hissed angrily and jumped on the closet, bristled like a brush. I put on my uniform in a rush, swallowed a stimulant pill, combed my hair quickly, and ran out, trying not to wake Sue. I didn't have time for breakfast.

Dr. McCave was waiting at the headquarters. Judging by the dark circles under his eyes, he didn't sleep at all, which wouldn't be the first time for him.

"I have the DNA test result," he said as soon as he saw me. "I took them with a traditional method and the probing of tissues method. They didn't like it, of course, but they had no say about it."

"And?"

"As we thought. They're doppelgangers. The only exception is Ray Munro. They sent me his tissue samples from the hospital. He still needs to stay there and I think we should send someone to guard him."

"We will," I assured him. "But how could you cheat a DNA test?"

"Not the test, just a sample. Usually, a smear from the mouth is taken. Doppelgangers have the salivary gland of the original one implanted, so to speak... This means you have to bypass the immune barrier, but that can be done today. A piece of skin, on arm or thigh, is also usually transplanted. "

"What about fingerprints?"

"That's easy. Silicon linings. The retina scanner is deceived by contact lenses with a built-in design. As you can see, there's a way for everything."

He gave me printouts of the results.

"What about Hampton's autopsy?" I asked

"As you thought, he died as a result of suffocation. He must have been using the breathing stimulant for a long time. Other stimulants too, anyway. In truth, my findings suggest that he shouldn't have been alive for a long time. A medical phenomenon, you might say. In my opinion, Brel did him a favor. Such a life is not life, it's a life sentence for torture."

I thought about my conversation with Hampton and the experiences I had, but I kept it to myself.

"What about Brel?"

He coughed.

"Well, that's a problem. And not just what we've talked about. There's something wrong with him."

I stopped him with a wave of my hand.

"We'll talk about it later, okay? In the meantime, get some sleep, because you're barely on your feet, and I'll take care of the current business."

He smiled wryly.

"You're starting to sound more and more like Scott."

I didn't have time to contemplate on what he meant. There was already a signal from the commander's office about the incoming conversation, and I had to run there as soon as possible.

On the screen appeared a blurry image of citizen Hakat. The encrypted connections distorted the video, but there was nothing I could do about it.

"Hello, Leeta," Hakat said upon seeing me. "We have to talk."

"I know," I said. "Talking helps solve every problem."

"Even ones very large, or when there aren't any at all."

I doubled my vigilance.

"The problem can be anything or nothing," I said. "The definition is up to us."

"The human being is always the key point."

"Although physically we don't resemble a key. The key has one ear."

"As we all know, we have two ears and one mouth."

"In order to hear twice as much as we say," I finished the bunk password and sighed deeply. "You suspected me, didn't you?"

"I don't trust anyone. That's why I'm still alive," Hakat said. "What's the situation?"

I sat down. The conversation could drag on.

"The WBI agents that have been sent to the Moon, except for one, are all doppelgangers," I began. "A man named Brel killed

Leon Beavis Hampton, then came to headquarters and surrendered. He's a clone, so it's a tough case. So far, he denies killing others and directing suspicions at a second clone named Fernando. We're looking for him. It's still unclear who killed Cable's lawyer. His death is probably not related to others..."

"Hold on. I know that Scott won your promotion as the deputy, despite lacking the necessary experience" the Chief of Arms interrupted me. "But where is he now? I told Sergeant Kunch I wanted to talk to the commander, and he called you. Why?"

In fact, I was expecting this question, he should have even started with it.

"Scott Cavanaugh is in the hospital," I said. The fake agents were trying to get something out of him.

"Oh. Do you know whether they succeeded?"

"I have no idea."

Hakat thought about it for a moment.

"Right, I understand now. Someone had to take command," he said at last. "It's best that it's you. I can't afford to let someone new be included in the investigation at this stage. Manage with the people you currently have."

"I'll try."

"Don't just try, do it. Listen carefully: Leon Beavis Hampton is not irreplaceable. Someone will take over Romain Corporation after him, but it won't be today or tomorrow. For now, you need to decipher the connection of this corporation with what is happening."

"Don't you feel bad about Mr. Hampton's death?" I asked quietly.

"There's no reason to feel bad about it. You haven't had a chance to get to know him as well as I have, and you feel sorry about him, but for no reason. You'll find out for yourself when you dig deeper into it. Anyway, you can't revive the dead, so there's nothing to think about, regrets or no regrets."

"Yes, of course... but let me remind you that we have provided all the files of Romain Corporation to the prosecutor's office and then what? They stopped at a fine."

"Do you think I don't know that? Now ask yourself if Prosecutor Cable had any obligations to Hampton," here Hakat was undoubtedly right. "Either way, it's your playground now and your case needs to be resolved. And don't tell me that it's too early for you, because that much I know. Ready or not, you have to take care of it. I have to track the doping center and figure out the whole grid before they infiltrate the government."

In fact, I had to admit that such a danger exists. Since they were able to get through into the WBI, it meant that anything could be possible for them... whoever they are.

"Do you have any suspicions who is behind all this?" I asked.

"I have suspicions, but I can't justify them. I need to gather evidence," he moved his hand across his head and sighed. "Don't think that I have it easy, Leeta. Sometimes even I don't know what to do."

I was reminded of something.

"Brel said that Dr. Oenas was responsible for cloning at Laboratory F. Doppelganging isn't far from cloning. Maybe she'll know something... something that will help you track down this organization."

"Thank you for the hint. I'll talk to her. Good luck, kid, and we're staying in touch."

I turned off the communicator and thought for a long time about what to do next. Then I gathered myself together, went into Scott's apartment, and sat down at his personal computer. He still had a copy of the data from both of attorney Cable's drives, both the business and private ones. I was quick to find the files I needed. As I expected, the Romain Corporation case wasn't even moved. It was put in the 'No Relation' folder, along with all the evidence we provided to the prosecutor's office. I don't remember most of the details anymore, but I decided to remind myself of them.

I was immediately struck by one thing: Hampton's association with the pharmaceutical concern Medcorp, which operates in Lunchester. The investigation into Medcorp was suspended despite strong evidence I was not aware of – and it was suspended immediately after the deaths of Silvana and Milton. And now I was able to find out why. They were the only witnesses to testify against the group. I froze. I didn't know that before. But Scott knew.

Why would he hide that even from me? Why would he at all? I started frantically looking through the material for answers, but I couldn't find them anywhere. Scott didn't make any side notes. I could only guess his motives, but the point was that I was unable to. It just didn't make sense.

Determined, I began looking through the contents of the computer until I found a password-protected partition. If the situation had been different, of course, I wouldn't have touched it. But now that Scott had the prospect of becoming a vegetable, or, best case scenario, a big child, and I found his new, completely unknown side, all my doubts went into the sidelines. I had the opportunity to test how good of a teacher Sue was, who introduced me to all the secrets of hacking.

After an hour of hard work, I managed to crack all the passwords. And I was struck dumb. The section contained documents that I didn't expect – financial statements, profitability schedules, stock lists, investment plans, stock quotes, and contracts with brokers... What was all this for? I scanned the documents and slowly began to understand why Scott was such a cheapskate when it came to personal expenses. I just didn't understand why he needed all this – until I came across a separate folder. It contained correspondence with the law firm Johnson & Strike. I felt a little uncomfortable looking through someone's letters, but since I've already gotten this far...

One of the letters turned out to be particularly interesting.

In connection with our agreement, we inform you that we have taken all necessary measures to ensure the safety of the materials you've sent to us. In the attachment, we send you a signed copy of the will submitted to our registry. If you have any objections, please contact us again.

Respectfully,

Johnson & Strike

I opened the attachment and read it:

I, Scott Cavanaugh, of healthy body and mind, decide the following:

In the event of my death, all my shares, bank account and movable property, with the exception of the property belonging to the Lunnar police department, are to be transferred to Alexa Ivanovsky-Cavanaugh, identification number HY76854BP. The following record is not subject to any legal reservations or restrictions.

This was very interesting. It seemed that Scott either did not break off contact with his ex-wife at all, or that at the very least he still loved her. Both meant he was hiding something from me. Although it's true that our relationship was not formal, I think it would have been polite for him to let me know about something so important. I suddenly felt like an idiot. After a while, less selfish feelings came to my attention. This Alexa was very important to Scott, and what if it was also the other way around? After all, I didn't know what made them break up. Maybe they spoke regularly by video link? And if so, maybe somewhere within reach of human activity – on Earth, on the Moon, in one of the orbiting cities – Alexa is living and waiting for a sign of life from Scott. Maybe she's even crying, thinking he's forgotten about her?

I had a name. And a connection. It was something. I looked at my watch and thought it was a 'decent' hour, so I called Susie.

"What's up, honey," the screen showed me Sue's pinkish, sleepy face. "Is it that important?"

"Probably. Do you have anything to write on? Note down the name. Alexa Ivanovsky-Cavanaugh, ID number HY76854BP. Track this woman down for me. Think of it as a task as per your contract with the police."

"When do you need it?" she asked shortly.

"Best if I have it by yesterday. But whenever you're able, is fine."

"Understood, Commander."

"Don't be a buffoon. We'll talk later."

I carefully closed all the files and sections in the private part of the computer. I learned everything I could, now I had to put this knowledge together into something useful.

XI

An explosion in the mines is nothing unusual. In addition to those caused by deliberate human activity, or the so-called blasting, there are also spontaneous explosions. On the Moon, however, there are no deposits of methane which would cause such a thing. According to geologists and selenologists, it never was there, because the lunar body was separated from the globe at a time when organic life wasn't yet there. And it was necessary for the formation of biological methane. There's also non-biological methane, but it will not be produced without active volcanoes. And lunar volcanoes have been dead for billions of years.

Even if at one point, unimaginably long ago, methane was trapped in the lunar reservoirs, it has long since 'evaporated'. The rocks of volcanic origin, and the Moon is mostly composed of such, are porous enough to have enough time for each gas to escape from them into space, literally sucked out by the prevailing vacuum on the surface. Low gravity wouldn't be able to contain it in the so-called bubble. However, lunar mines are also vulnerable to explosions, although not for natural reasons. The most common cause is damage to clean oxygen tanks. Under the right conditions, all it takes is a spark, ignition of the coal dust and rapid accumulation of gas products in a limited space.

When I was urgently called into the AMOS mine, already known to me by the documents, there was already an industrial guard, fire brigade and paramedics on the site.

"There are people left downstairs, in the first corridor," I was told by a frustrated foreman, changing into makeshift stretchers. "Three from my shift."

"We can't go down there yet," a woman in a firefighter's uniform squeezed through beside me. She wore a whole hoop of masks with closed air circulation "We make one move and everything collapses. We need to focus on those we can pull out right now."

"What about the others?" I called out to her.

"When we pull out the miners from corridors three and six, and ask to turn off the circuits of artificial gravity, it'll be worth a try!" she shouted from afar.

I understood why it was impossible right now. Direct rescue requires artificial gravity. Only when the firefighters pull out those they have any access to, can they use a method without gravity. It was an unsafe method, since turning off the gravity circuits immobilized the compressor, and the miners could run out of air before someone reached them. Sometimes, however, there was no other way.

I looked at those who were able to flee on time and those who had already been pulled out of the mine. Some of them were injured and were being examined by medics, others simply stood and were swearing loudly. I didn't pay attention to it given the situation. I hated swearing and, interestingly, since I started working at the station, my new colleagues have tried to keep language civilized in my presence. Sometimes, of course, it slipped away, but usually they apologized after.

"Hope you understand, this is the first time we have a lady from a nice house here," Dr. McCave said humorously, when we were talking about it once.

The miners' curses didn't catch my attention for a reason – I was searching for Monty. I felt a growing panic in me. The explosion could have been an attempt to kill my android after someone exposed him. Could that have happened? It was likely. Even the best plan has a margin of error that includes random, unpredictable events.

I pushed through a crowd of miners mixed with guards trying to bring in order, and reached the edge of the fault. At the bottom were surface buildings – three mining shafts, an output sorting plant, cehaus, scrubber and earthworks. The explosion occurred in shaft number two, miners from the other ones left the corridors without serious problems. The rescue operation took place around the emergency exits of mine number two, because the main corridor, along with the first one closest to it, was now a pile of rubble.

I looked with horror at the rock shards, arranged like in a giant 'jenga', a game I used to love to play. Was Monty there now? I didn't ask anyone because I knew in advance what answer I would hear. "People are dying in there and you're worried about a robot?" Unable to withstand the tension anymore, I pressed the call signal on the mobile communicator. He should pick it up through the collar with the transmitter – Sven Thorvald thought about everything.

It felt like centuries before I heard the communicator pinging. I felt such a relief that my legs trembled under me, and I didn't even have anything to support myself with.

"Can I do anything to help," I asked one of the medics who just approached me.

"Take over Wayland and grab a second stretcher," he replied briefly.

I dutifully changed the lifeguard pointed out to me, a boy who was literally stumbling from fatigue. He wasn't fit for such hard work, and in other circumstances I would have wondered who sent him to this disaster area at all.

For the next few hours, I was worked like a horse carrying wounded miners on a stretcher. The shaft area was too destroyed by the explosion to use a wheeled or sliding device, and the rotors couldn't fly under the domes. We had to rely on the strength of human muscles.

"I think that's everything," said Zara Tagliani, commander of the Lunnar fire brigade. She introduced herself to me next to the shaft when she saw me carrying the wounded with the medics, and there was a restrained assessment in her voice. "So far, two bodies and forty-six wounded. Now we have to take care of the first corridor."

She took out her messenger and called for technical support.

"Set the blockades and turn off the artificial pressurizers on the second shaft."

My heart hit harder. I didn't even feel my legs trembling with fatigue, and that my uniform was soaked with sweat. The quilting of my service biper at my belt just now caught my attention. I picked it up eagerly.

"I'm at a collapsed mine, support is unnecessary, I'll be back when I'm back," I said. Something suddenly came to my mind.

"Don't send people in there," I said to Zara Tagliani. "I'll try something that can save their work and minimize the danger."

She looked at me with obvious hesitation.

"Every moment matters. If you fail, you may be charged with causing harm to health and lives."

"It will only take a moment," I assured her.

I opened the communicator to establish connection with Monty's collar. For security reasons, we didn't have it set up for voice calls, but there was a different way. I started typing in Morse code dashes and dots, trying to make my message as brief as possible. After a while, the answer came, and I sighed. Monty was all right and had the opportunity to act.

"One more moment," I asked.

From a stream of dots and dashes, dripping from the messenger like virtual rain, I read the next message.

"Send your people and medics into the fourth emergency shaft," I said to Zera.

She wiped her dirty face with the sleeve of her ripped uniform and looked at me suspiciously.

"Are you play pirates? Morse code?"

"I know what I'm doing," I assured her. "There is an android there."

"So what? Mines are always full of robots."

"You don't get it. Not a robot, an android. He acts independently and is hellishly effective. He'll get the wounded out, you'll only pick them up."

She looked at me, slowly shaking her head.

"Well, if you're wrong..." she said, at last, and, without finishing her sentence, moved towards her subordinates waiting for orders.

I knew what she was going to say. That then she wouldn't want to be in my skin then.

I watched as huge, technician-controlled manbots, took off one after another blocks of the terrible 'jenga' carefully, so as not to break the entire structure and not to cause a second collapse. In conditions where pressure has returned to the Moon's normal, or one-sixth of the Earth, the shards of rock were lighter, but they still had weight and could kill a person by crushing them.

I almost screamed when the last of the slabs covering the emergency shaft moved, jostled from the inside and fell to the side, launching upwards a cloud of lunar dust. Although in artificial-gravity conditions it remained at the ground, it now caused a real problem. After a while I noticed a male silhouette in the gray mist, coming out of the shaft. It was Monty. He was carrying one of the miners. He passed him to the medical team and went back inside.

With struggle, I refrained myself from running over. What prevented me is the fact that I would get in the way of a rescue operation, so I just stood there and watched. I couldn't express how proud I was of my Android at that moment.

*****

The death toll from the blast increased by two people in the course of a day, and that was it. Initially, the AMOS management tried to convince us that the explosion was an accident, but very quickly it turned out that this was not the case. The analysis of records from Monty's recorder and the evidence we collected was carried out by our technical department, which worked effectively and accurately. As Scott said, this department was the greatest asset of the Lunnar police. For many years, technicians worked under the direction of Nana Tiburtas, who did not tolerate any shortcomings and always worked at the highest efficiency. If it weren't for this no longer young, likely even older than Scott woman, our lab wouldn't be what it is now.

Rosanda Merrick's department was taking care of direct investigation. The head of the economic department had personal motives to carefully examine everything, since she wanted to the killer of her man, so I knew she wouldn't miss anything. This time we had to work together properly, side by side, especially since she had the authority of economic inspection that I lacked, and I had a laboratory where the evidence was studied. Only together could we achieve our desired goal.

Monty's recorder contained interesting transcripts, although it took experts a long time to pull them out of the stream of irrelevant information. However, it soon became clear that there were activities in the mine that no one outside of it knew about. As to what kind of activity it was, the laboratory was the one to figure it out, because the miners interviewed by Merrick, as one could guess, were silent in solidarity.

Nana Tiburtas came to me personally with the results of the analysis, instead of just sending them to the computer. That alone said a lot. Normally she didn't want to move out of the lab.

"Sit down, please," I invited her. "What did your team discover that was so important, so much that you bothered to come to me personally?"

She put the prints on the table and smiled triumphantly

"A lot," she said. "You see, the AMOS mines have declared the extraction of chalkopyrite. Meanwhile, the company also extracts and processes another mineral, pyroxene. And they don't report it."

"Is that so important?" I felt stupid admitting it, but I really didn't understand.

"Yes," Nana confirmed. "You can get sodium from it, necessary in the production of 'golden rain' and other similar drugs as a catalyst. The issue is that, although in the production process it does not wear out, it nevertheless reacts with other materials, especially liquids, and eventually deteriorates, and recycling it means lost time and money, so it's better to buy it fresh..."

She paused for a moment when she saw my expression. She realized that I had a pale idea of chemistry in my power and she needed to be clearer.

"I'm not going to be giving you a lecture right now," she said. "All you need to know is that it needs to be replaced on a regular basis. Production was carried out in the mine workings. As the management wanted to hide such unconventional activity from the economic inspection, they stored the extracted sodium, already in the form of bars, in an unoperated area of the corridor. Damage to the fire system led to flooding of the storage compartment and the explosion."

"Coincidence?" I asked quietly.

"No way, we ruled that out from the beginning. I was there in person, I found traces of manipulation on the valves. That's not all. Just flooding the corridor with water wouldn't do anything. Shortly before the plant leaked, someone released kerosene from a sodium tank. This someone wanted the unfortunate to occur. You know, sodium is flooded with kerosene so it doesn't react with the air," she added. "You have all the evidence in these printouts."

I took them in my hand immediately, keeping my eyes on Nana.

"What about Monty's recordings?"

"They are very interesting. Using the algorithms of audio search engines, we have already found several hooks. The miners weren't too careful around your android. We have enough to bring charges against at least two people from the company's management and the head of the mine, who controlled all this."

Of course, this didn't explain everything. So it couldn't be enough.

"At best, we can accuse AMOS of illegal production and trade on the black market," I said after some thinking. "The managers will very easily wiggle themselves out of it, saying that they didn't know why their contractor uses metal sodium. And we're not going to prove otherwise. We have to uncover who caused the accident. And to do that, we need to find out what his motivation was. When can you give me a full analysis of the records from the recorder?"

Tiburtas counted on her fingers for a moment.

"In two days," she finally said. "The work is in full swing, can't do it any sooner. We're already working on it in three shifts, to not waste time."

"Okay. I believe that you are doing everything you can with your people."

"As we all do. If someone could at least say 'thank you'," she got up, said goodbye with a nod and left.

She passed Dr. McCave at the door, who, as he always did, entered feeling like he was entering his own home, and relaxed in the chair, stretching his legs as far as he could.

"You've sure gotten comfortable in boss's office," he notice.

"You know yourself that it's just a temporary agreement," I muttered.

"Don't joke about it. We both know that even if Scotty survives, he won't be back at work."

I looked at him gloomily. I liked him a lot, but sometimes he had the ability to irritate me immensely with his nihilism and an abnegation, something that wasn't fit for a doctor.

"Then they'll send someone to replace him. Once we're done with this investigation, I'm leaving this place faster than you can whistle Yankee Doodle."

He laughed.

"Girl, don't be so naive. Who in their right mind would willingly take on such a job? You should get used to it."

Maybe he was right. I felt terrible about it, but it seemed like I was going to replace Scott whether I wanted to or not.

"Do you have any messages for me?" I asked for a change of subject.

"Oh, yes," he said. "I know what's wrong with Brel, except for the fact that he won't live long, of course."

"So? What is it?"

"He is suffering from multiple personalities. He and Fernando Lopez are one person, but he doesn't realize it. It took a while before I realized this because I'm not a psychiatrist."

"So how did you figure it out?"

"We talked a lot. I noticed that his behavior changes at certain times, even the way he speaks and the way he uses words changes. I don't know what caused this change yet," he paused for a moment. "But it seems that someone was aware of it. And that this someone was taking advantage of it."

Someone, someone... still a hypothetical someone. We've been pursuing them from the beginning, and yet they continue escape us.

"Could they have gotten it surgically?" I asked.

"I don't see why not. Severing of the large commissure makes it so that each side of the person, left and right, has a different identification. Cyclical personality changes are more of a finesse thing, but since they studied the living brain at Laboratory F, who knows what they could've came up with."

I remembered the jars with still electroencephalogically active brains, and I started to feel sick.

"All in all, I just feel sorry for him," I whispered. "He was created to help achieve other people's goals. It never mattered what he thought or felt, what he wanted. It's understandable that in the end he killed Hampton, because this was the man who was the cause of all of his misfortunes. It's even strange that he didn't do it sooner."

"All right, I'm going to the hospital," the doctor stretched and got up from his chair. "I'll check on Scott."

I remembered something.

"There's a new doctor at the hospital. Jeannie McCave. Is that maybe your ex?"

He looked at me with his eyes wide open.

"You tell me that now?!"

I spread my hands helplessly.

"You know how it is, a lot of things happened…"

I couldn't say more because he wasn't there anymore. I looked at my watch wondering if I could already go home. It was eighteen, and I could barely see. Every sacrifice has its limits. I wasn't going to live at the headquarters like Scotty, whatever may happen.

At home I was greeted by warm dinner, cooked by Sue – pancakes with meat substitute, poured with Dutch sauce. Ever since my friend fell in love with Chris, she has also fallen in love with cooking, and is getting better and better at it, and I could always count on hot food after work.

"Sue, you've got golden hands," I said solemnly, eating pancakes and giving Sid some of the substitute. He loved it, although technically he shouldn't be eating it.

"I won't deny that," she laughed playfully.

"Of course. And by the way, did you learn anything about Alexa Ivanovsky-Cavanaugh?"

She sat in a chair opposite me, with a plate full of pancakes. As usual, she didn't deny anything herself so it wasn't surprising that she gained a good five kilograms again, but it didn't seem to bother her.

"You really gave me a good workout with this job," she said with a full mouth. "I searched through every corner of the virtual, but nowhere did I find such a combination of name and id number."

"So, we're not getting anything?"

She smiled proudly.

"You underestimate me. I started looking for a match with various diminutives. Finally, when I typed 'Lexi + Cavanaugh', the virtual spat out an old document. A photo from an old police chronicle with the caption: Scott Cavanaugh and his young wife Lexi at the administration of oath of the new police general."

I thought about it a little over my plate.

"It probably won't do us any good. Since there is nothing else..."

She swallowed such a large piece of the pancake that her eyes were popping out. She coughed it off, drank it down with some carbonated water from the bottle and continued.

"Well, I don't know. I took a snapshot of the girl's face on the photo, ran it through some aging programs, both backwards and forward, and tried to find a match."

"And?" I remained still with my fork raised.

"Nothing. This s very interesting, you know what I mean? How is it possible that there is almost no trace of this Lexi? And that's in our time, when the virtual is so overloaded with information that it takes someone with my qualifications to even dig through it? After all, we're not in the old ages, when everyone stored documents and photos in boxes, now they are stored in the cloud, and from there everything seeps into the virtual. Think about it, such anonymity is incredibly strange. This woman certainly existed. And all of a sudden, she's gone, just like that."

It was strange, indeed. Although, maybe not quite as much as it seemed.

"She could have done something, in a criminal sense. If you have enough money, you can hire someone to clear the traces of your existence. Someone like you. And then you buy yourself a new identity. If you make sure you don't stick out, it can work. Of course, all it takes is one stupid mistake to ruin the whole plan, such as a case that requires the confirmation of biometric data. If someone decided to throw that in one of the classified databases, everything could come out."

She nodded, chewing with delicacy.

"Did you check the police database?"

"Of course. In all the ones that are available from commander's level. Nothing. If this woman did something, it's not under her own name."

"Maybe throwing in a picture will give something? I'll give it to you in the morning. I downloaded this entire chronicle on my computer, but it started updating, in spite of me, so at this point all the data is unavailable."

I thought that was even for the better. I'll sleep a little before I have to work my brain cells again. I finished dinner, cleaned up after myself and went to the bathroom. For a moment I had a temptation to go crazy and take a water shower. In such buildings, each apartment had its own distribution of 'drinking water', which meant that from time to time it was possible to afford a short shower or even a small bath. The water was only seemingly wasted, as it all went to the treatment plants, like any household wastewater, and was reused. In any case, however, the distribution was small and had to be planned out.

In the end, I chose ordinary ozone spray. I've been taught saving since I was a child, and I couldn't get rid of Cynthia Lara's habits, even having cards full of points.

"Poverty is not just the state of the wallet, it's also a state of the mind," Scott once told me. "You can be poor with millions on your account, too afraid to touch them because 'someday you may run out'."

We weren't poor, but we weren't rich either, so the Laras taught all the kids to save, share what they had, and even fix broken things. It's something that can always come in handy.

I found Monty in my room. He sat on a corner chair, and on his knees rested Sid, curled up. It was amazing, but when the android returned after a few weeks of absence, my cat suddenly began to treat him friendlier than before. Maybe not as a family member, but home equipment that was taken away and which was unexpectedly found. He seemed to come to terms with his presence.

I lay down, and Monty joined me after a while. I hugged him around the neck. Only now have I realized how much I missed his presence by my side, his smell and touch of his cool cyberskin. I hugged his broad chest and fell asleep without any dreams.

This time, I was thankfully able to sleep until five in the morning, when my communicator forced me awake. Again, I had to dress up at lightning speed. Monty, without asking anything, made me a caffettino and smeared a few crackers with a soybean paste. I ate fast almost choking. Knowing the pace of things at the headquarters, I was fully aware that I may have no time for snacks later.

"Thank you, but you should dress up, too. Not in that, in the uniform. You'll be coming with me," I recommended. I wanted Monty to return to his role as my 'full-time bodyguard'.

I showed up at the headquarters even before the day shift. On duty sat a tired Corporal Barry Novak, who at my sight got up and muttered.

"Good morning, boss. The night was quiet, nothing exciting."

"Who called me then?"

"Senior constable Breitman. She brought some girl, very young, and they're waiting for you at the interrogation room."

"As if this couldn't wait..." not finishing my thought I went to the mentioned room.

I wasn't happy, and I had a great desire to rag on Yvonne Breitman for good morning, although on the other hand I had to admit to myself that such an experienced woman probably had good reason to wake me up. She wouldn't do it for any reason. A young girl... did she catch some 'illegal minor'? From time to time we encountered teenagers of both sexes, who managed to get to the Moon thanks to forged documents. Since the law prohibited minors from staying in Lunnar, we had to catch them and send them home as soon as possible. To my knowledge, there was only one exception. That's right...

I recognized her right away. She wasn't wearing a geisha costume or thick makeup, but it was Miniko, the governor's niece.

"This young lady came up to me on my routine patrol," Breitman filled me in. "She asked me to take her to the police station and call you."

"Child, what were you doing alone on the street at night, so far from home?" I turned to Miniko. "How did you get here?"

She raised her black like coal, round eyes, and looked at me. Wearing regular trousers and a sports hoodie with her hair tied in a ponytail, she looked like a schoolgirl who went for a jog before class.

"I had to see you," she said softly. "I want to tell you everything."

"What do you mean, 'everything'?" I sat in front of her, taking the smoothest and friendliest of expressions. "You should know that this room is constantly monitored and everything said is being recorded."

She didn't pay attention to that.

"It was Raiha who killed the prosecutor."

I was speechless.

"What are you talking about, child?"

"Please just listen to me. I can't stay silent anymore. I can't take it."

"Okay, tell me," I had no idea how I managed to stay somewhat calm.

"Reiha is the best step-mother under the sun. She really loved us, but she was afraid of uncle. She was incredibly afraid of him. She tried to confront him when he started sending us to the prosecutor's office... so that he would turn blind eye on him."

"Breitman, get out," I turned to the constable. And bring doctor McCave and Neil Slavik to the headquarters. As soon as possible."

When constable closed the door behind her, I looked at Miniko again. She sat with her hands on her knees, and looked at the floor.

"Go ahead," I encouraged her.

"Uncle said it was for our own good, because we would inherit everything from him. When he came to us, we thought that this is just what uncles do and we had to endure it... but the prosecutor was terrible. We were afraid of him. We cried every time uncle demanded us to go to him. Raiha was not at home when the prosecutor was killed. When she came back, she looked weird. She was drunk. She said this monster would never hurt us again, and she went to bed right away. And then we found out about... that murder."

"Miniko, my dear, are you sure of what you're saying?" I put my hand under her chin and lifted her face up. She was crying.

"Yes. I would've remained silent, but Reiha wants to kill uncle, and we... we love him. Despite everything. He's the only one left and he's good for us, but... he comes at night..."

"My child... how old are you? Really?"

"Thi... thirteen," she let out through her tears.

It was really too much. I felt like crying, but I had to remain calm and professional.

"What do you mean, she wants to kill governor Khamala?"

"Yes. Uncle has a meeting with the president of the Lunar Company today, and that's when she will do it. I don't know how, but I heard Reiha talking to someone through her communicator that my uncle is to not leave the conference room alive. Then she told us she was going to the hairdresser and left. Megumi stayed at home and is trying to call uncle, but I'm sure it won't work. Uncle doesn't carry his communicator outside, so that no killers can locate him through the signal. I sneaked out on the road, and from there I drove with a courier, whom guards sent for supplies. He doesn't know us because you know we're not allowed to go outside, and no one gets invited to the residence. I told him I was a maid and I had to do something very urgent in town."

"Do you know where this meeting will be?"

She shook her head, again with her eyes to the floor.

"Reiha said something about Luxembourg, but I don't know what kind of place it is."

It was good enough that I knew.

"Stay here for now," I recommended as I got up. "I'm going to send someone who will keep you company. I have to get to work. If you need something, ask. You know, we can't take you home right now."

She nodded. I rushed out of the interrogation room. The daily shift was starting to come to work, so I took everyone to the briefing room.

"Red alert," I declared. "Lieutenant Burns, get all the stormtroopers on their feet, they must be ready. Loaded weapons. Until further notice, no one leaves the headquarters without my orders. Constable Kent, officer Maru, there is a young girl in the interrogation room, Miniko Takahashi. Please take her to the guest house and keep an eye on her at all times. She is extremely valuable to us. The rest of you standby."

I locked myself in the office and started looking for data networks the way Sue taught me. Fortunately, I've already stumbled upon a place called Luxembourg. It was one of our 'high-risk objects' – a conference center, secured in every way, located very high, right under the dome protecting Lunnar. Only people from the VIP category had access to it, and not all of them. I really can't imagine how anyone could do a diversion there, but stranger things have happened.

Pretty quickly, I found protected information about the Lunnar conference at the summit and I was able to decipher it properly before McCave arrived at the office.

"Where is it burning?" he asked concretely.

"Everywhere," I replied briefly. "You'll find a young girl in the guesthouse. Carefully examine her and issue a health certificate. Do a detailed interview."

"Suspect or witness?"

"Actually, so far neither. More like a victim of a crime. Della Kent and Maru are with her."

He scratched his head with confusion.

"Will you tell me more?"

"Not yet," I closed the computer and got up. "I suspect that you and Maru are experiencing problems right now, but leave that for later. We have a crisis, and one that colony has never seen before."

"Are you managing?"

"I have to. We'll talk later."

I waited for the doctor to come out and fired up the red police line. With it, I was able to connect not only to any object in Lunnar, but also on Earth, but the rules limited its use to only absolutely exceptional situations. Like now.

I waited a while and the picture of the conference room and table was shown on the screen, behind which sat a dozen people of both sexes. Solo Khamala sat on the honor seat, in a navy blue suit. The sudden activation of the communication screen clearly surprised them because they looked into the camera without words.

"My name is Juliette Aneks, temporarily serving as the commander of the Lunnar police. Please close all the entrances to the room and do not open them to anyone, not even the most trusted people, until you are contacted again."

"What are you...?" Khamala exclaimed.

"Please trust me, Governor," I interrupted him coldly. "It concerns your life, and maybe the life of everyone present in the room."

I couldn't look at him. He seemed disgusting to me now, like an overgrown, slimy bug, and I felt like screaming everything in his face at once. But it had to wait.

One of the participants of the conference got up and turned something on the wall panel. There was a metallic clang, and an armored plate covered the door visible behind Khamala's back.

"You can be calm," he said, addressing the screen. "No one will come in here if we don't let them in."

"I'm coming to you with the intervention brigade. I'll explain everything in person," I did.

For a moment, I wondered if should get Judge Holstein involved in the case right now, but I decided to wait. I would have to spend too long explaining what's going on and every minute is precious. In the briefing room, a squad of stormtroopers was waiting for me. And with them, Monty.

*****

Once we arrived at Luxembourg, we were surprised by the dead silence of this place. It resembled a futuristic disc growing under the dome like a narrow stem. There were a few elevators but all of them non-functioning, so we used a fire-escape to get to the platform. No one responded to our attempts at contact. With great effort, we pushed through the entrance security, violating all possible security protocols. Alec Burns was backing me up tenaciously, and his subordinates guarded the area. We all risked losing the badge, but we wouldn't have figured out anything else. We had to get there.

When we finally got inside, to our relief, we didn't notice any signs of violent events. However, this relief didn't last long. We found the first security guard right next to the inside door. The others lay deeper in, giving the impression that everyone had simply collapsed where they were standing. No signs of conflict were found.

"Scan," I said, while with a quick motion pressing am ask with filter to my face.

"I have a spectrum of nitrous oxide, but not powerful enough to do any harm anymore," Alec said a short time later. "They were put to sleep."

The stormtroopers briefly inspected the people on the ground and moved them to one location. Two took up the repair of the elevator panel, the rest joined us. We went to the main conference room, where, according to the found document, the meeting took place. It was in the center of the disk and had its own infrastructure – its own temperature and load adjustment, an autonomous air purification system. It was like a fortress within a fortress.

We were ready for the attack before we entered. The sight of sleeping guards made us relax our attention, subconsciously taking for granted that everyone inside was asleep. That's why we let ourselves be surprised. There were only three attackers, but I immediately noticed that they must have been well trained. They moved like a deadly ballet, and for the first time I was able to observe how useful the stormtrooper's uniform is, light and yet durable like medieval armor.

Alec Burns covered me with his body. If he hadn't, I probably would have died without even knowing what had happened to me, because a rotating metal star hit his helmet with such force that he curled up, pressing me against a wall. One of the star's rays crashed into the outside of the helmet. It didn't break through, but the kinetic energy of the impact, which happened directly between his eyes, momentarily stunned the stormtrooper. I struggled to push the inert weight aside and stood face to face with a fury wielding two knives. She was moving fast, too fast for me to reach for a gun or even dodge.

Something whistled in the air, and a split second later I saw the assailant, dressed in a one-piece tight hooded jumpsuit, struggled within the iron grip of my android. Monty assimilated well the knowledge given to him by our instructor, he was able to take on such a stranglehold that no one in the world would've been able to free themselves from him. However, the woman kept trying – she probably had no idea who she was dealing with.

I went over and with a firm motion I tore her hood off her head.

"Calm down, please," I said.

"You don't understand anything!" Raiha screamed.

"On the contrary, I know enough to guess the rest. Solo Khamala led two orphaned girls to the governor's residence. He used them, and knowing the tastes of Prosecutor Cable, he also took advantage of them to corrupt him. But what was your role? Why didn't you just report it to relevant services?"

Reiha stopped twitching.

"It'll sound unconvincing, but I didn't know anything about it for a long time. Solo hired me to be the girls' teacher, but made me stay at the other end of the residence. I was to not spoil them. When I found out the truth, he raped me and said I was his concubine from now on. He swore that if I did anything, if I said a single word, he would use his contacts to kill my whole family. I knew he was capable of it. But he underestimated me. I came up with a plan to pay him back, as well as this prosecutor."

During this speech, Monty was able to handcuff her and put both knives in a proof bag. It was only then that he leaned over Burns, who had already begun to show signs of life. He took the star and put it in the bag as well.

"Lieutenant, can you hear me?" Monty asked.

Alec woke up and placed his hand on his head. He swore disgustingly.

"Will you repeat it before the court?" I turned to Reiha.

She had a crooked mouth in a grimace resembling a smile.

"Anything you'd want me to. But I don't know who I'm going to testify against."

"Commander, here!" I heard the voice of one of the stormtroopers. "The electrical room!"

I rushed into the room from which the hall's machinery was controlled. The stormtrooper pointed his finger at the control panel. The lid was removed and paths of connections flickered inside. I didn't need to be an engineer to be able to say that something was added to them, and it looked like a very complex device.

"Don't move," I stopped the stormtrooper. I looked at the indicators. If I was able to read them correctly, the course was reversed – instead of oxygenating the closed room, the machine was removing the air from it. I threw myself into the internal monitoring register. On the monitors you could see the participants of the conference – some half-lying on the table, others on the floor. Some had seizures, others were immobile, curled up in an embryonic position.

"Get someone to open the internal security!" I screamed into the microphone.

One of the people lying on the floor was moving clumsily. He was crawling to the control panel. I left the monitors and went back to the electrical room.

"It's too late, too late…" Raiha sang behind my back. I felt like hitting her, but instead I turned on my communicator and dialed Sven Thorvald's number, praying in the spirit of all the forgotten gods of humanity that the connection would work this time.

Fortunately, it worked.

"What's going on? I don't have time," the grumpy voice of the engineer sounded from the communicator.

"You need time for this, it is highest priority. The sabotage of machinery by switching the connections in the panel, reversing the phase of oxygenation systems and air purification in an enclosed room. How do you stop it?"

"Show me the panel."

I directed the messenger's camera to the panel.

"The indicators!"

I obediently moved the device.

"The pressure will soon cross the critical threshold," Sven said. "There's no time for finesse. It's a parasitic pin, only the second time I've seen one in my entire life."

"What?"

"Doesn't matter! You have to smash those connected thingies immediately."

"Everyone, get back!" I recommended.

I pulled my service weapon out of the holster and emptied the entire magazine into the panel without even thinking about what would happen if I got hit by a ricochet. An explosion erupted, sparks were released from the dashboard, and the air was filled with burnt plastic. The gentle noise of the air-removal apparatus gave way to a terrible grind, and then it was quiet.

I ran back to the observation room. To my great relief, I saw that the armored plates went up, admittedly only a dozen centimeters or so, but still. I found the emergency buttons and activated the mechanism of opening the double door. The sound of footsteps approached from somewhere behind me. Stormtroopers launched the elevators, and a medical team appeared on the platform, which they called.

"What about those two attackers?" I asked.

"They're dead. We weren't able to take them alive," Alec said grimly. He had just removed his helmet, damaged by the rotating star, revealing the face of a dark-haired man with gray eyes. His forehead was bleeding, so the helmet didn't quite do its job. One of the rescuers stopped by and started examining his head.

"Help the medics," I recommended to the stormtroopers and connected with base. "Captain Jaros, please put all units on their feet and send at least three to the hospital. They are to protect people who are about to be taken there, and at the same time ensure that they do not contact anyone until further notice. Is that clear?"

"Yes, Commander. Understood," the stormtrooper commander said briefly, and hung up.

There's no denying it, I got myself into quite a mess. If I make one wrong move, it will not end on degradation. I'm sending the police on the most important people in Lunnar, like they're a bunch of thugs. Although if I understood correctly, that's basically what they were. The image in my head was horrific. What would I give now for Scott to be with me and take that burden on his own shoulders.

"How are they?" I asked the rescuers who were transporting the first victims on moving stretchers.

"Severe hypoxia probably damaged the lungs," he said. "Two have symptoms of a heart attack, one woman is dead. All need to be taken to the hospital as soon as possible. We called an extra ambulance."

"Do what's best. How is my man?"

"He's fine, a bandage will be enough. It's a shallow wound."

"Lieutenant Burns, you and Monty are coming back to the headquarters with me," I said to Alec. "We're taking the detainee with us, of course," I turned on the communicator again. "Headquarters, are there any free detectives?"

"Sergeant Kunch has just returned," Stevens, one of the team's new acquisitions, told me.

"Send him to Luxembourg immediately. He'll know where it is. He should take the technicians with him. Actually, put him on the line."

"What is it, boss?" I heard Kunch's voice after a short while.

"Take forensic experts and go with them to Luxembourg. You'll investigate the whole place carefully. Local security guards will help you. Now, listen carefully. You're going to copy any and all data you'll come across, but discreetly. Do you understand?"

"At a facility of such high classifications of secrecy? You're taking a lot of risks."

"I have to. You'll find out for yourself why it was necessary, but not right now."

"All right. You're the one responsible for everything, not me."

He certainly wasn't convinced, but he wasn't going to disobey me. That was to be expected, Kunch was the kind of man who could be trusted in any situation. And I couldn't just split myself in two.

At the headquarters I found, first of all, the doctor waiting for me at the office, extremely outraged. I was also surprised to see Judge Holstein sitting in one of the seats. I stopped at the doorstep.

"Did something happen?" I asked uncertainly.

"Do you even need to ask?! Why didn't you tell me right away what hell this little girl went through? A man shouldn't have been examining her! Not even touching her!"

I felt stupid. I really did not think about that. I haven't dealt with a similar problem before, it doesn't happen very often nowadays.

"All right, all right," the judge said. "You'll deal with your own issues at a more appropriate time. Right now, we must focus on what's the most important. Dr. McCave notified me of governor Khamala's repeated violations of the law. I've already issued an arrest warrant and sent a request to Earth to gather the board of directors. Do you have anything to add?"

I took a deep breath and sat down at the table.

"Yes," I said, trying to make my voice sound calm and professional. "I've just returned from the Luxembourg Convention Centre. There was an attempted assassination of the governor and the representatives of the Lunar Company. According to my information, one person died at the scene, the rest were taken to the hospital. The perpetrator of the attack, Reiha Kato, is under our arrest. But that is not all. Judge Holstein, all the evidence points to the governor's connection with the Romain Corporation scandal and the illegal share buyback case. As well as the murders by contracts."

Vincent Holstein looked at me with moderate curiosity. He wasn't surprised by much. He was already very old. From what I knew, he spent at least fifty years in Lunnar, and he was older than he admitted. He probably would have retired a long time ago, if it had been easier to find someone to take his place.

"Do you have proof?"

"I think I do. I miss a few pieces of the puzzle, but I should have them in a few days."

"I understand. I will wait. Governor Khamala is to remain under arrest. Allegations that are sexual in nature are very serious. If you add criminal charges to that, he's not getting out of it."

"I hope so. When I think of these girls, I have the desire to strangle him with my own hands."

"I wouldn't recommend that."

The judge put two sheets of computer foil on desk, bearing the service seals.

"Please take care of Megumi and Miniko Takahashi until someone from Earth arrives. I expect a full report on everything you have discovered as soon as possible. The earth will demand all of the details and you'll have to prepare for a heavy hearing."

It meant that I had to temporarily, like Scott, literally live at the headquarters. At least until I complete the report, of course. I've never done this before, but it had to be done. No one could replace me at this job. And to make matters worse, there was no one who could help me.

*****

I was sitting neck-deep in material from the laboratory to review when I got a text message from Sue.

"When should I make dinner?"

"I won't be there for diner, I don't know when I'll be back," I replied.

"Do you want me to send you a picture of Mrs. Cavanaugh to your computer? My equipment is up and running smoothly."

"Send it. I'll look through the police database in my spare time."

These moments of spare time seemed like they were going to be few, but curiosity was stronger at that moment than the sense of duty. I couldn't wait to see what Scott's wife looked like. I turned on the mail download and waited impatiently. The computer screen flickered and then, pixel by pixel, began generating a three-dimensional photo of a young girl – a smiling, pretty, dark-haired woman with doe eyes.

I felt as if ground was escaping from under my feet.

It was Number One, looking at me from the computer screen.

XII

That's something I didn't expect. In truth, I was convinced that Scott's wife had committed a serious crime, and he, using his contacts, allowed her to change her identity. I wouldn't have blamed him for that, of course. Love encourages people to do worse things. But this...

My brain began working at highest speed. Selecting Number One is something of paramount importance. When it became clear that, by all available parameters, the best candidate for the position was Alexa Cavanaugh, she was forced to divorce her husband and traces of her former life were destroyed. Since then she was supposed to be Number One, and that's the end of it.

Yes, she gave up her husband, but she kept the baby with her. Was this poor boy, killed by the attackers, also Scott's son? From a legal point of view, he couldn't have been, but the law is not always decisive in such cases.

Scott's will made more sense now. The position of Number One was not for life. After their term expires, the one who occupied it returned to their former identity and received severance pay, which allowed them to start a new life. But that doesn't mean they no longer had to worry about anything, just like that. The pay-off was, as far as I knew, rather moderate. Not that it was little, but it was not a fortune. Scott packed all the money in stocks so that his wife could one day live without worry. He must have loved her very much.

I felt a rush of, not so much jealousy, but sadness. In that case, who was I to Scott? A moment of oblivion? A way to pass the time? His interest in my person could be explained in various ways, although I had to honestly admit that I was the one who took the first step, not him. After a while, I realized something else.

Scotty had made various financial operations, and it was pretty clever. He knew how the stock market worked and certainly followed the quotes on a regular basis. That's how he caught the trail of Mr. X, who had been trying for years to take control of the Lunar Company. Everything indicated that he had suspicions to who he was, but had to remain silent without any concrete evidence. As commander of the lunar police, he could pre-emptively arrest anyone and investigate anyone, even if he had no evidence, only clues. And yet he was silent as a grave, even though people were dying, and a hired killer wandered the city's streets.

There could only be one answer. And it's terribly logical. The Governor's office was not a life-sentence either. Control of the Lunar Company would have been a source of fortune and power that would reach all the way to Earth. Only that people in political positions were not allowed to trade shares, so it was necessary to act cautiously, use 'poles' and have people on your side in corporate boards. And have discussions with them occasionally.

I took the data crystal which Kunch had left on my desk. Even a cursory acquaintance with the stolen documents convinced me that I was on the right track. Delving into the contents of the crystal again, I came across a mention of Health Industries and again I experienced revelation. I left the reader and sent a call to Citizen Hakat.

"I hope it's important," he growled, as he appeared on screen after long minutes. He looked very dissatisfied and worried at the same time.

"Code 87205B789," I said, thus bypassing the questioning of the bunk password.

"A92750K342," he replied.

"Look into Health Industries. They have a network of gyms and wellness clubs on the Moon. If I'm right, this corporation was responsible for selecting candidates for doppelganging. With detailed biological parameters, they were able to select the most suitable people for the purposes of criminal organizations."

"Do you have proof?" he asked after a while.

"I will send everything in a copy of the official report requested by Judge Holstein. Along with Governor Khamala's full dossier."

"You better do that quickly."

The screen turned off. Why 'quick'? What was happening? I didn't know something again, but I didn't have time to think about that. I went back to work.

At lunchtime, as I was hastily eating soybean stew with groats, Rosanda Merrick checked in on me.

"Have you looked at the logs from that anroid's recorder?" she asked.

I nodded and swallowed the last spoon of the meal.

"Technicians have optimized the records with algorithms, so I have all the key information sorted. You're probably talking about Thomas Sanderson's killer, right?"

She sighed. At that moment she looked tired and discouraged.

"I wasn't able to find him. However, my department has gathered evidence of a conspiracy to illegally acquire AMOS by Romain Corporation. It's something."

"And I've got the rest," I threw the right data on the computer. "See this? This is a text transcript of conversations recorded by Monty. I've highlighted excerpts showing that the sentence on your man was issued by the chief of the mine, Gulab Paliavi, when Sanderson got a lead on the sodium processing plant. I've already sent a patrol for him."

She seemed a little re-animated.

"I'll tell you something. I know why someone caused the explosion."

"You do?" indeed, the case about the motives of the perpetrator still didn't get enough attention from us. Too much happened at once.

"One of the AMOS miners involved in the clandestine pyroxene mining previously worked for Romain Corporation. In that exact mine in which you've made your first arrests at the time. Unfortunately, I don't know the name."

I nearly fell off my chair. That I also did not immediately take this possibility into account!

"He knew about Monty!"

"It looks like it. The attack was aimed at the android, not the people. Except that they didn't predict his endurance. And they wrongly calculated the force of the explosion because they didn't take into account the secondary reaction. That is, the fire produced by hydrogen and the shock wave, which transferred kinetic energy to other corridors. Whoever developed the plan is certainly not a chemist."

"Are you?" I looked at Merrick with interest. I felt like she knew too much about that for a cop.

She smiled.

"To tell you the truth, I studied physics, but at some point I came to the conclusion that I would not achieve anything in this industry. But what I learned back then can be helpful in my work. The economic police must have some kind of knowledge."

She patted my hand and got up.

"I'm going back to my job. I hope you let me know when they bring this fucker in. I want to interrogate him in person."

"Of course."

For the first time since she found herself with her people at the Lunnar police headquarters, I felt a thread of agreement between us. It's like the ice is melting, which we don't even know why split us. Before I went back to the report, I thought we could even be good friends if we gave ourselves a chance.

*****

I hired Thorvald to investigate the installation at the Luxembourg electrical room. Chris agreed to delegate him for a day, though not very willingly. He was probably the only person in Lunnar who didn't care about this case, which wasn't just any. Not every day is the governor of the colony arrested like an ordinary criminal, along with high-ranking officials from a dozen corporations. The scandal was indescribable, although few regular people knew what it was really about.

The board of directors of the Lunar Company, for obvious reasons, furiously demanded explanations from the police, and after receiving them, appointed new managers as soon as possible and thus closed the case. No one likes to admit that they've been led by the nose for years, and the losses caused by this have been in the billions of pepes. It's always better to hide the screw-up, so that the knowledge of how big it is doesn't spread. And so, the representatives of the company were silent, the police too, since that's what was required for the good of the investigation, and all the others tried to add their own story to the scraps of information.

Lunnar, like any small community, literally lives on gossip. In addition to the official news, there are even two independent writings which couldn't be described as anything but 'tabloids'. Their main goal was to accommodate all kinds of gossip, journalistic ducks and generally unverified news, but effective. So it's not surprising that the arrest of the governor and a dozen of the most influential industrialists was a real golden goose for them. In less than two weeks, readers were plied with so many conspiracy theories and pulled out of thin air 'facts', that it was surprising how no one went crazy from all of it yet.

As for me, I was not particularly worried about this media storm. I'm even glad that none of the editors of these works comprehended the actual scale of the case. The more nonsense they wrote in their articles and press notes, the higher the probability that even if they do write something that's true by chance, it will be lost amongst the piles of nonsense and lies. And the residents of the colony had a circus like never before

Sven described to me exactly the type of sabotage of the electrical room, and brought the report to me personally.

"Can you explain to me that this is actually a 'parasitic pin'?" I asked, taking a piece of computer foil from him.

"A circuit that takes energy from a specific device, at the same time taking complete control over it," he said. "Usually they are quite primitive, but this one was really well made. You wouldn't have broken it yourself in time. I only know one person who knows how to do it. His name is Wu Thang, but I don't know anything about him being in Lunnar."

I didn't tell him that one of the killers who was shot was identified as Wu Thang, an electrician from the Herbert Rail plant that produces integrated circuits for precision cameras. The other was his colleague. How did she convince them to cooperate? Bribes? Intimidation? Unfortunately, neither of them are going to talk again. I preferred to be silent, too. For some time now, I have come to believe that it's best to speak as little as possible and only when absolutely necessary. Anyway, Sven didn't ask about anything. He was in a hurry to go back to the construction zone, and in fact the case of the explosion in Luxembourg was not his concern at all. He wasn't interested in politics.

The victims of Reiha's revenge were still in the hospital. The vacuum damaged their lungs some to the point that a transplant was needed. Governor Khamala suffered no less than they did because his health was complicated by a sudden stroke, hemiparesis and near-total loss of the ability to speak. He has not yet been able to be transported, and although, according to doctors, his condition improved somewhat overnight, he could not be questioned yet, neither by me nor the special staff sent from Earth.

I didn't like any of it because some the assault squads now had to monitor the hospital for three shifts. It was true that prisoners should have been taken under the control of a special unit at the order of the headquarters, but that could only happen if the doctors agreed. And it didn't seem like it was going to happen for now. For me, it meant that I had to remain at the station for twenty-four hours a day, and I don't know for how long. Overcoming moral resistance, I took Scott's apartment for this time – so I could finally have somewhere to get some sleep. If it wasn't for Monty, it would be very hard for me to do all this. The presence of an android by my side was priceless, and I could no longer imagine how I would live without him. He helped me with my daily activities, he made breakfast, embraced me when I needed it... and brought the news from the hospital where I sent him every morning.

"Unfortunately, some things we can't just jump over," McCave said when he came to the inspector's office one day to drink a cafe with me and talk. "A doctor could have the maximum possible qualifications, but he can't treat the patient with a snap of his fingers. You have to wait."

I gave him some yeast cookies, which he loved.

"Have you learned anything new about Scotty?" he asked.

I bit the cookie and shook my head with sadness.

"Unfortunately, there is no improvement. "

"Well, he's got ten days left, and then they'll turn off the machine," he sighed.

"They can do that?"

"Of course, this is included in the legislation and in the medical code. You can't keep someone with a damage brain in vegetable state indefinitely. You have to understand that. I know that it's hard on you, but there's nothing more you can do."

I wasn't sure myself if it really was that hard on me. Recent discoveries have shown me that I didn't know Scott at all, but rather that Inspector Cavanaugh, who was stuck in my head and heart, never existed. The real one was a stranger to me, and I had the impression that I had never had the opportunity to meet him. However, I did feel sadness, maybe not one that was overwhelming, since it was suppressed by my resentment, but significant.

"Without him, nothing will be the same."

"Just like without anyone else. You have to come to terms with what happened and move on. You have just proven that you can become a worthy replacement for your master, even at a very difficult time. I know there was something more between you two, but you'll get through it. You won't die from a broken heart."

I remembered Maru's gloomy expression, who for two days barely spoke and was completely extinguished.

"Your wife... she came here for you?"

The doctor sighed and took the next cookie off the plate.

"It's... hard to explain," he replied. "The law forbids us from official relationships, but no one can interfere in our feelings. You see, Leeta, I thought Jeannie decided to forget me... after we were separated. She could have married someone in her class, had a baby... she loves children very much. I didn't think she'd follow me here after all these years."

"Maybe it just took her years to figure out how she really feels about you. When she decided she couldn't forget you, she decided to come. It was definitely a difficult decision, but she dared to be with you again."

"She didn't contact me right away because she found out about Maru. I don't think she knew how to do it, and wanted to think about it all."

I got up, took the bottle out of the closet, and poured him a drink.

"How did Kendra react to the news that your ex-wife had found you?"

He took a greedy drink. I barely wet my lips. In fact, I don't like alcohol, but it does some good in certain situations.

"Badly. She immediately packed up and moved out, not even giving me time to explain the matter. Leeta, I didn't want to hurt her. I really didn't want to. I feel remorseful that this is how it ended."

I understood that. This situation would have overwhelmed anyone.

He pushed the empty vessel towards me. I poured him a little more.

"I have a simple question: which one of them do you love?"

He coughed.

"That's supposed to be a simple question? I think you're making fun of me. I'm more confused than ever before. I don't know what to do."

"I can't help you. I'm ignorant about these types of issues myself."

"I'm afraid that everyone is in some way. Even the biggest Casanova in the world."

He emptied the glass to the bottom and went out, passing gasping Hallie in the doorway.

"Boss, there's a fight in prison, in the square!"

"What?!" I looked at the clock.

Our cellblock did not have multi-person cells, but the people locked in it were entitled to two hours of leisure once a day. The videoart prison yard was located in the middle of the prison block, with different clocks for each section, understandably.

Currently it was section B that had their 'free time', which was for temporary detention. For the first time since I've been there, overcrowded.

"Monty, follow me!" I yelled. "Hallie, go get stormtroopers currently on their shift!"

"Yes, ma'am!"

As soon as I could, I got to the elevators and went down to the prison level. On the spot it turned out that the help of stormtroopers was no longer needed. A scuffle broke out between Reiha and the mine chief, and other participants joined the entertainment without worrying about the conflict. The guards managed to separate them before I arrived, although that did not mean that the fight itself was done. Both women continued to throw nasty curses at each other, and the most colorful of accusations, still trying to reach each other.

"To the solitary confinement, both of them" I ordered. "Separate ones, of course. The rest – back to their cells. That's enough for the walk."

"Mrs. Commander, we have a deceased," one of the guards said unexpectedly.

As if we didn't have enough trouble, I complained in my head. I looked in his direction. He looked at me as if alarmingly, warning me... I got closer.

On the slabs of the yard lay a short Asian man. His prison jumpsuit was stained with blood, but his narrow eyes jerked to me with a silent plea for help. He forced himself with difficulty to not scream from pain.

"Need a medical team and technicians at the cell block," I said to the messenger. "Murder at the prison yard."

I stood on the other side of the one on the ground, hiding him from the eyes of fellow inmates together with the security guard.

Other guards, assisted by the visiting stormtroopers, quickly brought the detainees back to their cells, and the two rioters were locked in separate confinement rooms. I kneeled down next to the lying man and took his hand.

"Hand in there," I whispered. "Who attacked you?"

"I... didn't see," he whispered with difficulty. "But I know... who made them..."

"Who?"

"Chief... Paliavi..."

Someone pushed me aside. It was Dr. McCave.

"What are you...?"

"Shh..." I whispered. "No one can know that he is alive."

He nodded slightly.

"To the morgue," he ordered the paramedics. "I'll be there soon."

Medics, who have been working in the police for a while, were not surprised. They packed the wounded in a black bag for corpses, put him on a trolley and went with their cargo to the elevator.

"Good work," I said softly to the guard. "How did you figure it out?"

"I didn't figure anything out. He asked me when I leaned over him to declare him dead," he said. "I just realized that it must be important."

"Good work," I repeated.

"Thank you, commander," he saluted, clearly proud of himself, and returned to his duties.

"Collect all traces," I instructed the technicians. "I have to interrogate the witnesses."

I knew in advance what would come of it. The detainees were miners and employees of the AMOS administration, they knew each other very well and... No one saw anything, no one heard anything. Traces of blood wouldn't help, because at the time of the attack all were crowded in the corner where the guards pushed them. However, I ordered that those who had a bloodied body or clothing be separated, and after several hours of work with the virtualization scanner, I identified three who, according to the spray, could have carried out the attack.

I didn't expect anyone to admit it, and of course no one did. Being aware that in each interrogation room there are nozzles with a soft version of the truth serum, they were simply silent, squeezing their teeth. Many people study this technique in case they come into conflict with the law, others implant neutralizing implants preventively – in short, and they exercise their right to silence. Eventually, I ordered them to lock up those three, double the guards and not let them go to the yard. Only then did I go to the police morgue.

The young Asian, the victim of the attack, lay on a camp bed placed in the autopsy room, under an IV. He was already bandaged and clearly calmer. Kelly McCave cleaned up his tools with a gloomy expression.

"How is he?" I asked.

"Not terrible. He was lucky. He was stabbed, but the blade slipped on his rib."

"Did the technicians find the crime weapon?"

"Yes. Narrow blade from cemented carbide, not detected by the scanners, but damn it, the detainees could have simply been searched, the old way. Those idiots of ours, I mean our guard, did some nice work, since one of the detainees managed to smuggle a sharp tool into custody..."

"What's your name?" I sat next to the makeshift examination couch on a three-legged chair and smiled to the wounded to comfort him.

"Peter Wang, licensed front miner."

"So please tell me, Mr. Wang, why did you accuse Chief Palavi of ordering the murder of your person."

The miner changed his position and moaned from pain while doing so.

"Commander, ma'am, I'll tell you everything."

"That's what I'm hoping for."

"I was the one who reported to the commander that the new robot was actually an android and that it was probably sent there to spy on us. I've known him since I worked for Romain Corporation. I didn't want him to screw me up. From the beginning, they hired me to do this business for the extraction and processing of pyroxene. I needed the money. Do you know how much that bitch paid?"

He stopped for a while, breathing heavily. Then he continued.

"I happened to find out, while in arrest here, that Sanderson's death was planned in cold blood. He said too much to Bruce Niven, his roommate at the hotel. I heard him arguing with Henry Klein. He said it was supposed to end at Sanderson's addiction to 'golden rain' and that it was the only reason he was persuaded. I made a mistake, I began to explain to them that there is no longer a point in hiding Paliavi or her puppy from their dirty work... I thought they would understand..."

"You could've paid for it with your life," I muttered not without compassion. "For now, they're convinced you're dead. I'll wait for their next step."

"You don't have to wait," he interrupted me impatiently. "I know what's going to happen next. When the doctor was sewing me up, I put it all together."

"What do you mean, exactly?"

"Check the medical records of those who were with me, but carefully, up to a few years back. I bet one of them will have previous psychiatric treatment."

I raised my eyebrows in disbelief.

"Blah blah blah," McCave spoke. "People are not allowed into the mines after psychiatric episodes."

"That's right. That's why I'm telling you to check them carefully, because this information will be hidden. Good enough to not be seen during a cursory check, but also badly enough to be pulled by a virtualist. All those who do left business, they hire people like that on purpose. They do at Romain Corporation, too. Subsequently, it can always be explained that the employment office didn't check it thoroughly and that it's not the fault of the management that the worker suddenly had mental problems. And that, for no reason at all, they stabbed somebody."

It made a lot of sense. The longer I thought about it, the more so. The chief of the mines orders the killer, and then provokes a fight with a cellmate to distract the guards...

"Will you repeat this before the court?"

"Of course. Do you think I have anything left to lose? If any of them go free, I'm going to die anyway."

"For now they don't know you're alive. That's just in case. We don't know how deep the corruption goes. Please relax. I'll find you a safe place."

He didn't look convinced I could protect him, but he didn't say anything else.

"I'll put him in our patient ward for now," the doctor said. "It's empty right now. Just get someone to look after him, because I'm not going to do that. Unlike many, I have a personal life."

"You have so much of it now that it would be enough for two," I remarked. "Don't worry, I'll take care of it. I'm going back to the office for now. I have a lot of work to do."

I ran into Hallie at the office, wandering around aimlessly, as always.

"You have a guest, boss," she said cheerfully. "It's that young one from colonel Sitris. She's waiting in front of your office, boss."

"Is that so? Then please bring us two caffettinos and some cookies. Double time, miss Trent!"

The sight of Mabel made me very happy, although I didn't have time to socialize now. Ah, what the hell, I thought, a moment of relaxation improves performance, and I also needed something back from life.

"How's your new life, my good friend?" I asked while we exchanged warm hugs.

"You know what, better than I thought," she pulled up a chair. "It turns out that I'm able to adapt. At first it was hard, I won't lie... but the colonel is an amazing woman. She helped me through my training and took care of me like an older sister."

A 'hedged' hairstyle and no makeup surprisingly fit her face – or maybe the facial expression were more important? She had a sense of security and strength, and the field uniform looked like she was born in it. What happened to the exquisite, luxury-loving floressa?

"And when all this ends, will you return to your old life?" I asked another question.

Our messenger brought a tray of caffettinos and cookies. Mabel took her cup and thanked her.

"I don't know," she answered to my question. "Probably not. You see, I took a soldier's oath. Semper Fi. There is hardly any turning back from that."

Holly put the cookies on the table, deliberately dragging this simple action so she could overhear as much as possible.

"Miss Trent, that will be enough," I said to her. "Now please order a large lunch for us. I'll keep sergeant Rochester here for a few more hours."

Mabel smiled with approval and lifted the mug to her mouth. For the first time in a long time we were able to talk to each other and she enjoyed it as much as I did. That mattered.

"Well, tell me," I encouraged her. "I'm very curious about how the first months in the military look like."

*****

Only after a month of hard work were we able to unload everything we had and collect all the indictments. One of them was actually, logically, completely superfluous, because it concerned Leon Beavis Hampton, who was still resting in the police freezer. However, the law also requires that the act be brought before the court, as it is closely related to the prosecution of the entire corporation. When we got to the end, I literally fell on my face and had enough of everything – but I could talk about myself with pride that I passed the fire test. And finally, I could go back home and sleep in my own bed.

Sue opened the door before I could use the remote control. She smiled from ear to ear, and held Sid under her arm. Our cat had an ugly habit of going out the hallway and had to be well protected when the door opened.

"Why are you so happy and dolled up? Is Chris here?" I asked, went into the apartment and looked around. Monty went behind me. Sue handed him Sid, who puffed up with offence, and then climbed over the android's shoulder, sat comfortably there like on moving furniture and from there followed us with his emerald eyes.

"No," my roommate said. "Not Chris."

Citizen Hakat came out of the living room politely. He seemed slimmer to me, and as if he was older than the last time I saw him. He looked tired.

"Hello, Leeta," he said. "How are you?"

"Not too bad, thank you," I replied with surprise. "What fury sent you here? Is Venus casting a shadow over Earth again?"

He shook his head.

"The sound of the sea drowns out the cry of the innocent," he replied with the passcode. "It's really me, Leeta. And it looks like I'm going to stay here longer."

"How's that?"

"Sit down at the table, both of you," Sue interrupted us vigorously. "It'll get cold. We'll talk at the table. Today we have soy chops in spicy sauce and baked dumplings."

Who would resist such an invitation, especially if for more than a month they were sentenced to a diet from a cheap restaurant's delivery? I hastily changed my uniform to a homemade dress, washed my hands and sat down at the table, immediately starting to eat. Citizen Hakat sat across from me, next to his niece, and ate tastefully, telling us both at the same time what we didn't know.

The Doppelgate case, as it was called, shocked the entire Central Island. Although citizen Hakat eventually figured out the entire anarchist organization, he was still found guilty of shameful negligence and appeared before the island's internal court. Doppelgangers managed to mix well and get a lot of classified information, so cleaning up this mess seems like was going to take years. In the end, Hakat was demoted and stripped of his position as Chief of Arms, but in gratitude for a nonetheless successful job, he was sent to the Moon, as the new governor, instead of Khamala, who was currently in death row on Earth.

"Well, he deserved such judgment," I commented on these revelations. "Scotty suspected him for a long time, but he had no proof. And he really did not know how to get to a government official in such a high office."

Citizen Hakat, now Governor Karl Stanton, twisted his mouth in a sarcastic smile.

"You're wrong, Leeta," he said. "This stubborn mule didn't suspect Khamala at all. Not for a minute. He suspected me. "

The fork slipped out of my hand and hit the floor with a metal rumble. I looked stunned at the man sitting in front of me, and I could not gather my thoughts. It was so simple and so crazy at the same time.... Hakat must be destroyed, the words ringed in my head, words which should have made me think a long time ago. It seems I'm not as smart as he thought.

"Are you serious?" I blurted out

"As serious as can be. Didn't you know? It was against me that he gathered evidence. I knew about it, but it was even to my benefit since I had nothing on my conscience, nothing to find and use against me."

"So, he was wasting his time," I muttered.

"Not at all. It was thanks to this idiotic obsession that he followed in the footsteps of an organization that uses doppelgangers. Not wanting to cooperate with me at the time, he was always a law enforcement officer, but he was still trying to get through to me. Poor old bastard... before he died, he believed that I was responsible for the accident in which his sister died. In some strange way, it gave his life meaning."

I thought about whether to tell him about Scott's will and that I know Number One's identity. In the end, however, I decided to remain silent. I'm entitled to my secrets, too. I will protect the last will of my mentor and lover, and when the time comes, I will make sure it's seen through. I owe it to him. In his own way, he loved me, even if he didn't tell me everything.

And I loved him too. He was the first person I really cared about, and I knew he would stay in my heart forever. Just like how I'll stay on the Moon forever. This is my place. Grim and claustrophobic. Deprived of faith, hope and love.

But it's mine.

EPILOGUE

I'm standing on the observation deck. Below there is a panorama like one from a fairy-tale – a beautiful, colorfully lit city full of fanciful buildings. Some of them are hotels, others are entertainment venues. Between them there are wide slates of free space, converted into videoart parks, playgrounds and sweet – as well as salty pools 'under the naked sky'.

"How much did all this cost?" I ask Chris quietly, who is standing next to me, embracing Selenaport with a very loving look of an accomplished artist. I've never seen him so happy.

"Don't even ask," he replies. "The dome itself is worth more than half of Lunnar. But it'll pay itself off, relatively quickly."

I look up. Under the perfect imitation of the blue-pink sky, decorated with lazily flowing clouds, fly birds. Their shouting and twitter fills Selenoport with the sounds of nature. At the moment, we are the only ones enjoying the sounds. The opening ceremony will take place in two days, and then the first guests will arrive here. The service is cleaning up the interiors, the videoart technicians are doing final configuration of the machineries, making the illusion as believable as it can be. While it doesn't seem like it could be any better that seems to be their goal.

"Do you know who was the pioneer, and, of course, the first videoart theorist?" I ask Chris and, without waiting for an answer, continue. "A writer from long ago, probably from the twentieth century, Stanislaw Lem. He wrote the novel 'The Magellanic Cloud'[10], in which he accurately described the idea of linking holography with material props."

"He must have been ahead of his era."

"Oh, yes. Few took him seriously at the time. He was also the first to describe the electronic reader with all its functions, recording information in crystals, speech synthesizer, spray clothing and a number of other technical solutions. It was not possible to build these things then, but time showed that it's all possible."

Chris is silent for a moment.

"Every science fiction writer is in some ways, a poet," he says, at last. "And poets don't need to have technical skills to create

---

[10] „The Magellanic Cloud, Stanisław Lem, 1953 – Polish author, in the U.S known mainly for "Solaris", he proceeded even Star Trek.

something unimaginable for ordinary people. And the realization of their ideas is the expertise of engineers. Ones like me."

"As if you're not a fantasist... I've never seen a bigger dreamer than you. If it wasn't for that, you wouldn't have reached this far."

He's smiling, satisfied. It's true, if he had listened to Cynthia Lara's teachings, he would have become a technician in precise mechanics workshops at best. He did not hesitate to follow his dreams, and so he got to his dream university, completed it and eventually became the chief engineer of the construction of this wonderful place. True, he was helped by a few lucky coincidences, but if it were not for his determination and diligence, he would have achieved nothing.

"What are you going to do now?" I finally ask.

"I'm waiting for a new appointment. It probably won't be as great as this, but who knows?"

"Mabel is staying here, too. Now, as we did before, we're meeting regularly, although the topics of our discussions are quite different."

"Life can be a surprise. When you begin to walk on any path, you never know where it will lead or end."

Oh, yes, I've had the opportunity to experience that many times. My life has changed so much that at some point I didn't even believe that something like this was possible.

"Where would you like to work now?" I'm asking.

"The pinnacle of my dreams is the Martian station," he replies. "But I don't know if I can get into this team. Anyway," he adds, "I promise that I will spend every vacation with you guys, here."

"Really?"

"Of course. You're both the closest people to me. And I like Lunnar. Plus, I'll have a reason to visit Selenoport and see how it's doing."

Laughing, I give him a light nudge to the side.

"I'll take your word for it, brother. Okay, I need to get back to work. I have a stack of reports to fill in. It's not easy being the commander."

"I knew you would get an official nomination. You deserved it."

I kiss him warmly, hug him, and bury my cheek in his light hair. For a moment, I feel like before, when we lived together, and the world seemed so beautiful to us, without worries or serious problems. Then I move away, and Lunnar comes back, with all its gloomy secrets.

"See you later, Chris," I say, and go towards the elevator.

The technicians' cabin leads me down, where amongst the last scaffoldings, which are currently being taken down by the manbots, stands a police slider. Paul Hidalgo, senior constable since a few days ago, is smiling from behind the wheel.

In the back of the car, dressed in his assistant's uniform, waiting for me, is Monty.

THE END